THE MAIDEN SHIP

MICHELINE RYCKMAN

Dedicated to Hannah.

This ship was constructed when you were born,

yet did not sail until you were grown.

Table of Contents

THE *four* KINGDOMS

Prologue

Dain watched the waves flip up between the wooden cracks of the boardwalk as he counted his steps by twos. The air smelled of salt and fish. He hated fish. Leaning back, he tried again to loose his fingers, but his father's grasp remained unyielding.

If only he could free himself. If only he could run.

The pace quickened, and Dain lifted his chin in response to a more urgent tug on his arm. Looking ahead, he spied it— the green-and-gold galleon. Their new home . . . The mainmast climbed to the salmon skies, and the sails hung larger than clouds. The ship bobbed impatiently on the harbor waves like it couldn't wait to take him away. Dain tried to keep the quiver from his lip as he read the dark, sprawling letters inlaid along the freshly painted flank: *The Maiden.*

The gossip of the manor staff had been rampant for weeks prior to Dain's departure. Even Nurse Lydia had partaken in the whisperings. He'd been squatting beneath the workbench, stolen sweet roll in hand, when she'd entered the kitchens with the upstairs maid. Her beryl eyes had been wide, and he remembered the insistent tone of her voice.

"My brother works the twilight shifts at the harbor, and

you know he's always been trustworthy. He told me that *The Maiden's* been docked in Aalta for decades, and despite years of weather, the ship remains the same. Never a mark of wear on it."

Nurse Lydia swiped one hand over the top of the other—a superstitious sign Dain had seen her do countless times before. She added another for what seemed like good measure as she leaned in toward the maid. "But that's not the most unsettling part. On nights when the three moons are full, many a watchman has spied a figure floating around those decks. Some believe it's the departed soul of Mariette Ulsman—she was a victim of the grisly Pier Three Murders. They say her ghost remains to seek revenge."

The maid dropped her armload of linens to raise slim fingers up to her mouth. "Do you really believe that? Then . . . why would the master buy it?"

Nurse Lydia's bright copper curls bounced as she shook her head. "He hasn't been right since the mistress died. He's told everyone he needs that ship for his business"—she squinted her eyes, and lowered her voice further—"but I'd swear there's more to it than that."

After the mention of his mother's death, Dain had lost interest. It had been too hard to listen to others talk about her. He'd even dropped the sweet roll as he'd quietly crawled away. The ghost story, however, had not been so easily abandoned, and now it preyed upon his mind as he topped the boarding plank.

His father promptly dropped his hand to leave Dain standing alone among the bustling crew. All around him, whistles blew, crates crashed, men shouted, and gulls cried. The noise deafened him. The smell of fish gagged him. Knees wobbling, he fixated on his father's retreating back, and vaguely wondered how it would feel to call him "Captain."

His father was known as the merchant king of Aalta; he was *the* aristocratic businessman on high, and while the man had studied ships, he'd never been aboard one. The same went for Dain, and even worse, it seemed his first might be haunted.

A breeze whipped around him as he clenched his fists open and closed. His nails began to bite into his skin, but he ignored the sting as he watched his father's form disappear in the throng. Dain's urge to run returned. Maybe he still had time to get back to Lydia.

Just as he turned back toward the plank, a figure stepped in front of him.

His gaze started at the man's boots, then traveled the long distance up, passing over his green-and-gold tunic, to look into the sailor's charcoal eyes. Dain was a full nine years old, and Lydia had told him recently how much he'd grown, but right now, faced with this giant, he felt like a mouse.

The sailor was *massive*. His ebony skin glistened in the

spring sunshine, and his long, black dreadlocks swayed behind his shoulders as he chuckled. His laugh was rich, textured and deep. The sound reminded Dain of his mother's favorite fabric, a plum velveteen.

"Are ye the Captain's lad?"

Dain swallowed, but didn't respond.

A knowing smile spread wide across the giant's face. "I'm Morgan Crouse, yer father's first mate. Ye can call me Mo. And I'm here to tell ye, there ain't a thing to fear about *The Maiden*, lad. She's a worthy mistress. Ye may not believe it now, but she'll soon feel like home to us all." He bent low, hands resting on his knees as he looked Dain directly in the eye. "Maybe ye need to explore a bit?"

Like a key springing a lock, the man's kind words and invitation moved Dain to speak. "Do you mean—is it safe?"

The sailor stood, sweeping his arms open in a wide, welcoming arc. "Aye lad, entirely safe. Take a look around. Yer free to fly wherever ye please."

Dain's lip stopped quivering, his fists loosed, and his eyes began to dart from prow to stern. Then, he bolted. He could hear the sailor's laugh grow distant behind him as he ran.

For a time, Dain forgot about the manor. He forgot about Nurse Lydia, the haunted tales, the noise, and even the smell of fish. He scaled every unoccupied ladder, finding that some led to upper decks while others led to the quarters below. He flew down long corridors lined with doorways. He couldn't resist the knobs, nor the fresh bunks that begged him to bounce and the open portholes that tempted him to holler. The empty hull made his voice echo, and the free-hanging hammocks swung with the waves. It was a long while before he surfaced on deck again, but when he did, Dain ditched his boots and dodged sailors, ropes, and riggings as he slid his socked feet along the polished decks.

The big sailor had been right. *The Maiden* wasn't so bad—

A few glides led him to the bow, where he noticed a great statue of a lady fixed upon the prow. Why had he not seen her before? Her hair streamed back behind her in long, wooden waves, and like everything else on board, her details were fresh and realistically crafted. Dain marveled at how each part of the ship was in perfect condition. Even the barnacles that scaled the hulls of every other vessel in the harbor seemed to shy away from clinging to *The Maiden*. As he continued to stare at the wooden maid's solemnly carved features, he realized that she reminded him of someone. A storybook character, perhaps? His chest tightened, Nurse Lydia had always been good at telling stories—he'd spent countless hours on her knee while she'd brought tale after tale to life. Like his mother, those days were now gone . . .

The wind tousled his hair, and Dain's chest loosed a little as his gaze broke from the wooden maid to follow a breeze-blown gull toward the horizon. The distant salmon skies dipped over the rim of the sea, and for the first time since boarding, he wondered where the waves might take him.

Chapter 1

Dain squinted at the bare bit of stubble along the sharp line of his jaw. The small cabin mirror tilted with the waves. Bending his head to match the angle, he rubbed at his chin and wondered if anyone would call him a sailor worth his salt. After eight long years aboard *The Maiden*, Mo's long-ago words had never come to pass—Dain had never felt at home.

Gull cries pierced the cabin walls.

Hurriedly splashing water over his face, Dain reminded himself that there was no need to dwell on the past any longer. Today, if everything went according to plan, he'd soon have a true place to belong.

* * *

The first mate stood at the helm, wheel in hand, as he tested the winds, referred to his compass, and periodically called orders to his men. His pale green tunic was trimmed with gold, matching *The Maiden's* colors. Every officer wore gold and green, including the captain—it was a mark of their station aboard the ship.

Dain snaked his way through the busy throng to stand by Mo's side. Turning, he saw the small, rugged island of Tallooj just beyond a teeming bay. The cove was cluttered with colorful ships from all four corners of the known world, and the distant hum of people wove itself into the chorus of gull cries above. As *The Maiden* drew nigh, the briny air filled with scents of spice, livestock, sweat, and fish. Dain still hated fish, but the scents of civilization were welcome. Rubbing at his nose, he looked beyond the harbor to the small, thatched-roofed town nestled among the island hills. If the sparse tales were true, Port Tallooj was nothing to write home about, but no matter how much a sailor loved the open waves, he eventually longed for land. Even land like this one.

Shifting his attention to Mo, Dain saw that the first mate was looking down at him, appraising. "Ye know lad, I do believe the sea has gone and scrubbed away that boy I once knew, and in his place it's left behind a tried-and-true sailor."

He smiled up at Mo. Even now, with Dain on the brink of adulthood, the man still towered over him. "You always know exactly what I need to hear, my friend."

A mischievous glint glimmered in Mo's eyes. "And now that yer a real sailor, ye'll be needing a nickname." Mo flipped his compass twice in his palm, as though pretending to mull the question over. "I think I'll call ye, 'The Lion of the Sea.'"

Dain snorted. "Has there ever been a time you didn't follow up a compliment with a poke, Morgan Crouse? I'm the farthest thing there is from a lion."

The breeze shuffled around them playfully. It tugged Dain's hair free from its leather tie, and the wild blond strands flew fast into his face.

Mo burst into a peal of rich, velvet laughter.

Dain didn't even bother trying to tame his hair—the irony was too perfect. He simply defended his locks. "I'll have you know, sir, that every time I've been back to Aalta, Lydia says that my wild hair is the perfect compliment to my stormy gray eyes."

"I think yer childhood nurse just loves ye too much to tell ye to get a haircut."

"Ah, not so, Mo. Lydia isn't afraid to speak her mind about anything." This time it was Dain's turn to give Mo a mischievous look, and he added a wink through his hair for good measure. "I think you'd find her a formidable match."

Mo's deep baritone filled with further mirth. "Are ye trying to set me up, lad?"

Dain crossed his arms over his chest. "Me? Play matchmaker? I know nothing of courtship, sir."

Mo clapped Dain on the back, following his gaze. "Never

a truer word was spoken."

Dain tried to look insulted, but he couldn't commit. Mo's statement was truer than true—he had no experience with women.

The man squeezed his shoulder. "Eager for some leave, lad?"

Dain shoved at his tangled mat of hair, but the wind resisted by pushing it right back into his face. "Yes, but this is not just regular leave for me, Mo. This is it. This is my chance. Maybe I'll buy an inn—or a farm, who knows. But soon, very soon, I'll finally be off this ship. "

The big sailor's hand dropped away. "Aye, lad. I suppose. Ye've had yer plans set a long while, and I expect that ye'll do good by them." Mo cleared his throat roughly before he changed the subject. "A word of caution, though. Tallooj is a tough port. Be on yer toes."

Dain fingered the dagger at his belt. "I've heard the crew talk, and you've taught me well. I'll be fine."

The first mate slipped into a knowing chuckle. Dain thought perhaps he heard a hint of pride in his big friend's laughter. He looked up at Mo again. "I do wonder why my father chose to resupply here? There are certainly more desirable ports—some less than three hundred leagues."

Before Mo could reply, the air buffeted behind them. The sails grew full with the final gust needed to set *The Maiden* well into port. As soon as the wind settled, Mo blew the whistle and sent the crew flying fast to trim the sails and weigh anchor.

The first mate kept his eyes ahead. "Ye came on deck just in time to lend me the favor of the winds, lad. Now we're properly set to port."

Dain wasn't surprised that the first mate had dodged his question about Tallooj—the man rarely commented on the captain's decisions—but Dain wasn't pleased with the alternate response. "I think you need to leave off on that superstition, Mo. The crew is starting to believe you. I can't have the mates thinking I'm some kind of phenomenon." Dain issued the words in a jesting fashion, but in truth, it really was beginning to get uncomfortable. If even a glimpse of a storm threatened, the sailors were there to practically drag him up on deck as their good luck charm. One sailor had even had the audacity to wake him up in the middle of the night. The thing was, his presence seemed to work every time—the weather always settled when he was up there. All coincidence, surely, but the crew's faith in him was escalating, and the superstition was getting out of hand. Most concerningly, Dain knew that the minute it didn't work, he was going to be the one to blame.

Mo gave another velvet laugh before blowing the whistle and loudly commanding the rowboats down. Once the order was obeyed, the first mate leaned his massive form toward Dain. "I'm convinced that there's never any harm in a little something to believe in."

Dain rolled his eyes. "You know, with all those wise phrases you have stored up inside that head of yours, you'd make a great carnival act."

The first mate gave a loud bark. "There may be coin in that idea, lad."

A shift in crew movements called attention to the fact that the captain was now up on deck.

Dain's fists clenched, and his back instinctively stiffened. Since the death of his mother, Dain's father had become an unrelenting tutor. The studies he imposed on Dain were rigorous, mistakes were unacceptable, and errors usually resulted in discipline. When the captain wasn't drilling or disciplining him, the man remained aloof and indifferent, typically cooped up alone in his chambers poring over maps, books, and ledgers. Besides merchant-related business, Dain never quite understood what his father studied. What he did know was that whatever occupied his time had and always would be more important to him than his own son. Dain couldn't wait to be rid of him.

Captain Alloway's voice carried across the decks. "Are we secure, Mr. Crouse?"

Mo's voice carried further. "Aye, Captain, the crew should already have the boats waiting."

"Thank you. I will be on the first one out to port. Appoint

the appropriate guard, and follow directly with the cargo."

"Aye, Captain."

Willing his fingers to relax, Dain nodded a goodbye to Mo, then stepped down to the lower deck to follow his father.

The captain rounded on him. "Where exactly are you headed?"

The abrupt assault caused Dain to stammer. "Well— Captain, I have earned my leave and—"

"Not this time, sailor. Port Tallooj is no place for a boy." His father turned sharply, making for the ladder. Several crew members clambered to help their captain down, and in mere seconds he was out of sight.

Dain stood for a moment in stunned silence. A boy?

After months at sea, working hard to earn this leave, Dain wasn't going to stand for this exclusion, and he definitely wasn't going to stand for being called a *boy*. Fists clenched once more, he lunged for the ladder, but anger blinded him to the pile of rope at his feet. His right boot tip caught the coil with full force, and Dain tumbled headlong into one of the busy sailors. There was some jesting and hearty laughter from those nearby as the older sailor slammed to the deck with a groan and Dain flew back hard in the opposite direction.

The prostrate man growled loudly. "Ye need to start seeing what's right in front of yer nose, lad."

The closest sailors yelped in good-humored agreement.

When Dain managed to get to his feet, a strong hand latched upon his arm. He turned to see Mo, holding him fast. "Yer father knows what's best for ye, lad."

Dain wrenched his arm loose and rounded on the first mate. "My father is barely half a man these days, with even less of a heart. He knows nothing." Dain knew he should stop, but he couldn't help himself. "This was it, Mo. It'll be months before the next port. My cargo will be spoiled, and I'll lose everything I've worked for. This was my chance to leave this bobbing prison. This was my chance to start fresh and build a real life. A life far away from *The Maiden,* and far away from my father." He spit his last words out like venom—he didn't care who heard.

Mo's response was soft. "I am truly sorry, lad. I'll take yer wares into Tallooj myself. I've not the same ways as ye when it comes to merchandising, but I'll do my best. I wish I could do more, but it's my place to enforce the captain's orders. And it's yer place to follow them."

Dain threw his hands in the air. "Damn his orders, Mo!"

Turning on his heel, Dain stalked below deck and slammed the door of his cabin. Crumpling onto the bunk, he pulled his hands over his hot face. Morgan Crouse didn't deserve those words. The first mate had been nothing but a true friend and mentor these past eight years. The man had stayed the course, never leaving *The Maiden,* never leaving Dain, but he couldn't go back up on deck and apologize. His pride pricked too sharply. And he knew that no amount of pleading would sway Mo's resolve. The first mate was an obedient sailor to the core. The man lived by a code, never wavering. Plus, there wouldn't be a rowboat left to sneak after them, and it was a long swim to the pier.

His father often excluded him from leave. It was an act that infuriated Dain, a scene all too common across the years. And at seventeen, Dain was no longer a boy. The age excuse just didn't cut it.

Snatching the dagger strapped to his hip, Dain repeatedly drove the blade into the target on the wall at the end of his bunk. His mind churned with every pitch. Mo would be lucky to get half the coin Dain had hoped for—everyone knew Tallooj was a tough sell. All his well-laid plans, all his hard work, simply dashed. It would take another year or more to earn enough again to buy his way into a new life. With one final throw, he embedded the point of the dagger straight into the center of the hand-drawn bullseye. The perfect hit did little to ease his frustration. Throwing himself down on the bunk, Dain gave in to a fitful sleep.

Lately, his dreams had launched him on long, treacherous adventures. Chaos and danger reigned over them, and in these dreamscapes Dain traveled to foreign lands where he was always seeking, always searching. The dreams made him feel like he'd lost something long ago and was desperate to find it again.

On rare occasions, they would permit him a destination. Today, they planted him in a garden, where he happened upon his mother. She was standing in the starlight, surrounded by a grove of cultured trees. Her feet were bare in the grass, and her gaze was locked upon the figure of a man carved out of stone. Despite all outward appearances, Dain knew the statue was no simple ornament, and as he joined his mother to stare, his mind flashed to the wooden maid fixed upon the prow.

Chapter 2

Tep, tep. Swish.

Dain opened his eyes. The room tilted as he tried to tune into the noise outside his cabin door.

Tep, tep. Swish.

Footfalls.

Tep, tep. Swish.

The noise now encouraged him fully upright in his bunk. *The Maiden* had had her fair share of attempted theft and piracy over the years, and Dain knew better than to ignore new or unfamiliar sounds.

The steps stopped.

He could tell via the porthole that he'd slept the day away. The last gleam of twilight quickly faded as the light of the three moons began to filter in through the glass.

The door hinges creaked.

Dain lunged for the wall. His hand clasped on the hilt of

his dagger just as a figure emerged, silhouetted in the frame. He had no time to quietly free the blade, so he plastered himself against the paneling and held his breath.

The form did not advance. Instead, he heard a heavy shuffle of fabric on the wooden floor, and then a soft female voice whispering his name. "Dain?"

A woman? Onboard the ship?

"Dain—?"

"Who are you?" So much for staying hidden.

The woman didn't answer. Instead, she walked over to the hanging oil lantern, groped for the flint, and lit it.

A warm glow filled the small room as Dain focused. The first thing he saw was the woman's heavily embroidered gown of green and gold. It made him think of all the history lessons he'd suffered through as a boy. The fashion was old, but the woman was not. Dain's stomach flipped as her features caught the light. He had seen beautiful women before, but she— nothing compared. Her hair fell in silky auburn waves behind her shoulders, and her bright, azure eyes glinted above high cheekbones. She had a strong, perfectly aligned nose that pointed straight down toward her full lips, and Dain's first thoughts about her mouth were not appropriate. When she smiled, his knees nearly gave out.

Dain rubbed at his face and eyes roughly, but after drawing his hand away, the lady remained. The craziest thing of all was that he thought he knew exactly who she was—or what she had been.

As though she'd read his mind, the maiden's smile broadened. "Thank goodness you know me. I feared you would not. Please, take my hand." She offered it.

Dain recoiled from her touch as every ghost story ever told about *The Maiden* crashed back into his skull. "Why—why are you haunting me?"

The lady dropped her hand and laughed. It didn't sound joyful. "I am no ghost, Dain. I do not haunt. You have known me for years." The woman looked down at herself, and then up again. "Perhaps not in this form, but it is I. And I've waited beyond two lifetimes in this prison for someone like you."

Pity stirred as he stared into the maiden's alluring, sea-blue gaze. The word prison resonated. Dain noticed that his hand still held the hilt of his dagger. Leaving it plunged in the wall, he leaned forward. The familiarity of her features struck him again, and he froze. Caught between trusting his senses and the need for rational proof, Dain felt the call of nature come to his aid.

He waved his hand apologetically. "Will you excuse me, my lady? I've slept the day away and I am in need—" He indicated the door.

At first she looked confused, and then her eyes widened in recognition. "Oh, certainly, my apologies." Stepping aside, she let him pass.

Dain walked smoothly by, but once he was out in the hall, he darted for the deck.

Three sailors—Casper, Dev, and Trait—had been left behind for clean-up and guard duty. Obviously, they hadn't taken their job too seriously tonight. Empty rum bottles were scattered about their prone bodies as they snored loudly in the moonslight. The drinking must have begun early. Dain rolled his eyes. He contemplated waking the drunkards, but then decided it would only complicate matters. Easing his pace, he walked quietly to the prow. He wasn't surprised to find it empty, and he bet the others had not noticed since they were well and truly drowned in rum. Visiting the poop deck before returning below gave Dain a few moments to think it through. Mo always said that most men thought best there.

Alive. The wooden maiden was alive, and breathing, and in his cabin. How in all the kingdoms was this possible? Either he'd gone mad, or it was—magic? The history books his father had supplied as required reading made vague references to the mystical, but those days, true or not, were now centuries past. Today, few believed in the existence of magic—or at most, as the devoted followers of the Orthane taught, magic had died when the Selteez left the four kingdoms. Dain had never been religious, but the wooden maid's sudden transformation had him grasping for any kind of explanation, rational or not.

Dain stood, adjusted his breeches, and then dipped his entire head in a nearby rain barrel. The cold hit him like a tidal wave, the sensation fully confirming that he was not dreaming.

Once he'd wiped at his face and smoothed down his wet, matted mane, Dain reached to finger his dagger. It startled him to find nothing there, and he realized that he'd left the blade buried in the cabin wall. Probably not the wisest decision under the circumstances. The maid didn't seem threatening, but as Mo would say, "Folk ain't always what they seem." Apparently Dain could live by the things Mo said, because he suddenly recalled another: "Ye rarely find what yer looking for at the top of a barrel—more often than not, it's at the bottom."

Drawing a steadying breath, Dain made his way back below deck.

* * *

The maiden stood gazing out the cabin porthole, her moons-lit features flawless, her auburn hair glowing. She was still here, still entirely real. His stomach fluttered, causing him to hesitate before re-entering the cabin. As he allowed his gaze to linger on her face a few moments longer, the same familiarity that had always struck him about her features played again upon his senses. Whom did she remind him of?

Dain finally worked up the courage to announce himself. "Ahem. I brought some cheese and apples. I thought you might be hungry, my lady?"

The beauty turned her distant gaze towards him. "Please, call me Ileana. And thank you for the offer, but I never hunger. Not for food . . . You must be famished though. Come, sit, eat." She motioned him toward the bunk. "There is so much to tell—and I have only until dawn."

Why did she have to be so beautiful? Dain sat on the bunk, and watched the maiden seat herself opposite. He tried to smooth back his crazy mop of hair, but the sweat on his palms caused his hands to snag in the damp tangles. It took a lot of tugging to disengage himself, and when he finally freed his fingers, he knew his face was bright red. This entire experience was bizarre, but the worst of it was how awkwardly intimate it felt to sit so close to a woman. Obviously, he'd sat above her countless evenings on the prow, but now she was made flesh. Living, breathing, gorgeous flesh, and he didn't know where to look. Every time her lashes fluttered, or he glanced at her full lips, his face warmed, and his insides flipped. And it wasn't only her appearance that played on his senses—she smelled like sweet oak and warm sea breezes, both scents equally enticing and distracting. He felt like a fool. Wriggling further back into the bunk, Dain hoped she hadn't noticed.

The maiden seemed nonplussed. In fact when she finally spoke again, her voice sounded remote. "So many years, so much time has passed—my story feels lost to even me."

Dain offered her a question, trying to distract himself.

"How long have you been attached to this ship?" The minute the words were out of his mouth, he groaned inwardly, realizing their indelicacy. He definitely needed some lessons on how to talk to women, magical or not.

Again, though, the maiden seemed unaffected. She raised her perfect chin as though calculating. "From what I can ascertain, it has been nearly 220 years since I was imprisoned."

This revelation gave Dain a small jolt. It was hard to reconcile the youthful beauty before him with the age she had just given.

Her small sigh meant she'd noted his surprise. "The curse prevents me from aging, and I do not hunger or have any other physical need. Yet, my spirit grows old, my soul wearies, and my heart ever longs. I'm not certain how my mind remains intact, but perhaps that is part of the curse as well."

A sympathetic lump formed in his throat. "Who cursed you, my lady?"

She blinked back the silver now lining her azure eyes. "Ileana, please call me Ileana. I will answer that question, I promise you, but perhaps I should start from the beginning?"

Dain nodded, and then grabbed an apple as he watched her lean back more comfortably against the opposite side of the bunk. The gold of her gown glittered in the lantern light as her voice assumed a storyteller's lilt. Her tone was not conversational, and Dain wondered if she used it to ease her obvious sorrow. Perhaps she wanted to separate herself from the past, to control her emotions.

"It was love. Tangible, authentic, honest love. It came to me unexpectedly, as true things often do, in the form of a man named Elden Grayspire. He was honorable, moral, and brave—and a commoner. The head game hunter to the crown, he supplied the meat that filled our noble bellies, but he was a servant, nothing more. I took little notice of him until . . . the accident.

"Every year, a royal hunting party was held during autumn's peak season. The entire court attended, and the queen rode ahead of them all. Rectlor, the high chancellor and palace governor, oversaw the proceedings, but Elden directed us to the game. He'd been stalking an albino stag for weeks prior to the event, and as expected, he led the party directly in its path. It was customary for the monarch to draw first, but instead of running, as prey commonly do, the animal turned toward the queen in a crazed frenzy. My mother's mount panicked, and she was thrown to the feet of the stag."

"Wait," Dain interrupted. "Your mother? Your mother is a queen?"

The maiden dipped her head gracefully. "Yes, Queen Illyian of Derchar."

Dain's mind raced. Derchar? Right, the former northernmost of the four kingdoms. Ernham, in whose waters they currently sailed, was the middle, and then Iandior and Zaal comprised the two Southern lands. However, the Northern realm was no longer called Derchar—the kingdom had been overthrown a couple hundred years ago and renamed Dorthane. The next thought struck Dain hardest of all, because if the lady sitting before him now was who she said she was, then that made her—he stared at the woman intently. His jaw went slack. Now he understood why her wooden features had always been so familiar. "You are *the* Princess Ileana? The Lost Princess?" It seemed unbelievable, but she confirmed his deduction with a nod.

Dain began to babble. "Every child knows your story. It's a tale that has been passed down for generations. My old nurse, Lydia, told me the tale numerous times when I was small—she always gave it a different ending, but everyone knows how you mysteriously disappeared, how countless portraits circulated throughout the four kingdoms, and how for over twenty years the Queen of Derchar searched for you in vain. Those portraits can still be found hanging throughout the four kingdoms. They're everywhere. Inns, collector's homes, libraries; your tale—your face is legendary."

"Yes, all true. Yet legend fades, reality wears away, and now I am only a bedtime story. A fairytale. No doubt there's all manner of conjectures told about what truly happened, but may I tell you the real account?"

"Of course. Apologies, my lady—er—I mean, your highness." The revelation of her fantastic identity humbled Dain. There was no questioning the truth of her claim after he recalled the portraits—their every feature was identical. This wooden maid turned flesh was undoubtedly The Lost Princess.

"Please, just call me Ileana. After so much solitude, it will be good to be called by my name."

Dain felt awkward at the request, but she looked so earnest that he nodded in agreement. Her responsive smile made him forget everything except her lips. Snatching up his fruit again, he dropped his eyes from her mouth and started munching fast. He thought he heard a small giggle. The sound made him cringe and hope, beyond hope, that she was only laughing at his eating habits.

The princess smoothed her gown before resuming her tale. "As I mentioned, the queen was thrown from her mount to the feet of the stag. I was relatively close by in the procession of riders, and I watched in terror as the beast's hooves rose in the air above her. It seemed as though everyone froze—all except Elden, who leaped from his horse and threw himself between the white stag and my mother. Confused, the beast flailed backward and somehow missed them both. Eyes wide and nostrils flaring, it fled wildly away into the woods. While we all continued to hold our breath, Elden stood and reached to assist the queen. The high chancellor recovered quickly, dismounted, and roughly removed the huntsman. Intense words were exchanged before Elden obediently stepped back. After the fact, Rectlor was rewarded for assisting the queen while Elden Grayspire was whipped and demoted for leading her majesty into danger."

The princess took a deep breath and began fiddling with the ends of her auburn hair. Dain could tell the tale was difficult for her to recount. And he had been right about her tone—when she resumed talking, the minstrel flair was even more pronounced, as if she had stepped farther away from her history.

"I felt beholden to the huntsman for saving my mother. And though none would acknowledge his act of bravery, I was determined to do so. Bringing a healer, I sought him after the whipping. He was alone, in a small cottage at the edge of the royal woods. His wounds were deep, crusted with blood and starting to fester. It took hours of cleaning and stitching. The huntsman was much younger than he'd seemed. He was fresh-faced and handsome . . . The healer and I visited his cabin daily until we knew he was out of danger.

"During those visits, Elden and I talked. He was uncommonly educated, witty, and kindhearted. I had heard how his skills were renowned, but he was modest about the tales. Through these exchanges, a mutual respect grew. I convinced myself that my actions were only recompense for the way he had been treated, but days quickly turned to weeks, and I began to visit the huntsman on my own. No one knew of my sojourns—I never even told the healer that I had returned.

"That winter, Elden and I spent every free moment together. His companionship unlocked my heart, and as that door opened, it revealed how much I had been missing." Ileana drew a long breath. "Wealth can procure many things in this world, but Elden was the first person in my life to give real meaning to the things it cannot buy.

"As spring approached and court life resumed, it became increasingly difficult for me to find time away. Yet I could not live without my huntsman, and so, in my youthful naivety, I determined to tell my mother."

She shifted uncomfortably, the distanced tone of her voice cracking for a moment.

"The choice was unwise.

"The chasm of our stations was insurmountable, and my mother would not hear of it. As heir to the throne of Derchar, I had duties. I was expected to take a royal consort of considerable political advantage. According to her, my time and my attentions were wasted on a commoner. She forbade our love.

"However, we could not stay apart. We stole fleeting moments together, and we never realized that we were under surveillance. When the queen heard of our disobedience, she gave the governor free rein to *deal with* my huntsman. The events that followed—went beyond all natural law."

Dain couldn't help whispering the word. "Magic."

The princess stood. "Indeed."

Dain silently watched her pace the tiny cabin, the long train of her gown dragging and swimming behind her as she moved.

Tep, tep. Swish.

As he watched her chew on her bottom lip, he imagined how being bound in wood for centuries must make one long for movement—for freedom. He could understand, to some small degree. He'd been bound in his own way to *The Maiden* for eight years, and he couldn't wait to be free of the ship.

Ileana stopped, and turned her gaze on him in earnest. "Dain, you have been so sheltered—so protected—and what I now share will irrevocably change all that you have ever known. Two centuries I have waited, and for the last eight years I have watched you grow up happy. Or happier than most, at least." Ileana hung her head. "I so wish there was another way . . ."

He was confused by her words, but beyond that, Dain felt nothing he would've expected to given the impossible situation. Perhaps the lack of fear stemmed from the overall fantasy of it. As the princess had pointed out herself, it all rang out like a fairytale, a mere bedtime story. The only response that came to him was another Mo-inspired phrase. "Mo always says that it's fear and fear alone that binds a man from living." He felt like he'd managed the big sailor's accent particularly well this time.

The princess's shoulders relaxed, and she gave him a small smile. "From the prow, I have often heard the wisdom of your first mate."

"Yes, he's full of it, and full of unmentionable phrases alongside." Dain laughed, and then caught himself mid-wink. By Orthane, he spent far too much time with sailors. Clearing his throat, he once again hoped she hadn't noticed his awkwardness. Trying to redeem himself, he leaned forward and asked, "Please, will you continue?"

Her beautiful brow knit. "Dain, you know a world without magic. I have seen this world, its emptiness, everywhere the ship has gone. But magic did not simply disappear from the four kingdoms. It did not fade away, nor was it lost. It was *stolen.*"

Chapter 3

The night wore on, the tale stretching for hours, yet Ileana's voice never grew hoarse. She relayed in detail how Rectlor had long set his mind on obtaining rule over Derchar, how the white stag had been no accident, and how he had imprisoned her huntsman. He'd also demanded she take him as her royal consort in exchange for Elden's life. After she'd refused, the high chancellor had had her secretly abducted. Ileana told of fear-filled weeks in captivity, where her huntsman was tortured before her eyes and she was mercilessly abused.

Despite the darkness of the tale, her storyteller's lilt did not falter. "After countless months, Rectlor had Elden and I conveyed to a stale underground tomb. Worn carvings featuring the conquests of Dorthane Loremight crawled across the walls, and unnatural shadows crept in every corner. I had never felt so cold, so afraid. My beloved was fastened to the top of a sarcophagus. He was bloodied, unconscious, barely breathing. All I could do was sob while the henchman held me fast.

"It had been weeks since I'd seen the high chancellor, and when he finally arrived, his appearance was considerably altered. Rectlor's youthful vigor had been restored—his shoulders were now wide, and his back was no longer bent. The gray once lacing his hair and beard had disappeared, and his eyes were no longer dull. The irises now shone a menacing amber. He was dressed in robes the color of twilight, with silver trimming every edge, and the entire affect made him nefariously handsome. As he strode toward Elden, the shadows in the tomb sprang to life, swathing Rectlor in darkness. The cold intensified, and my fear grew thicker still.

"I had never witnessed magic before that night. It had begun disappearing from the four kingdoms long before even I was born, if you can imagine that. Yet, from what I knew, it was obvious that the magic before me in that tomb was not the same kind my predecessors had wielded. It was wrong, twisted and maligned. I could feel an ugliness in it, a palpable evil."

Ileana explained how she was offered another chance to recant, and to accept Rectlor as consort, but she refused. She knew she was a disposable pawn, simply a tool to make the path to conquest easier for him. She told Rectlor that she would never give her kingdom over to his evil, but he mocked her words and pointed to her huntsman, saying, "Your kingdom already belongs to me, as will all kingdoms in time. And your fate will be worse than death—you will spend an eternity of living without him."

After relating this, she struggled to speak for some time. Dain tried to be patient during the extended silence, but at this point, he was so desperate to know the rest of the tale that he couldn't resist urging her on. "So he separated you both permanently? You here on the ship, and Elden—somewhere else?"

She swallowed visibly, and for the first time in a while her bard's tone faltered. "His words terrified me, despite all he'd already done. Even during those weeks of despairing abuse and torture, I had felt nothing akin. Everything was going to be taken from me. And by everything I mean Elden. He was the love of my life, the family I had never truly had. He was the home of my heart."

Dain watched as several tears cascaded down the princess's cheeks. He resisted the urge to reach out and comfort her, guessing that the sympathy might only make her feel worse.

Wiping at her face, Ileana straightened her shoulders and lifted her chin. She was royalty indeed. "My captors held me fast. All I could do was scream. I screamed and screamed until my throat was so dry, so raw, that all sound was lost. And while

I screamed, Rectlor sang. It was a symphony of horror. As his frightfully enchanting tenor rose, the cold blackness snaked away to encase itself around Elden's limp form. It happened fast—as soon as the cloud enveloped him, it fled, and left behind was a man made of stone."

Dain leaned forward fast. "Did you say a *man made of stone?*"

She looked surprised by his sudden interruption, but managed an even response. "Yes, why?"

"Umm—not important. My apologies, Princess—I mean, Ileana."

The princess looked as if she might question him further, but after a quick glance at the porthole, she continued her story. "I marveled at Rectlor's unnatural strength as he lifted the stone statue off the sarcophagus to set it upright. It was an exact replica of Elden, dressed in impeccable hunting gear. His sword was at his side, his bow at his back. He even looked as though he might be quietly stalking his prey. Then the governor turned his gaze toward me. His song rose again, and the shadows gathered once more.

"The henchmen released me when I became enveloped in the darkness. Violent shivers wracked my frame as I reached for my huntsman, but though I strained, I could not move toward him—my feet had gone painfully rigid. They felt hard, solid. It was not the coldness of stone, but the brittle stiffness of wood. In seconds, I was trapped within a body of oak. I could neither speak, nor feel, nor move, but I could see and I could hear. The high chancellor smiled as he advanced toward my immobile form. He reached for my shoulders, and then he leaned in to kiss my wooden lips." The princess absently brought her fingers up to touch her mouth. "It has been the only time during this damned curse that I've ever been grateful not to feel."

Her hands dropped and her brow creased. "Elden was placed in the gardens of his private chateau. I was removed and fastened to the prow of this ship, a ship that Rectlor had commissioned for the queen. He said the wooden statue was crafted in my honor. My mother was artfully deceived, and set out upon my prison in search of me, with the assurance that her kingdom was in safe hands while she was gone.

Ileana looked exhausted as she turned again toward the cabin porthole. Light glimmered on the horizon. Her tone became urgent. "Listen to me, Dain. Dawn approaches. My time is running short. This story is not only about me. It is about hundreds of thousands more. There are people, past and present, whose lives, like Elden's and mine, have been taken from them. Those who survive today are driven from their homes, doomed to live on the run. And Rectlor is at the center of it all."

"Rectlor lives? Wouldn't he be a corpse by now?"

"Like me, magic sustains him. He still rules in Derchar."

"That's impossible. There's been a long string of dictators in Dorthane since the occupation." Dain was starting to question whether the princess was sane after all.

Ileana's face flushed. "Yes, and all of them have been Rectlor. It will take too long to explain. Listen, we must work together to stop him. We must save those who remain. We need to find the safe haven."

"The safe what?"

"The safe haven. I don't know exactly where it is, but I do know it exists, and I believe it is somewhere north. The people there need to know about Rectlor. Only they can help us."

"Sail *The Maiden* north? We have no trade routes up there—it would take months. Plus, winter is setting in, and the seas will be treacherous. How in all the four kingdoms can I convince my father to do that? And if I somehow did, where would we even look?" Dain splayed his hands for emphasis. "You told me that magic was stolen. How? By whom?"

Ileana gently took his hands in her own. "I want to explain everything, but my time is up. Please, find the safe haven. I cannot do this without you. I am rarely in human form. The fate of so many rests in our hands. In fact, the fate of the four kingdoms may as well. In a month, when the three moons are next full, I'll take on flesh again, and we will talk more." With that, she dropped his hands and fled.

For a moment, Dain sat motionless. Then he gave chase, but she had gotten such a head start that he couldn't see her, only hear her fading footsteps from ahead. By the time he reached the prow, dawn had struck.

Fumbled steps sounded behind him. Dain turned to see Dev teetering his way. "What ye running amok for, lad?"

From the squint of the man's eyes, Dain could tell that the light of dawn was seriously hurting his head. Dain took a deep breath and crossed his arms over his chest as he lied. "It's nothing, Dev. I thought the crew was back."

"No lad, they aren't due until tomorrow eve."

Dain nodded in response, and then watched as the sailor shuffled, in a tilted fashion, toward the poop deck. Bending over the rail again, Dain gazed down at the very solid form of the wooden maid upon the prow. He couldn't help wondering if she'd even been real . . . She looked exactly the same as before.

He heard the other sailors beginning to stir, and Dain knew he needed a few moments to reflect before being able to interact. Grabbing a bucket of rainwater for washing, Dain made his way back down to his cabin. Once inside, he set the bucket down, and retrieved his dagger from the wall. While his fingers played over the hilt, his mind scrambled through the night's events. He had momentarily questioned the princess's sanity, but now he was starting to wonder if maybe it was he who had gone mad.

No, she had held his hands in her own. They had been warm, *real*. His eyes instinctively fell back to the bunk where he'd sat all night beside the princess. Something he hadn't noticed earlier caught his eye on top of the blankets. Drawing near, he sheathed his dagger, retrieved the small item, and held it up in the morning sunlight.

A key. And fastened around the head was a piece of gold-and-green ribbon.

It didn't look large enough for a door, so it was probably intended for a small chest or drawer. Unless it was meant to unlock something far away, the only person on this ship who owned lockable storage was his father. Perhaps Dain would find more answers there? He doubted much could be found in his father's belongings besides merchant files and ledgers, but he had to assume the princess left it for more reasons than just the proof of her existence.

Pocketing the key, Dain decided to wait until nightfall. Dev and the others would have a list of chores left behind by Mo, and since Dain had slept away the day before, he knew he'd be expected to help out. And even though the captain was his father, they'd still question Dain rummaging around in his quarters.

* * *

The first mate had indeed left an extensive workload, and

the day was spent sanding, painting, cleaning, and rearranging the cargo hold for new provisions. While Dain worked, the curious key weighed heavily in his pocket.

Autumn was well on its way to the waters of the middle kingdom, but the evenings were still comfortably warm. And after a day of labor, Dev and Casper gathered up a large amount of cold foods for the group to share together up on deck. They all ate ravenously in the lantern light, and it was only a matter of minutes before they were through.

Dain noted that Trait mostly filled his gullet with rum. However, it seemed the more he drank, the better he sang. The sailor's deep baritone now belted out "Willow's Chase," while Casper accompanied him with loud stomps and Dev played shrilly on a flute.

Through wildest nights and darkest skies
Willow raced among the cries
Tempted fates and forest's dye
Feeding plains and open sky
Undulated fearsome yells
Turning slow she faced the swell
Darkened faces, clothed unseen
Grasping hands, clawing fiends

As men called ho,
Feet beat the ground
She dodged the grasping lo
She dodged the grasping lo

Earthen soil crashing high
Willow gasped an eerie cry
Depthless seas, and rugged coasts
Pillars, spires, and common hosts
Undulated fearsome yells
Turning slow she faced the swell
Darkened faces, clothed unseen
Grasping hands, clawing fiends

As men called ho,
Feet beat the ground
She dodged the grasping lo
She dodged the grasping lo

As men called ho,
Feet beat the ground
She dodged the grasping lo
She dodged the grasping lo

Dain didn't have a musical bone in his body, but he relished the melodies, and always inquired about the origins when he heard a new one. Mo had once told him that song was essential to a sailor's soul, because months at sea can turn any mind afloat. Dain believed it. The music always anchored his heart and reminded him of home. Though tonight, instead of easing Dain's mind, the lyrics of this first tune pricked at him meanly. The sensation was far from pleasant. The story of the song brought back Ileana's words about lives being taken, about people on the run. Putting a hand in his pocket, he fingered the tiny key, flipping it over and over until Trait slurred into a new number. It was a Zaalish ballad called "As We Linger," and Dain released a sigh of relief.

Standing, he moved away from the lantern-lit circle. Looking up, he watched the stars sputter to life in the night sky, each speck birthed in tiny protest against the darkness. Dain knew the others wouldn't think twice as he made his way toward the prow—he'd sat upon the bowsprit most evenings since he was small.

Climbing above the wooden maid, Dain listened to Trait's low ballad sail through the salty night air, and he caught snatches of other tunes coming from the neighboring ships as well. He swallowed. It was awkward to talk to a statue, but the words managed to tip off his tongue as a long, low note peeled from Dev's flute.

"After so long at sea, I wonder if you find music even more necessary than I do?"

Chapter 4

Since *The Maiden* had set sail all those years ago, Old Toff had always been on board. Many of the crew had come and gone, but, like Mo, Toff had become a permanent fixture. The spectacled, silver-haired man had not always been a sailor. He actually referred to his past as his "previous lives," and apparently, in one of those lives, he'd learned to pick locks. On a calm afternoon, a little over a year ago, Toff had taken it upon himself to teach Dain some tricks of the trade. He'd since had little cause to put Toff's lessons to use, but he remembered the fundamentals. However, those basics were proving far less effective on the door to his father's quarters than he hoped. Lack of sleep was probably an added disadvantage. Dain knew he should probably be in bed like the others, but the princess's tales and the small key in his pocket demanded otherwise.

Adjusting the lantern at his feet, and rubbing at his eyes one more time, Dain determinedly began again. He didn't know how much time had passed when he finally heard that one satisfying click. Old Toff called it *the quench*. The door finally creaked open, and a disappointed sigh escaped Dain's lips. He wouldn't even get to let the old man in on his secret success. After another moment of thought, he supposed this might just be the unavoidable nature of the trade. Being a criminal must be a very lonely profession indeed. Dain silently vowed to not make this kind of thing a habit.

His palm was sweating as he held the lantern up to survey the familiar, mahogany-paneled space. The main door opened directly into the captain's office. A large, oaken desk stood bolted in the center of the room, and extensive cabinetry lined the walls from top to bottom on either side. Near the back of the room stood two doors. The left was curtained, leading to the captain's sleeping quarters, and the right was an open arch that framed a glimpse of a small dining room. The farthest wall boasted three large, diamond-hatched windows, through which Dain could see the stars.

The room smelled like his father, all ink and crisp linen. The scent did nothing to ease his nerves. In and out, quick as a whip, that's what he needed to be. No one would ever know.

Fishing into his tunic pocket for the princess's key, Dain quickly got to work. He tried the key in all the obvious places first—the desk drawers and a couple cupboards—but none fit. Wandering the room quietly, he looked in cabinets and carefully shuffled through crates and bookshelves, but no other lockable container could be found. Ready to quit, Dain stifled a yawn, and then suddenly remembered the large wooden chest he'd seen beside his father's bed the few times he'd been there. Pushing the doorway curtain aside, he wandered into the captain's sleeping chamber. The chest sat nestled in the back corner, nearly hidden by the huge four-poster that took up most of the room. The chest wasn't locked, but there was no point leaving anything unexplored. Once the heavy lid was lifted, Dain held up the lantern to see that it was full of extra bedding. Setting the light at his feet, he rummaged blindly through the linens. To his surprise, he felt his hand grasp the top edge of a smaller chest. Pulling hard, he yanked the box up through the weight of the bedding, and set it down with a clunk on the floorboards. As he sat, he fingered the delicate lock fastened on the front. He knew the captain kept every copper he had strapped to his person, so why hide this?

Pulling the key from his tunic once again, he tried it in the lock. The fit was instant. The lock sprang.

Dain hesitated, palms sweating again.

What if he didn't want to see what was inside? What if it was something incriminating? His father had always been respectable, but the captain never did anything without a reason.

A sudden resentful snort escaped Dain. The captain

probably even felt he had a reason for keeping Dain away from Port Tallooj. This chest, though—it might have been hidden and locked for good reason. A reason Dain didn't want to know. He felt his expression sour. It must have been the sleep deprivation. His father, he reminded himself, had little room for much else in his life besides schooling, trade contracts, and ledgers.

Dain flipped open the lid.

Intense, stormy gray eyes stared up at him from inside the chest. Blonde, untamed curls framed a pretty oval face. It had been nine long years since he had seen that face anywhere else besides his dreams. Dain's back stiffened as he carefully picked up the ornately framed portrait, holding it close to the lantern. His mother's mouth curved up in a small smile. The smile did little to soften her eyes, but he still felt a warmth in her expression, and Dain's body relaxed as he held her gaze.

He'd only been eight years old when she passed. A sudden, unknown illness had ravaged her body, and within a matter of weeks, she was simply gone. Lydia said she'd fought tooth and nail to stay alive, but Orthane had been intent on calling her home. The notoriously superstitious nurse was also vaguely religious, and though Dain didn't really believe in anything divine, he had still felt some comfort in Lydia's words.

Other than the clarity of her deathbed and a few other vague snippets like her favorite fabric, Dain's memories of his mother were now fleeting. Thoughts of her felt like entombed bats swarming in a disturbed flurry—when he tried to reach out and grab one, he couldn't quite get a firm hold.

It was customary for the gentry of Zaal to give over their child's primary care to a nurse, followed by a governess or tutor in later years. Hence, his mother's interaction with him may have been minimal. Perhaps that was the reason why he could barely form a decent memory? Dain shrugged—the memory loss had always been an enigma. He wished he remembered more of her, and far less of his father.

Reluctantly setting aside the portrait, Dain turned his attention back to the remainder of the chest's contents. There was a handkerchief embroidered with his mother's initials, some dried wildflowers, a few pieces of jewelry, and a pair of gloves that smelled faintly of stale lavender. The smell reminded him of something. Alloway Manor, perhaps—home. Underneath it all, wrapped in a swath of plum-colored velvet, was a heavy book. Dain unwrapped the thick volume, and read the title scrawled across the front in hand-drawn, calligraphic lettering: *The Journal of Alis Lin Alloway.*

The diary creaked harshly. The musty tang rising up from the old book made him acutely aware that he was invading someone's private history. He couldn't stop. She hadn't only been his father's wife, she'd also been *his* mother. This was his first opportunity to get to know the woman he could barely remember, the one who so often walked his dreams.

Bang, bang, stomp.

Thud, thud, thud.

Voices rang out from up on deck.

Dain was on his feet in seconds, heart beating fast as he quickly replaced the book and the rest of the chest's contents. He secured the lock before shoving the box back down through the linens. As he ran for the door, he realized that he couldn't lock the captain's quarters without a key—this was a detail he'd overlooked when breaking in. Hopefully, no one would notice. Hand wrapped tightly around the hilt of his dagger, Dain shut the door behind him and dashed for the main deck.

The scene that greeted him above was unlike anything he'd seen before. Chaos reigned among burning lanterns. Crew members swarmed up the rope ladders and over the deck edge, looking like petrified sewer rats. Most were bloodied, bruised, and beaten. Toff and two other men scrambled up, half dragging, half carrying the captain's limp, blood-soaked form. Mo followed directly behind them, hauling the unconscious body of a boy under one arm. He heard the first mate try to raise his voice above the panic, but no one paid attention to his words, not even Dain. Instead, he ran straight to where they had dropped his father.

Old Toff knelt battered and breathless by the captain's

side.

His father's clothing was drenched crimson from what looked like lacerated claw marks crisscrossing his abdomen and chest. Gory red innards spilled from some of the larger gashes, and Dain tried to imagine what manner of animal could have done this. Did predators even exist on an island that small? Bile rose and burnt his throat as the hysteria raging on around him grew more intense. The mania was contagious, and he began to shake Toff. "Get the Captain to his quarters, get the Captain to his quarters!"

The old man ignored him for a few moments before suddenly jerking Dain down on one knee, where he gave him a solid smack to the cheek. "There's no use, boy, he's gone. Get your able body to the helm. Help the first mate gain control, and get *The Maiden* out of the harbor. NOW." He shoved Dain away roughly and remained panting, kneeling by the dead man's legs.

Stunned, Dain staggered through the madness toward the helm. Men cried out on all sides, some screaming for help, others to sail away. All Dain could see was red. The iron tang of blood filled his nostrils to the exclusion of all else. How could this have come to pass? What was happening? When he reached the wheel, he saw Mo's whistle dangling from the topmost handle. An unexpectedly cold gust of wind slammed into Dain's face. It stung nearly as much as Toff's smack, but it cleared his head. Grasping the whistle, he blew loud and hard. The shrill peal rang high above the frenzy, and every head snapped in his direction.

"All hands on deck! Hoist the anchor and make full sail. Move!" Dain's voice never wavered as he hurled a tirade of further direct orders. There was only a moment of hesitation before those who were able roused themselves with purpose to the tasks they knew so well. Dain watched the frantic bustle of activity, hardly breathing. Mo, Toff, and the captain's body were no longer in view.

* * *

He was roused by a gentle shake to his shoulder. Bright autumn sunshine shattered his vision as he yawned. The crisp morning air bit at his lungs.

"Morning, sir. Yer needed in the captain's quarters." Dev stood over him, wringing a clenched cap between his palms.

Dain rubbed his eyes, shoving his mop of hair out of his face. "Dev, did you just call me, *sir*?"

"Aye, Captain."

Dain's head snapped up. Had he heard Dev correctly? Captain? He must have been mistaken. Then the night's events flooded back—the chaos, the blood, his father. When had he fallen asleep? He staggered quickly to his feet. Dev reached out to assist him, and Dain gladly accepted the steadying hand.

"Dev, nothing pursues us?"

"No, sir, ye got us far from—whatever that was. The winds listen to ye, and the sea pays heed. We are clear."

Dain the good luck charm had struck again. It seemed the crew had most definitely taken to believing Mo over the years. Plenty of sailors had talismans or superstitious rituals, but Dain had no interest in being one of them. Yet, while the faith-filled confidence Dev exuded made Dain uncomfortable, he supposed, under the circumstances, as Mo had said, a little something to believe in couldn't hurt.

"Sailor, you have the helm, until Mo—er—Mr. Crouse returns."

"Aye, Captain."

He didn't bother to think on the title, nor question the man further. The answers he sought did not lie with Dev—they awaited him in the captain's quarters.

Chapter 5

Dain stared at the hulking form half bent over the captain's desk. He watched as the man itched his dark, scruffy chin with enormous fingers, and Dain wondered what kind of tale Mo had to tell. After a moment he entered, walked around the desk, and sat down tentatively in the chair. Mo's eyes remained fixed on the wooden desktop. He appeared at a loss for words.

Dain broke the silence. "What happened?"

Clearing his throat, Morgan Crouse stood upright and started to pace. "Well lad, it seems yer father got mixed up with the wrong folk—"

Dain couldn't understand why his back stiffened at Mo's words, or why his normal tone of address suddenly became formal. "Are you suggesting my father was involved in something disreputable?"

"No, lad, no." Mo waved his hands as if to signal Dain to

stop, and then began fiddling with the golden hoop in his left ear. "It might simply be that yer father didn't know who he'd gotten himself mixed up with. Ye see, he was always searching for something. I can't rightly say what that was—ye know I never pry. I do know he sought out some unsavory folk over the years, and last night was no different. He set out from the inn saying he had a private meeting. Like always, I just watched him go. Old Toff, on the other hand, took a mind to follow him. Most of the crew were just finishing up their grub, ready to head out for an evening of fun, when Toff returned to warn us that the captain was in grave danger."

The first mate stopped pacing, leaning onto the desk again and bending low to look Dain level in the eye. His charcoal gaze was wide. "The crew and I followed Old Toff through the dark streets until we came upon an empty grain shack. We heard shouting within, yer father's voice among it. Bursting in, we found him tied to a post, already bleeding out. The room was bitter cold, and three tall forms, dressed in crimson robes, surrounded him. When yer father spied us, he called out a warning, but the cloaked figures moved fast. In mere seconds, yer father was already dead. Then the building became a slaughterhouse. It was like nothing I've ever seen before. The robed ones moved like lighting. They were wild red streaks across yer vision, and they lashed out, slashing constantly with large, clawed hands. There were only three of them, but sailors fell at my feet fast. The . . . demons were so quick that I don't think one of us ever laid a hand on them. I hollered for those near enough to grab the captain's body and run. It was all we could do, lad—run."

Mo stood and began pacing again. "They chased us through the streets, maiming those they could snag, and killing those they caught. Most of the townfolk were indoors for the night, but I don't doubt that many heard the screams, and some were caught unawares. The monsters only slowed when we reached the sea. I swear to ye, lad, I never would have believed such a tale if I hadn't seen it with my own eyes. Along with yer father, we lost a dozen of our crew, and just as many more of them are injured." Morgan Crouse stopped moving and sagged against the desk, dropping his head into one hand. "I'm so sorry for yer loss, and for the others."

Dain's stomach clenched. He knew every word must be true. Mo never spun tall tales. His fists began to pump. Dead? A dozen dead? To be honest, he didn't know how to feel about the loss of his father. But the crew—so many had families with wives and children waiting for them back home in Aalta. Turning his face away, Dain focused on the windows behind him.

The morning sunshine sliced through the diamond panes in harsh, fractured rays of light. Rising from his chair, Dain walked toward the glow. He heard a small sob escape Mo, and his mind began to whir. He'd just inherited his father's estates, and by default that meant he was now captain of *The Maiden*. Suddenly, Dain was responsible for far more than just himself. There was no time for him to mourn. He swallowed, shoving the losses deep down beside his older sorrows. Then he turned to his first mate. "Thank you for your account, Mr. Crouse. I assume the captain's body is properly stowed in the hold?" Dain had no idea how, but his voice sounded almost exactly like his father's as he spoke the words.

Mo looked up. His dark face was wet with tears. "Aye, Captain."

For a brief second, Dain felt like a child again. He wanted to run. He wanted to fly from the grief in Mo's eyes, and the grief clawing up the depths he'd dug inside himself. The full force of his circumstances crashed into him further still when he realized that he couldn't run, not from any of it—he was trapped. Trapped in the life he'd spent nearly a decade trying to buy his way out of.

A throb started in his temple. Mo must have noticed the change in his countenance, because the man's expression of grief turned to concern, and he moved toward Dain. Holding up a hand to stop the man's advance, Dain firmly issued the necessary orders through clenched teeth. This time, he sounded even more like his father. "We sail for Zaal. My father's body will be returned home. Once we arrive, we will impose extended leave for the traumatized sailors, and compensate the families there who've lost loved ones. Set a course, see to the wounded, and send those who are able-bodied, one at a time, to me. I will record their versions of the story. My father's murder will be registered and investigated once we reach Aalta. I mean to make sure it's a crystal-clear account." Dain paused momentarily. "Also, set a watch rotation at the stern and in the crow's nest. We don't want any unexpected visitors overtaking us at sea."

"Aye Captain." Mo took a step toward him again, but Dain's hand remained firmly raised, and the first mate halted, reconsidering. Instead, he motioned toward a crate on the floor. "Any belongings that were still on yer father's person when he died are in there."

Dain didn't look at the crate, and he didn't meet Mo's gaze either. His eyes remained firmly fixed ahead.

The imposed formality in Mo's voice drained away. "Remember lad, there's no coffin in yer heart. Those feelings inside of you will never perish. They'll only stay hidden from sight until they ruin ye, or find themselves a nasty way out. I am here for ye—we all are. I hope ye can see that?"

All Dain could manage was a blank nod in response. Then he dismissed his first mate with a wave of his upraised hand.

* * *

Dain spent hours taking detailed notes as each sailor

57

recounted the events from Port Tallooj. All the stories lined up. Phrases like "black demons," "faceless devils," and "dark hunters" were threaded through every account. It was mid-day before the last sailor left.

Dragging both hands over the top of his head, Dain momentarily smoothed his mane, sinking back exhausted in the chair. The whole event was dark and confusing, loaded with unanswered questions despite the multiple accounts. No one knew who the red-robed figures were, nor what the captain had been searching for. The only sailor Dain hadn't questioned yet was Old Toff. He hoped the man might know more, but Mo had warned that he wasn't sufficiently recovered.

Gazing around the mahogany room, Dain held his breath as another urge to run pierced his gut. He tried to suppress it, but his mind schemed on without his consent. Plans rushed through, elaborate ways to sneak off at the next port. Dain quickly pushed up and away from the desk. He tried to channel some physical energy into convincing himself that he wasn't that selfish. Arching his back, and stretching his leanly muscled arms high above his head, he warred against himself. He couldn't abandon *The Maiden's* crew or the hundreds of others employed by the Alloway Trading Company, and he definitely couldn't leave the wooden princess to her plight. Shaking his long fingers, Dain tried to refocus on the task at hand. It was important that he begin searching his father's files—there was a chance they might hold more clues to what had happened that night. As he rolled his shoulders and took a step toward the cabinetry, the air in the room became stifling. Sweat beaded on his forehead, and Dain's resolve faded. He ran for the door.

* * *

More than a dozen injured men were laid out in the hull. The ship's infirmary had been too small to hold them. Some rested on hammocks, some on stretchers, and some on the floor. Dain cringed inwardly as he noted the claw marks along jawlines, forearms, and other body parts not visibly bandaged. His fists were tight as he walked among the wounded, awkwardly offering a smile or a word of encouragement to each of the men. One frantic sailor yanked at his arm as he passed, and Dain knelt to hold the man's hand while he sobbed out his version of the story.

None of this was right.

Trait was tending to the wounded as best he could, but the sailor was no healer. He mostly offered rum to the wounded to ease the pain, taking swigs of the golden liquid himself in between patients. Trait said it settled his nerves, and Dain didn't blame him.

As he moved through the wounded again, Dain realized that his father had never hired a proper ship's healer in all the years they'd sailed. He'd need to remedy that soon.

Toff appeared to be recovering. He lay snoring, soundly

drowned in rum. The bandages wrapping his head and torso weren't as extensive as many of the others', but Dain still wondered how he'd missed seeing the old man's injuries the night before.

Leaving Trait to his nursing, Dain made his way to the main deck. The wind picked up when he surfaced. It ruffled his hair, forcing him, like always, to constantly push the wild strands from his eyes.

The sailors on duty looked tired. Dain knew most of them were pulling double duty for the sake of the injured, and he could sense their fear and loss. He saw it in the strain of their faces and the width of their ever-watchful eyes. He wished he could turn back time.

Making several rounds on deck, Dain made polite inquiries after each sailor, and marveled at how they, considering his age, seemed to readily accept his new position as captain. Despite the recent horrors, they responded easily, treating him with proper respect. Reflecting as he strolled, Dain decided that few of these men would oppose Morgan Crouse—the man was too well-loved, and everyone knew the first mate would stick to his code by supporting Dain as captain without question. The thought was comforting and frightening at the same time. He was now responsible for all of them.

After attending to a few course details with the helmsman on duty, Dain gazed briefly toward the bow, where he knew the wooden maiden stared fixedly at the horizon. The insistent sea breeze seemed to give him a little shove in her direction, but Dain held his ground. The princess had been imprisoned for two centuries, and he hated the fact that he would now be prolonging that incarceration, but he had no choice. It was imperative that he bury his father in Aalta, investigate the murders, and restore his traumatized crew to their homes. Plus, the Alloway Trading Company would need attention. His father's business empire needed to be put into the right hands, and those hands were not his.

Dain's brow creased. His rounds throughout the ship had brought horror, but they'd also brought clarity. He could do this. He could do it the same way he'd done everything else since he was nine. Somehow, he'd pull all this off, and though he knew nothing about magic, he'd also find a way to set the wooden princess free. Once freed, she'd be able to seek out the mysterious safe haven, and set her own world right as well. Perhaps then, if the winds favored him, he'd still have the opportunity to pursue the life he'd always wanted. Turning, Dain headed for his old cabin. He fervently hoped that moving his personal belongings to his father's old quarters might make him feel more like, well, a captain.

* * *

Dain walked straight into his old cabin only to stagger back fast as a shrill, high-pitched scream pierced his ears.

"Get out!"

After the loud command ceased, Dain released his squint and focused. Furious hazel eyes, framed by a freckled face, glared at him over the top of a haphazardly arranged armload of bedsheets. Short, chestnut hair stuck out in every direction around her head and—*her?*

Dain gaped.

The girl stamped her foot hard behind the bedsheets. "I said, get out. Do you have no regard for what is right in front of your face?"

At that, Dain's shock was replaced by anger. He pointed firmly around the small room. "Out? I'll have you know these are my quarters—if anyone should be leaving, it's you. Who are you, and what are you doing in my cabin?"

The girl's face only reddened further. Then, a determined look of fury crossed her brow. To his utter disbelief, she dropped the bedsheets to free up her hands, entirely exposing her naked form as she shoved him, with full force, back into the hall. The cabin door followed fast in his face.

Dain was standing stock still, nose to the door, when Dev and Casper came around the hall bend carrying sacks full of rations.

"Ahoy lad, ye look as though ye've seen a ghost—er—pardon, I mean to say, everything alright, Captain?"

Dain barely noted Casper's casual address. Actually, he

nearly replied in kind— but he quickly bit his tongue. His response came out awkwardly clipped. "Not a ghost. Thank you, Casper. I'm fine."

The sailor didn't look convinced. "Well sir, if yer needing us, we'll be just below in the galley. Cook got injured last night, so we'll be handling the grub for a time."

Dain nodded blankly as he moved aside to let them squeeze by. After they disappeared, he considered knocking on the cabin door, but the thought instantly made his cheeks grow hot. It might be best to seek answers elsewhere.

He knew the first mate would be found in the cargo hold, assessing their supplies and rations. The unexpected flight from Tallooj would have left them low on provisions. *The Maiden* would need to take port again soon to restock for the journey to Aalta.

Dain's walk below gave him time to think. He'd forgotten about the boy, the one that Mo had dragged up on deck with him during the night of the attack. Turns out *she* wasn't a boy after all. By the time Dain reached the cargo hold, his jaw was clenched tight. Not only had Mo brought an unauthorized person onboard, he'd failed to share the entire story. As a result, the first mate had placed his new captain in a compromising position.

"Mr. Crouse, may I have a word?" His father's voice had returned again.

The sailors assisting Mo excused themselves to the other end of the hold.

Mo stepped out from behind a large stack of crates, dusting his hands on his tunic. "Aye, Captain."

The formal address managed to loosen Dain's jaw slightly. He wasn't sure he'd ever get used to Mo calling him that. "It appears as though we have an unexpected guest onboard?"

"Aye sir. Ye mean the lad?"

Dain barely nodded.

"He came aboard last night with the crew. He was knocked on the head hard, trampled in the chase. I set him in yer old quarters to sleep it off. I would have introduced ye at dinner this eve. Mind ye, he isn't a guest—yer father hired him on as a new cabin boy."

Dain stepped closer to Mo. "The lad . . . is not a lad."

Mo gave Dain a confused look. He was obviously unaware, which meant the rest of the crew wouldn't suspect either. Dain dragged his fingers through his tangled mop of hair. One day, he'd need the locks shorn—he was fairly sure he looked nothing like a proper captain.

Mo twisted the hoop in his ear. "Ye mean to say—?"

"Yes, Mr. Crouse."

"And ye found this out how?"

Dain felt his face flush, and Mo's smooth laugh rang out strong.

The sound felt somehow shocking in the moment, though not unwelcome against the rage of recent events. It was hard to stay angry with Mo. Still, Dain crossed his arms with purpose over his chest. "Mr. Crouse, your failure to impart that news to me this morning caused unnecessary grievance to both parties. I ask that in the future, you divulge all such pertinent information to me forthwith."

"Aye, Captain." Mo's tone held even more amusement now.

"Have my personal belongings conveyed as soon as possible. And tonight, bring the *cabin boy* discreetly to my quarters. We will decide what to do with our newest crew member then." Dain groaned inwardly. His new tone was beginning to grate on his own nerves—he couldn't stand the thought of what it must sound like to the rest of the crew. He had been thrust into the life of his father, but in all the four kingdoms, why this need to imitate the man?

"Aye, Captain."

Chapter 6

D ain reluctantly picked up the box sitting at the foot of the captain's—*his* desk. He knew it wouldn't be easy to go through his father's personal belongings, but after a thorough search of all the available official ledgers and files, Dain had come up empty-handed. His father had kept impeccable business records, but they held no clue as to what had happened in Port Tallooj. Dain hoped the crate might at least offer up a couple of answers.

As he set the box up on the desk, Dain noticed the crimson stains throughout its contents. Mo had obviously worked hard to clean most of it away, but blood is blood, and some inevitable residue remained. The sight should have made him uneasy, but thankfully the more threatening emotions stayed safely locked down.

Directly on top of the stack was the leather money belt his father had kept strapped to his person at all times. Opening the latch and lifting the flap, he found it brimming with coin. It was more money than Dain had ever seen in one place. And even so, he knew it was only a small taste of his inheritance—the rest resided in Aalta, securely stashed in the vaults of the Alloway Trading Company. He might be an orphan, but he was far from an impoverished one. The thought gave him no comfort. At least the full purse told him one thing—the robed murderers had not been after money.

The next three items in the crate were not as enlightening: a pocket watch, some trade contracts with attached paperwork, and a rather dull, unsheathed dagger. At the bottom of the container lay a compass and a small tin. The compass was curiously designed, its interior ornately decorated with wildflower motifs. When Dain examined it more closely, he found the instrument faulty. The arrow didn't settle north at all; instead, it flitted in jagged circles like a lost moth. One minute it pointed directly at him, the next toward the prow, and then toward the crew's quarters. Even after he gave it a solid shake, it continued flipping between the three locales with rapid fluidity. Pitching it back into the crate, he reached for the last item. It looked like a beaten-up chew box, but Dain had never known his father to use tobacco. Prying the lid off, he locked his gaze on the contents in distress.

So much for being safely locked down . . .

A small, chubby, gray-eyed face smiled up at him, fuzzy

blond hair wreathing the round head like a dandelion halo. Dain's gut tightened. His father, the indifferent captain of his formative years, had carried a baby portrait in his pocket all this time—a portrait of Dain. The horror of his father's mutilated form flashed across his vision, and the tang of blood stung his nostrils again as he recalled the screams of the lacerated sailors. Then the wind, the darkness, the fleeing, sailing away. So many were dead . . .

A solid knock at the door made Dain jump. He nearly dropped the portrait as he scrambled to replace the lid. Taking a deep breath, he set the tin in the side drawer of the desk, away from view. After another steadying exhale and an internal shove at the barely-dammed flood of emotion inside himself, Dain lifted his chin toward the door. "Enter."

His face must have looked pale, because when Mo opened the door, his eyes fell from Dain to the crate and back again. He didn't want to give the first mate time to ask. "Good evening, Mr. Crouse. what can I do for you?"

Mo didn't miss a step. "Evening, Captain. I've brought the new—er—cabin boy as you requested."

How could he have forgotten? Clearing his throat, Dain's tone became more formal. "Of course, Mr. Crouse, my apologies. Please come in."

Once Mo's mammoth form was through the door, Dain saw the slight figure following close behind. The girl was dressed in a loose patchwork tunic, with torn breeches and no shoes. She wore a weathered cap pulled down low over her forehead to better hide her features. He could only guess at her age—perhaps a year or two younger than he was? Her eyes were respectfully fixed on the ground, and in this state she looked every bit the part of a common cabin boy. Dain's ears burned as he recalled their meeting earlier that day. He may have inadvertently walked in on the girl, but it had been his cabin—how could he have known she'd be there? In return, she'd been rude and insubordinate. An indignant sort of anger crept up Dain's neck, and as it stretched along his clenched jaw he realized that it felt . . . satisfying. At the very least, it was a safer emotional release than what he'd just experienced when he saw the baby portrait in his father's belongings. He didn't have time for sorrow or mourning; those kinds of emotions might rob him of his ability to function. And if he was really truthful, he was afraid of exploring all the loss.

Mo's voice interrupted his thoughts. "Captain, may I introduce ye to Sable. The new hire yer father picked up in Tallooj."

At this, the girl slowly raised her face to greet him properly, but when her gaze met Dain's, she staggered back a step. "You—"

Dain watched the girl's expression flip from shock, to rage, to embarrassment, and back to shock again. Then he lifted his chin, looking down his nose at the girl as he crossed his arms over his chest. "Sable, is it? Apparently, we've already met." He spied Mo out of the corner of his eye, and saw a hint of reprimand in the man's expression, but he ignored it.

The girl, however, did not back down. Instead, she stiffened her back as straight and tall as she could manage. Her voice was full of mock civility, almost like she knew his own tone was fake. "Yes, *Captain*, apparently we have. And what do you intend to do with me?"

She spoke the common tongue well, only a mild Ernhamian accent edging her words. However, her mockery grated along his frayed nerves like coarse sand. Leaning forward across the desk, he couldn't keep the growl from his voice. "The brig comes to mind."

The girl bristled visibly. Mo cleared his throat, and Dain's head snapped toward the first mate. "You have a better suggestion, Mr. Crouse?"

Mo's response was patient, gentle even. "Aye, sir. As ye know, *The Maiden* is in dire need of hands. So many have been lost or injured. It'd be a sad waste of labor to keep Sable idle."

Dain knew every word of this was true, but his pride, coupled with the desperate need to let off steam, wouldn't allow him to back down that easily. "So, you are suggesting that we let this *girl* parade around the ship pretending to be a boy, while our crew remains unaware? I will not lie to my men, Mr.

Crouse. That's the last thing they need right now. My father failed them by hiding too much. I will not." His conviction wouldn't last long though, because the truth was he was already hiding things. He'd told no one about the cursed princess, or the safe haven, or breaking into his father's chambers to find the journal—

"Aye, Captain, I agree that honesty is often the best policy, but I'm certain yer father had good reason for keeping things hid. He may have gotten mixed up in something real bad in Tallooj, but he was an honorable man. And even honorable men keep secrets for the safety of those they love."

Dain's teeth ground together. Damn this man. He pulled wisdom out of the air like a Zaalish fisherman pulled catch from the sea. Dain had no choice but to concede. "Very well, Mr. Crouse, but the girl works just as hard as anyone. There will be no concessions made for her sex. She remains discreet, and careful. She can have my old quarters for privacy reasons, but you will be in charge of keeping an eye on her." Dain gave the girl what he hoped was a reprimanding glare.

Sable squared her shoulders, glaring back. "I don't need Mr. Crouse or anyone else keeping an eye on me." The girl turned to the first mate. "Female sailors exist, do they not, Mr. Crouse?"

Mo looked amused and mildly impressed. "Indeed they do, lass. They are few and far between, but I've never had a complaint about any I sailed with."

Dain gave the first mate a warning look, but this time Mo ignored him.

Mimicking his earlier pose, Sable crossed her arms over her chest and looked down her nose at him. "Well, Captain, it's settled. There will be no secrets after all. The crew will know exactly who I am. They'll find I'm hardworking, stronger than I look, and that above all, I can take care of myself."

For some reason Dain didn't doubt her claims, but his hackles were still raised. "Fine, take care of yourself, but not only will you have regular shifts on deck, you'll also see to all the cabin duties you were hired for in the first place. Starting with cleaning my quarters tomorrow. And, just so you have advance notice, when we reach Aalta, your term with us ends. Your wages will be remitted, and we will no longer be responsible for you."

The girl didn't look pleased about the last remark, because her shoulders slumped slightly. "We are going to Aalta? But, I need to get back—I left something behind in Tallooj."

Mo reentered the conversation. "Perhaps by then, your wages will be enough to buy ye passage back home."

Sable faced Mo, and Dain noticed that her expression had softened. He almost thought she looked pretty—almost.

"Tallooj is not my home, Mr. Crouse." Her voice cracked. "But there is something important there that I need to retrieve."

Dain was vaguely disappointed that she was no longer barking at him. Her sudden, more vulnerable state was setting him off balance the same way the miniature baby portrait had done earlier. To compensate, he made his tone even colder than before. "I'm sure you'll find a way back, but it is none our concern." He turned his focus back to Mo. "Mr. Crouse, please take our new cabin girl to the cargo hold. There is a shipment of various clothing items down there. Find her some proper and presentable work clothes. She begins at dawn." Then he waved his hand heatedly at them both. "Dismissed."

It looked as though Mo might say something more, but instead he simply nodded and headed for the door.

Sable gave Dain one final, side-eyed glare before following fast on the first mate's heel.

Once alone, Dain careened around the room. By Orthane, he didn't have time for another problem, and this girl was shaping up to be just that. What had his father been thinking when he hired her? Shoving his hands firmly into his tunic, he paced in circles. The tips of his fingers repeatedly brushed up against the cool metal in his right pocket. When he finally came to a stop, he pulled out the small, delicately wrought key, and held it up to the lantern light. It was time to take his mind off things—perhaps some light reading might do the trick.

Chapter 7

Before retiring for an evening with his mother's journal, Dain took a few turns in the twilight up on deck. Sharp, crystalline stars wreathed the three crescent moons. Dain looked down to watch the nocturnal lights reflect off the dancing waves beneath the hull, thinking about the days ahead. They would take port in Ernham's largest bay, Eandor Vid, the day after tomorrow to resupply. From there, he'd attend to unfinished merchant business, procure a healer if possible, and dispatch letters of apology to several regular trade centers that would be expecting them. The lack of routes and merchandise would induce a minor loss of profit before winter—it was something his father would have avoided at all costs, but Dain knew it was more important to get back to Aalta.

Pulling his eyes from the waters, he climbed to sit at his usual perch on the bowsprit above the wooden maid. He knew a captain couldn't remain idly lounging in the starlight for long, so he whispered quickly into the wind, relaying the details of the past few days. He hoped the princess could hear the regret in his voice well enough to understand why they now sailed for Aalta.

* * *

The bedding had been changed, but the familiar ink and crisp linen smell of his father still clung faintly to the room. Dain would have expected the scent to make him sad, but instead it just irritated him. Pulling his mother's journal into his lap, he tried to ignore the aroma as he fingered the edges of the well-worn volume. It struck him that this might be the first time in a very long while that he'd felt the presence of both his parents in the same room, however phantasmic. Shifting uncomfortably, Dain rubbed at his nose as he cracked open the large tome to the first page. It was mostly blank except for a few hand-drawn wildflowers. Running his fingers over the designs, he wondered if his mother had enjoyed art.

The next page was a surprise. Dain had anticipated finding a dated entry with a paragraph about the weather, or an account of the previous night's dinner party, but nothing of the sort graced the surface of the thick, yellowing paper. The page was covered in foreign diagrams, symbols, and scrawled paragraphs. Some things were written in the common tongue, some in Zaalish, and others in a pictorial language Dain had never seen. He focused in on a handwritten note in the margin.

Learning to read and decipher the Selt hieroglyphs has opened up more than I hoped. The language takes time to master. One glyph can have numerous meanings, depending on its placement. After I grasped the basics, it flowed more easily. I've only managed to locate one incantation book in this ancient script, but it has led to important discoveries.

Incantation book? Selt hieroglyphs?

Dain read on sporadically, skimming and flipping quickly through the pages. They were filled with more drawings and annotations on subjects such as herbs and their uses, healing enchantments, all manner of charms, divinations for illusions and glamours, astrological charts, curses, alchemy, conjuring, transformation, omens, and prophetic visions. The lists went on and on. He paused with a start when he came across a note that contained his name.

Dain is now four—he shows an ever-increasing aptitude in two specific areas of study. These might be not his only talents, but time will tell. I hope that as he grows, I'll have gathered enough information to protect him. The Stalkers are tireless, never ceasing. I have only evaded them thus far because my knowledge exceeds most. He's going to need everything I can offer to keep him safe.

Dain dropped the journal in his lap. Talents? Stalkers? Keep him safe?

It took a few deep breaths before he could pick up the diary again. The entry continued on with an exposition about his mother's plans to collect, record, study, and restore Selt history and culture. Dain didn't quite understand what Selts were, but from the context of her words, they seemed to be some kind of magical race—a race his mother believed she and he were somehow a part of. Dain rubbed at his face. If he had come across this journal a week ago, he would have inevitably drawn the conclusion that his mother had been mad, but after what had happened with the wooden princess . . . His mother's written word now stood before him as more proof, a scholar's evidence in fact, that some form of magic existed in the present day.

What struck him further was the notion that his father had owned this book. His father had known. Mo's words crept back. *Even honorable men keep secrets for the safety of those they love.*

Though Dain understood little of what he read, he continued scouring the pages, devouring as much of the journal as he could before sleep claimed him.

* * *

He strolled peacefully alongside his mother as the bright summer sunshine warmed his skin. The sky was a richer coral than usual, and the surrounding fields were covered, end to end, in a rainbow of blooms. His mother held his hand. He was a child again, and she smiled down at him. "Do you know why wildflowers are the most beautiful blossoms of all, my son?"

Dain shook his little head.

Soft waxen curls blew forward in the breeze as she lifted her storm-gray eyes to gaze out over the sea of petals. "Wildflowers are the loveliest of all because they grow in uncultivated soil, in those hard, rugged places where no one expects them to flourish. They are resilient in ways a garden bloom could never be. People are the same, son—the most exquisite souls are those who survive where others cannot. They root themselves, along with their companions, wherever they are, and they thrive."

Then more memories flew, cascading over his mind like a flood from a broken dam. Through the long, dark hours before the dawn, dreams shone bright, and Dain's memories returned.

He woke curled in a ball. He wasn't crying, but sweat drenched every inch of his body. It was almost like he'd just finished a training skirmish with Mo. He was so tired he felt like he hadn't slept at all, but even awake, the memories were no longer evasive. They did not fade like dreams did.

With shock and surprise, he found he could now recall his mother as clearly as his father from those childhood days. Dain remembered her stern, yet kind smile, her rare laugh, her discipline, and her wisdom. He also recalled her frequent trips away from home. She had been slightly more available to him than his father, but she had still been greatly absent. Why was he remembering this now? Had the journal triggered something? Or maybe it was some kind of magic?

Dain started to cough, the type of cough you get when you run outside in the winter for too long. It seared his lungs. Amidst the fit, he grabbed for water from the bucket near the nightstand, and as he stretched for it, more memories tumbled. He remembered being very small, sitting on the floor outside the large white double doors of his mother's manor apartment. He'd been waiting for her to come out and play. It had felt like hours. After a time, Lydia had appeared to fetch him away, but he'd resisted so loud and long that his mother eventually emerged. Her hair had been wild, and her eyes glassy. She'd given him a firm, though not unkind, look as she picked him up and handed him directly to Lydia. He'd cried all the way back to the nursery. What had she been doing behind those closed doors all day? With the journal's insights, Dain thought he could hazard a guess.

Scooping up handfuls of water, Dain splashed them into his mouth and over his face. He swallowed hard to ease the wheezing cough. His arms trembled with the effort. Setting himself back on the edge of the bed, he began sifting through his newly recovered recollections. The first question to arise was why nothing in the archives of his childhood hinted at magic. Apparently, Alis Alloway had kept that knowledge a well-guarded secret. He wondered when his father had found out—or had he known before? Had that brought them together? More questions rose, blossoming out from those.

Hanging his head in his hand, Dain forced himself to staunch the flow. The sun was rising, and he needed to be up on deck. Amidst the chaos of morning activity, few sailors would pay him heed, and that meant he could steal a little time with the wooden maid before he took the helm. Obviously, the princess had known about his mother, and she'd wanted him to know as well. She wouldn't be capable of giving him answers right now, but maybe talking it out at her side would somehow make things clearer.

Dain's knees wobbled as he stood. Why was he still so exhausted? He'd planned to take the helm today, but now he wasn't even sure he'd make it up on deck. Looking down at himself, he realized that he'd been so consumed with his mother's journal that he'd slept in his clothes. The garments were a sticky, sweaty mess.

Stripping down, he washed. The stiff leadenness of his limbs slowly melted with the movement. After, he leaned on the wall as he scoured his father's cabinet. It was time to dress like a captain. He selected a crisp, green linen shirt, a gold-trimmed tunic, and a pair of snug black breeches that tucked neatly into a polished set of matching boots. He completed the ensemble with a leather belt his father had purchased from an Ernhamian vendor years ago. It was decorated in gold studs, with a built-in sheath for his dagger and a useful pouch created to hold everyday items. The clothes were slightly larger around the waist than Dain would have liked, but the belt served to hold everything in place.

On wobbly legs, he made his way up on the deck.

The wind seemed to linger around him more heavily today, pushing against him like the weight of a dozen blankets, soft but insistent. The air felt moist, damp, and hot, all at the same time. These sensations made his skin prick, and he felt like he was being followed. When he turned to look behind, though, he saw that no one paid him heed. Every hand on deck was intent upon their duties, the morning shift change foremost in their minds. Trying to shake off the feeling, Dain quickened his pace, moving as fast as his worn limbs could bear, hastening across the swaying ship to the bow. He eagerly leaned forward on the railing toward the wooden princess. His voice was low. "I remember her."

"Remember who?"

Dain turned fast at the unexpected voice over his right shoulder. Leaning casually against the bottom of the foremast was Sable. She was dressed in a simple, gray wool frock, cinched around her tiny waist with a laced leather corset. Her cropped chestnut hair was tied back from her face with a turban-style scarf. This freed her features, and revealed the full force of her heavily lashed hazel gaze. Dain's initial surprise quickly turned to irritation. The anger that had rolled out in her presence yesterday started to return, but his voice still sounded tired. "None of your business. Return to your duties, and bear in mind that the next time you address your captain with such familiarity, it will result in discipline."

Sable sneered in response, and pushed away from the mast.

As she moved to leave, Dain caught sight of a half-hidden pendant just under the top of her frock. The design looked familiar. Grabbing her arm to stop her retreat, Dain snatched at it to get a closer look. She resisted, trying to break away, but he held her fast. With the necklace between his fingers, Dain bent to study the pendant. "Where did you get this?"

The girl tried to wrench her arm free. "None of *your* business, Captain."

Dain tightened his grip, his face only inches from hers. "Everything on this ship is my business. Answer me, or the brig becomes your home for the remainder of this voyage."

Her mouth was clenched in a tight grimace, and Dain realized he was probably hurting her arm. He eased his grip, but didn't entirely let her go. Her voice cracked. "It was my father's. It's the only thing I have left of him. I don't know where he got it."

At that, Dain released her.

As he watched the girl scramble away, he noticed that the animosity that had felt so satisfying yesterday didn't quite hold the same sway today. He sighed—not only had he been acting like an angry fool, he'd just hurt and alienated the newest member of his crew. If he wasn't careful, he'd turn out to be no better a captain than his father. Straightening his shirt sleeves and adjusting his tunic, Dain set aside the lingering curiosity about Sable's necklace and his need to talk to the wooden princess, and made his way toward the helm. Thankfully, the exhaustion in his limbs was starting to ebb away.

While Dain's father had been alive, Mo had been in charge of everything concerned with sailing *The Maiden*. And the first mate still stood at his usual post by the helm, several sailors ringing him. Men always gathered in Morgan Crouse's presence—he was the kind of man everyone wanted to be near. And no matter who they were, the giant welcomed them openly to his side.

Mo noticed Dain's approach. "Ahoy, Captain. Yer abroad early. What can I do for ye?"

Dain smiled at each sailor before turning to Mo and willing his voice into a more natural tone. "I'll be taking the helm, Mr. Crouse. I have some other important duties I was hoping you could attend to today?"

A mild look of surprise crossed the first mate's features, but always the professional, he barely skipped a beat. "Aye Captain, to be sure. Would ye be willing to take a moment to

84

brief me in private?" Mo cheerfully waved the surrounding sailors back to work.

Drawing close to the first mate, Dain once again noted how big this man truly was. Mo stood nearly a head-and-a-half taller than him, and almost twice as broad. This dark giant was strong enough to snap a man's neck with one fist, and yet he was the one person in all the four kingdoms that Dain knew he never needed to fear.

With most ears now out of listening range, Dain decided to drop all pretence of formal address. It was an immense relief to hear his own voice again. "Mo, I know that my father had little to do with sailing *The Maiden*, but I hope, with what you've taught me, you'll trust me to take on more of that responsibility. I understand that I'm still young, but you've always said that the best way to learn is through experience. And I'd like my crew to get to know me as a hands-on captain. I know they haven't complained about my leadership because of your standing and support, but I would still appreciate the chance to earn their respect on my own."

Mo's face softened as he gazed down at Dain, flashing one of his all-knowing smiles. "Lad, do ye not remember what ye did on that night in Port Tallooj?"

"I'm not sure what you mean."

"Yer merit was earned that night. Ye got us away, ye saved us. That is the reason none have rallied against yer leadership.

It has nothing to do with me, lad."

Dain had repressed a lot of that night, avoiding the intruding thoughts. It remained a blur of action and dark seas. He never imagined he could have made such an impact. Fingering the dagger at his belt, Dain cleared his throat. "Well—I—"

Mo chuckled, and then gave him a hard clap on the back. "Plus, it helps that yer as lucky as a hare's arse when it comes to the skies and the sea. Now, before ye list my duties and send me sailing, can I ask ye one thing?"

Dain nodded.

"Ye seem more yerself this morning, but are ye alright, lad?"

Dain knew the question ran deep with true concern—the emotional force behind it made him want to tell Mo everything, but he held his tongue. He wouldn't even know where to begin. Instead, he replied as truthfully as he could. "Perhaps today is a little better, but I think—I think the rest will take some time to sort out."

Chapter 8

Retiring to his quarters before dinner, Dain washed, changed his clothes, and then retrieved his mother's journal. Spending the day at the helm had been satisfactory. The winds blew true, the seas gave way, and to everyone's great relief, *The Maiden* remained free of pursuers. If the favorable conditions kept up, Dain even thought they might reach Eandor Vid ahead of schedule.

Setting the heavy volume down on his desk, he scoured through the tome. He was certain that the symbol etched on Sable's pendant had been pictured here—somewhere. He finally found it near the end of the volume. Taking in the page, he traced the design with his finger. A circle ringed the outside edge, and a bar of three triangles ran across the center. Above the triangles was the outline of a bird in flight, and below, a set of four smaller circles intertwined. He was starting to read the note scrawled beneath the drawing when a knock sounded at the door.

Dain replied without a glance. "Enter."

Someone limped their way into the room, but Dain's eyes remained transfixed on the page.

A gravelly voice snapped. "Well, thank Orthane, you finally know."

Dain's head whipped up.

Old Toff stood on the other side of the desk. His long, fuzzy white hair poked out from under a red woolen cap. The hat only half-covered the lopsided headdress wrapped around his wounded forehead. The old man's shirt was loosely rumpled across his bandaged injuries, but he looked much better than yesterday. In fact, he looked almost spry.

Closing the volume with feigned nonchalance, Dain internally reprimanded himself for being so careless. "Know what?"

"Relax, Captain. I know." Toff let out a cracked laugh, and yanked at his silver beard. "Honestly, I'm relieved. I wasn't sure having it all come from me would've been the best."

Dain tried to school his expression. "I don't understand."

Toff pointed a crooked finger at him. "I know about your mother." Then he waggled his finger at the book with a semi-toothless grin. "Let me rephrase that; I *knew* your mother."

Dain was beginning to get used to surprises, but he failed entirely at keeping his face blank this time. He snatched the volume off the desk. "I'm glad you're on your feet, sailor," he said, recovering. "Apparently, we have more than Tallooj to discuss this evening." Turning swiftly, he left the room, and securely stowed the journal away in his sleeping quarters. When he returned, Mo had arrived as well.

The archway to the right of his office space led to a small, mahogany-lined room, furnished with a simple dining set that was firmly bolted to the floor. The room was bare of decoration except for a large map of the four kingdoms secured high on the farthest wall.

The table seated six, but only the three of them would dine tonight. Still, it was heaped with a generous amount of warm food, and Dain invited the others to take a seat. He'd eaten very little in the last couple of days, and no matter how curious he was about Toff's account, or this apparent connection to his mother, Dain needed food first. Adding a decent portion of the saucy meat, mashed potatoes, and cheese to his plate, he encouraged the others to do the same.

Mo took nearly three times Dain's generous plateful. Toff, on the other hand, only grabbed a few pieces of cheese, and then he sat back, resting his pale, flinty eyes on them both.

Dain wondered at the old man's behavior—until he took his first mouthful.

The potatoes tasted like they'd been boiled in lye. Dain knew the flavor, because Nurse Lydia had once disciplined his errant tongue with a bar of it. The vaguely chicken-like sauce was somehow worse, nearly impossible to describe. He considered spitting the food out, but decided against it for reasons of propriety.

Old Toff was bent halfway over in a vain attempt to stifle his laughter. Dain knew his lips must be screwed up fiercely as he chewed. He couldn't even swallow without the assistance of several large mouthfuls of water.

Tears streamed from Toff's eyes as he turned to watch Mo follow up Dain's reaction with similar theatrics. The old man gasped for air. "It's the worst food you ever tasted, am I right? Casper and Dev have been running the galley since Cook was injured. I'd say they need replacing, don't you?"

Dain guzzled the remainder of his water while Mo tried to recover from his mouthful amidst a choking spell. Toff's observation was an understatement.

After he'd rallied sufficiently, Mo said, "Ye never saw fit to warn us?"

"Now where would the fun be in that, sir?" Old Toff cackled hard, only to grab at his torso mid-laugh and wince. "Ouch. Damn ribs."

Mo tossed a hunk of cheese at Toff's head. "Serves ye right, ye old bastard."

Dain looked down at his plate in disgust. "Toff's right, we need to find some replacement cooks as soon as possible."

Toff cackled hard again—the old man's laugh was so contagious that it was only seconds before all three of them were howling despite the predicament, though Toff intermittently cried out in pain amid the mirth.

While laughter felt good, Dain was confused by the day's complexity. He'd woken this morning to an exhausting flood of melancholy memories, quarreled with Sable, experienced a full, satisfactory day of work, and now was at a meal with old friends, where he could barely contain his merriment. Did loss always birth such inexplicable tumults of emotion? Right, loss. That thing he'd been refusing to explore of late. Actually, he'd refused to explore it for most of his life. He'd never truly mourned the loss of his mother, but as they said, time heals. It seemed the span of years and the new peace of remembrance were starting to ease those older sorrows. His father's murder and the loss of so much of the crew, on the other hand, was shrouded in a mountain of mystery and responsibility. He didn't know when he'd have an opportunity to mourn that. On top of it all was the issue of the existence of magic, and the wooden princess's plight. He supposed it was no wonder he was on a bit of an emotional ride. With these sobering thoughts, Dain rubbed at his eyes as he watched the others finish up their final guffaws.

Once settled, Toff spoke first. "Well, Captain, sit back, enjoy your cheese, and I'll attempt to answer the questions I know are burning a hole in your skull."

Dain couldn't help smiling again. Picking up a piece of cheese, he tipped it toward Toff, gesturing for him to speak.

"First off, I need to apologize for smacking you the other night, Captain. I hope you understand, circumstances being what they were—"

Dain watched Mo's brows draw together. Before the senior officer had a chance to reprimand the old sailor, Dain interceded. "Forgiven. Honestly, it was probably exactly what I needed in that moment."

Toff snorted in agreement. Mo's expression darkened further, but he refrained from commenting.

Rubbing at his ribs, Toff dipped his chin to peer over his spectacles at them. "I suppose my tale starts long before Tallooj. As you are both aware, I was not always a sailor."

This time, it was Mo's turn to snort in agreement. The sound made Dain realize that the first mate would have known exactly how inexperienced Toff was when he first signed on, because he would have been in charge of the old man's training. Funny that Toff had even managed to get the position at all . . .

Toff gave Mo a crooked grin. "My upbringing was decent, but some bad personal choices landed me on the streets of Aalta at a young age. I made my living any way I could, gained myself some *skills* and a solid, tight-lipped reputation. Folk hired me for the kind of jobs that required stealth, a good sniffer, and a strong stomach. I was known as—"

Mo quickly interrupted. "Yes, yes, the Ghost of Aalta. We've all heard the tales, Toff, nigh on a thousand times." The first mate rolled his eyes theatrically. "Ye were the most famous assassin-thief Zaal has ever known. Now, let's skip the rest, and move on to yer account of Tallooj, shall we?"

Toff glared pointedly at Mo. "I've never known why the crew speaks so highly of you, Mr. Crouse. Your manners are ill met, sir."

Dain couldn't help chuckling. Mo and Toff had always had the kind of brotherly connection that ran deep enough to tease without restraint.

"But there's truly more to tell before I get to that part," the old man continued, "hence the reason for prefacing my story. It was my skill set that led Alis Alloway my way twenty years ago."

Dain noted the surprise on Mo's face—the expression was probably similar to his own from earlier. He had no idea where Toff's tale was going to take them, but he was starting to think that perhaps he should have filled Mo in on a few things this morning after all.

Rubbing at his ribs again, Old Toff got distracted as he scoured the table. "Got any rum around here, Captain?"

Dain sat back, shaking his head. Rum was not what they

needed during this conversation.

The old sailor shrugged. "Well, as I was saying, it was my particular set of skills that led your mother my way. Apparently, she'd done a fair bit of sniffing to track me down. I always made sure I was a hard fellow to find, but that Alis was a smart one." Toff looked thoughtful. "A pretty, albeit intense, little thing. She was newly married when I first met her, and far away from her end of town."

Dain wondered at Toff's familiar use of his mother's first name, but he asked something entirely different. "My father didn't accompany her?"

"No, sir. You see, your father knew nothing about me. And mark my words, Alis may have looked like a misplaced garden flower in my part of the city, but she was nothing of the sort. I tested her once, and I regretted it." The old man waved his hand with a chuckle. "But that's a story for another time. What you need to know right now, Captain, is that your mother hired me to be her eyes and ears in Aalta. She paid me handsomely to watch for signs of *them,* and she taught me everything I needed to know."

"Them?" Dain was pretty sure he knew the answer, but he asked anyway.

"Yes, them. They hunt her kind—er—your kind."

Mo's confused voice cut in. "Kind?"

Toff squinted at Dain. "You didn't tell him?"

"To be fair, I only recently discovered the fact myself. And I know little about the hunting part." Dain turned to the first mate. He didn't want to mention the princess, or the key. He hadn't asked permission to share her story with the others—she'd hidden her true nature for eight years aboard this ship, and he didn't know if she wished to remain a secret or not. "I came across a journal. It belonged to my mother, and apparently she was a scholar of—sorts."

Toff coughed.

Dain glanced at him irritably. "A scholar of—magic."

Mo's face went blank. He was obviously trying to decide whether Dain's mother had been a madwoman, or if the two of them were just pulling a prank.

Dain followed up fast. "Now, before you draw any conclusions, think back to Tallooj. You stated yourself that you had never seen anything like it before, the way those robed figures moved. Remember? What else could explain that night, except—perhaps—magic?"

"The captain's right, Mr. Crouse. Those demons we encountered in Tallooj, they were not human. Well, that's not entirely true—in fact, they used to be just like Alis Alloway herself."

Chapter 9

Mo stared at Dain intently. The first mate looked like a father searching his son's face for some sign of falsehood. Dain held his gaze. He knew the concept of magic was fantastical—he was still struggling to come to terms with the reality himself. However, there was no denying the evidence that had been presented to him over the past couple of days.

Mo's expression conceded. "I agree, those demons were oddly—skilled. I'll be hearing ye both out, but be warned, it'll take a fair bit of convincing to make me believe in magic."

Toff smacked a hand on the table. "I have been in your shoes, Mr. Crouse, but I promise it won't be long before you're a believer." The old man winked, took a swig of water, and then continued. "Now, those dark monsters we met with in Tallooj are known as stalkers. And stalkers aren't born, they're made. I can't say how or why, but Alis said every single one of them used to be human. There's no saying how many there are, but for over three hundred years, they have hunted the adept."

Dain knew his expression must have shown confusion, and perhaps Mo's had as well, because Toff gazed between them both as he explained further. "Alis called them that—it refers to people who are born with magical talents. According to her, there are all kinds of different talents among the adept. She said some people were healers, some controlled the weather, some talked to animals—the list was extensive, apparently." Toff waved a hand dismissively. "I didn't keep track."

Dain nodded to himself, recalling the endless catalog of magical talents he'd briefly perused in his mother's journal.

Toff rubbed at his ribs again. "Anyway, as I was saying, the stalkers hunt the adept, and one by one, over generations, those monsters have secretly stolen, drained, and tried to eliminate people with magic. When they don't drain them, they . . . turn them." Toff shivered. "Alis told me that the hunt began when the Selteez were summoned, by the goddess Orthane, far from the four kingdoms."

Mo interrupted again. "Now yer asking me to believe in the Goddess as well, old man?"

Toff pointed an accusatory finger at Mo. "Tsk, tsk. You made a promise to hear this out, *sir*."

The first mate refused to alter his sardonic expression, but he tipped his head in mock permission for Toff to resume.

The old sailor very deliberately pushed up his spectacles before carrying on. "Alis, along with her family before her, was one of the hunted her entire life. From the moment she was born, she was on the run with her folks. That girl never lived a moment of true peace, I don't believe, but as I said, she was clever. Through the years, she studied, developing ways of sniffing out the stalkers, even tricking them. It wasn't until love came knocking that she ever considered settling in one place. It was an enormous risk to make an attempt at a normal life. She took it though, and set up every possible precaution." Toff adjusted his tunic proudly. "*I* was one of those precautions. She taught me the signs—everything I needed to know. In a city the size of Aalta, it was necessary to have more than one nose to the ground, because those stalkers are slippery buggers.

"It was these signs that I caught wind of in Tallooj. I heard talk in the taverns, the inns, on the street—the butcher's youngest gone missing, the barmaid whining about lack of sleep due to nightmares, folk complaining about the cold snatches down by the storehouses. All these conversations might not seem noteworthy to the ordinary ear, especially not on their own, but I've had my sniffer on these marks for years. It's the reason I decided to follow your father that night." Toff's voice cracked, and he took another swig of water. "You sure you haven't got some rum around here, sir?"

Dain crossed his arms firmly over his chest, but he couldn't resist a small smile. "I'll wager Trait has a crate load of it waiting for you once you're back in his care."

"Right, well, best get this story over with fast then. My head feels like a battered coconut." The old man massaged his temples. "As you know, your father was a closed book. He kept to himself, sharing little with others. For the first while, he had me fooled. I figured him for a businessman through and through; he seemed to have little else in his head besides figures and contracts." Toff tapped the side of his nose. "But mark my words, Captain, I eventually know another sniffer when I see one."

"You're saying my father was like you, Toff?"

"Well, in a manner of speaking, yes. Oh, he never lived the life I did, but he had his nose to the ground at every port we dropped in. I saw it plain as day when we returned home to Aalta for the first time. You were still a young one, but the minute we landed on that shore, he changed. Every sense was on high alert. His eyes were peeled, his ears open and his nose out. He was always watching, constantly searching. I came to the conclusion that while your mother may have kept your father in the dark for most of their married life, she must have told him the truth before she died. My guess is that she risked the truth to protect you."

Dain raised an eyebrow. "My father was sniffing out

stalkers—to protect me?"

"That's exactly it. Like your mother, you were born with magic—"

Dain interrupted Toff. "Sorry Toff, but you must be confused—"

Toff interrupted him right back. "Let me finish, Captain. I believe your mother started your father on the path to protect you. I know it, deep in my bones. Ever wonder why your dad left Aalta for a life at sea? The man hated sailing, we all knew that. But he sailed for you." Toff waved his crooked pointer toward the ceiling. Dain wanted to interrupt again, wanted to object to the idea of himself being somehow magical, but all he could think about was the miniature portrait in this father's belongings. He remained silent as the old man continued. "I'd wager my last coin he couldn't keep you hid well enough from the stalkers in Aalta, so he sailed away, establishing a life on the move to keep you alive. Unbeknownst to you, yours became a life on the run, much like your mother's before you."

Dain let Toff's words slowly sink in. His childhood on *The Maiden*, Ileana's words, and some things he'd read in the journal seemed to come into sharper focus. He still wasn't able to bring himself to visit the possibility that he might possess some kind of magic, let alone that he was being hunted for it, but if his father thought it was true, then it explained a lot, including why the old captain had refused him leave at Port Tallooj. Still, it was all so—

Mo's dubious voice cut through Dain's thoughts. "Toff, how is it ye know this all so *deep in yer bones?*"

Toff looked uncomfortable. "Uhhh—well, that's difficult to explain, sir. Perhaps we ought to chat about the events in Tallooj now?"

"No." Dain gave the old man a firm glance. "I think it's a good question. I would also like to hear why you feel so certain about all these theories."

The old man swallowed visibly. "It's really just gut feeling, sir. I knew your mother well—her motives, her tactics."

"That doesn't exactly answer the question, sailor."

"I suppose not." The old man rubbed at his ribs in agitation, and then looked Dain straight in the eye. "You might as well know. I failed her, boy—er—Captain. I failed your mother. My sniffer was too slow. I was—I was too late."

"What are you talking about, Toff?"

His face went pale. "You deserve to know it now, I suppose—your mother didn't die of an illness or disease. She died because the stalkers got to her before I could. She saved you, though. She drew them away, confused them, and led them on a wild goose chase far outside the city limits of Aalta. In the end, she rattled them so much they had no idea what was up and what was down."

Dain heard admiration and sorrow mingle together in the

old man's wistful words.

"So damn smart, that girl . . ." Toff rubbed his eyes hard on his sleeves before he went on. "She'd left a difficult trail to follow. It took me nearly half a day to find her, and by the time I arrived, it was too late." The old man sniffed loudly as he lowered his gaze to the floor. "I alluded to it before, but when a stalker captures an adept, they typically drain them. I don't know how they do it, but they steal every last drop of magic from their victim's body. And according to Alis, those born with magic cannot survive long without its presence. Apparently, it's like any other essential organ—once removed, the adept dies."

Dain recalled Ileana's ominous statement about magic being stolen from the four kingdoms, and now, for the first time, he fully understood what she'd meant. It was far more horrible than he could've imagined.

Toff shifted in his chair, eyes still on the floor. "The stalkers were long gone by the time I reached her, so I brought her home to die with her family. Alis passed a couple weeks later." Old Toff finally looked up again. "Your mother's last request of me was that I do everything in my power to protect you, Captain. Maybe now you can understand why I drew the conclusion that she may have asked the same of your father."

Dain's throat was thick. "That's why you signed onto *The Maiden*? To follow me, to protect me for her sake?"

"Yes—it was easy to secure a position on board at the beginning, even with my lack of experience, because your father was having trouble collecting a real crew. The haunted tales from Aalta's harbor had all those stupid, superstitious sailors quivering in their boots."

Dain swallowed. If only Toff knew that the haunted tales had a truth behind them. The old man wouldn't be calling anyone stupid after that. Ileana must have been the "ghost," wandering the decks of *The Maiden* on those long-ago nights in Aalta.

Toff continued. "However, after Mr. Crouse signed up, everyone else followed." He looked up at Mo with a fuzzy, arched brow. "Seems people will follow you anywhere, Mr. Crouse."

Mo shrugged. The skepticism on his face had faded a little, and Dain noted a slight smile at the corner of his lips.

The old man rubbed at his eyes again before he looked directly at Dain. "Your mother—Alis was special. I never had children of my own, and she was the closest I ever came to having a daughter. I promise you, I will honor her wishes until I breathe no more."

Dain tried to find a way to reply to Toff's last statement, but Mo spoke up first. Though the first mate's expression had become less doubtful, his voice still betrayed his skepticism. "So, in Tallooj, the late captain was seeking out these . . . stalker demons then?"

Toff turned to Mo and adjusted his spectacles, his throat sounding even rougher than usual. "Well, yes and no. I'm certain he was on the lookout for them, but I believe he was actually searching for something else." Grim-faced, the old sailor leaned forward on the table. "You know as well as I, Mr. Crouse, that our dearly departed captain was always looking for something. Like you, I never really questioned it. I figured I had him pegged. Whatever he wanted didn't matter much to my mission anyway, and it could have been any manner of things. That night in Tallooj though, he was different, on higher alert. At first, I thought it was just because of the tell-tale stalker signs, but then he decided to go out.

"Knowing what I did, I couldn't let him wander off into the night alone, so I followed. Once he was in the street, he pulled out a compass. I'd no clue why he needed it to navigate Tallooj—the port isn't that big—but he referred to the instrument constantly. Then it happened. The air grew unnaturally cold. I knew what was coming, and so did the captain. I watched him pocket the compass and turn to escape up the street, but before he got anywhere near my hiding place, a flash of crimson crossed his path. They snatched him faster than I could blink, dragging him down the street and into that grain store. And as you then know, I shot back to the inn for help. The rest of my tale, I'd imagine, is the same as the others."

A moment of silence followed.

Several questions popped into Dain's mind, especially about the curious compass, but he only asked one out loud. "What exactly was my father looking for in Tallooj?"

The voice that answered behind him was small, almost inaudible. "He was looking for me."

Chapter 10

Dain twisted in his chair to see Sable standing in the doorway between the dining room and his office. She held a large wooden tray in her hands. Dain's fists clenched at the intrusion. He tried to reason with himself, because deep down, he didn't want a repeat of their quarrels from yesterday or this morning. It was difficult, but he kept the tone of his voice professional and fitting to his station. "How long have you been eavesdropping? And why didn't you knock on the office door before you entered my chambers?"

Sable didn't answer. She just gave him a side-eyed glance as she walked around to the end of the table, and sat herself opposite.

Her silent actions inflamed Dain. His anger blinded him yet again—this girl was an insufferable sneak. All will to control his temper was lost, and Dain threw an arm forcefully through the air. *"Be our guest."*

Sable nodded as though his invitation had been polite, which only incensed Dain's anger.

Mo and Toff said nothing. They simply watched Sable with expressions of interest and expectation. Their calm demeanors convicted Dain. Taking a few steadying breaths, Dain tried to reason away his anger. The girl wouldn't have revealed herself eavesdropping if she didn't have reason. Most people don't want to be caught red-handed in such an act. Crossing his arms over his chest, he leaned back in his chair and waited expectantly.

The girl pursed her lips, but remained silent as she lifted her arms to set the serving tray on her end of the table. Then she raised her hands above it, and proceeded to make several delicate signing motions over the top of the empty platter. The air around her hands seemed to warp in barely visible waves.

Dain didn't know how it happened, but one moment, the table was scattered with food and dishes, and the next, everything was piled on top of Sable's tray. It was a blink, a flash. It was—magic.

Mo stood up and backed away.

Like Dain, Toff remained seated, and the old man adjusted his spectacles again. "I should've known. The captain and the stalkers were searching for the same thing. That's why they snatched him—they wanted to find *you*."

Sable didn't look up. "It's true, but, they were not only

searching for me. They were also hunting for my brother, Tars."

Dain now understood the girl's need to return to the island port. She hadn't left something behind in Tallooj—she had left *someone*.

Everyone was quiet for a moment before Sable resumed talking, her voice quavering as she spoke. "I'm not sure how Captain Alloway found us, or how he even knew who we were, but he tracked us down on his first afternoon in Tallooj. He promised to help us get out. He told us there was a safe haven for people—people like us."

Dain interrupted brusquely. "Did you just say a safe haven?"

The girl nodded.

As he leaned over the table, an earnest edge invaded Dain's tone. "Is it real? Where is it?"

The other two sailors turned to stare at him with curiosity as Sable responded. "He didn't tell us where it was; he only said he could take us there. He said the stalkers couldn't reach it, neither by night or day. He told us it could become our—our home."

Dain leaned back in disappointment. His father's behavior was mystifying, and it made him wonder if Ileana had learned of this refuge from Captain Alloway himself. Maybe she'd overheard something? Perhaps the captain had made some secret confessions at the prow while she listened, or perhaps she was just better at picking locks than Dain. The possibilities were endless; either way, this new revelation made it much more likely that the safe haven did exist. When he looked up again, Sable's face had paled. Even the slate of freckles across her nose appeared dimmed.

She swallowed visibly. "Tars, he didn't believe the captain. Trust is not something we adept come by easily. My brother refused his help." She hung her head with a sigh. "He is good at hiding, my brother, better than I am. After Captain Alloway left us, Tars stashed me away for the night. Stalkers tend to do most of their hunting at night, and it was safer for us to hide separately; it splits the trail. Anyway, I didn't listen. I snuck away. I knew the risk, but I needed to find Captain Alloway again—I was tired of running." Her voice wavered. "He promised us safety. He told us we'd have a home, and I believed him. When I found him at Tablet's Inn, I begged him to help me find my brother, to help convince Tars to join us."

Tears now tumbled from her large, hazel eyes, and Dain found himself following the droplets over her cheeks. He watched each one soak, with silent grief, into the fabric of her blouse.

The girl wiped at the small rivers. "Before the captain left, he pulled out a bottle of Harborage, and rubbed the cream into my hair. I hadn't seen that kind of potion in years—he told me that his wife had made it long ago. She must have been an alchemist." When she noticed that everyone at the table looked confused, she clarified. "The potion confuses stalkers—it averts their gaze, for a time. Only an alchemist can create it." Then she shrugged, as though further explanation was unnecessary. "After he finished up with the potion, he introduced me to Mr. Crouse as the new cabin boy, and left me in the first mate's care while he set out to search for Tars."

Dain was dumbstruck. He knew the question would sound strange, but he asked anyway. "What did the bottle look like? The bottle that the potion was in."

"It was blue, with a cork stopper. The stuff smells rotten, but it did help keep me safer that night." The girl's eyes shifted earnestly to Dain's own. Her chest heaved. "You need to know, sir—you need to know that it was my fault your father went out that night. I was desperate." She covered her face with both hands, and it was hard to make out her next words. "Your father is dead, and so much of your crew. I don't even know if Tars is still alive, and it's all my fault. All of it—"

Toff cut in with a coaxing voice as he reached over to pat Sable's shoulder. "It's not your fault, girl. Captain Alloway made his own choices that night. He obviously wanted to help you, and your brother. He knew the risks to himself and his crew."

Listening to Sable assume responsibility for his father's

death, and watching her tears continue to fall, softened Dain. Like Toff, he found himself drawn to consoling her. "I think my father used that potion on me, several times. Although, he lied and told me it was hair conditioner. He said it would make me presentable before we went on leave. You are right—it smells like sewage."

Sable lowered her wet hands to look at him, but she didn't smile.

Dain surprised himself further as he continued. "Old Toff's correct. My father did make his own choices that night, and so did your brother. You are responsible for neither." Then he raised one eyebrow. "However, you are responsible for eavesdropping on a conversation you were not invited into."

Sable sat up straighter, and wiped her face on her sleeve. "Yes, Captain, it's true. I was eavesdropping, but not maliciously, nor with any ill intent. I was sent to clear your dishes, and I arrived early. I forgot to knock, and I noticed you were still engaged. I had planned to leave directly . . ." She averted her eyes. "Then—then you mentioned the stalkers. You talked about talents, and I hoped—" Throwing her hands in the air, she shook her head with a sigh. "I don't know what I hoped. Tars says I often act before I think."

Dain stared at her. The girl was different than she'd been in the days prior—her spunk remained, but her demeanor was changed. He supposed her anger had been a mask of sorts, worn to hide the fearful suffering beneath. Or it had been a release for the suffering. Either way, Dain realized he could relate, because he'd been doing the same thing himself. He was reminded of Mo's parting words the morning after the Tallooj attack. *There's no coffin in yer heart. Those feelings inside will never perish, only stay hid from sight until they ruin ye, or find themselves a nasty way out.* Mo had been right. He was always right.

The first mate hadn't moved away from the wall, nor spoken a word since Sable's tray performance. He now inched forward, looking down at Sable warily. "What ye just did there, lass—what was it exactly? Can ye do it again?"

Toff slapped a hand on his knee, cackling. "Aha! I told you, Mr. Crouse. I knew it wouldn't be long before you were a believer."

Mo raised a large hand at Toff. "Hush, sailor. I've no need of your jabbering, but what I do need is explaining and proof."

By the way she smiled, Dain could tell Sable liked Mo. The first mate even appeared to soothe her nerves, because her voice grew steadier as she explained. "Of course, Mr. Crouse, I'd be happy to tell you what I understand, but the only knowledge I have is what has been passed down through my parents to Tars." Sable waited for Mo to give a nod of acknowledgment before she continued. "I was told my magic is a form of conjuring. I can move things from one space to another, but it's limited. I need to have seen where the object is and where it is going in order to shift it." Sable glanced briefly at Dain. "It comes rather intuitively once you know what your talent is, but it requires strength to do it, almost like the magic is a real, physical part of me. Tars mentioned that in the past, most talents, especially things like alchemy, required extensive training. As you may have figured out, such training no longer exists." With that, the girl lifted her arms above the tray again. It looked like she was writing in space with her fingers. This time, the air around the platter warped, and then everything, platter included, simply vanished.

Mo stepped back, tilting his head. He didn't look afraid this time, only perplexed. The man was a marvel of steadfastness.

"I have moved it all to the galley," Sable explained. "Don't panic though, I know the room is empty. No one will have seen the tray appear, because all the clean-up has been left to me tonight. There are a few perks to being on the bottom rung of the crew."

Toff cleared his throat loudly, and then winced as he shifted in his seat. "Well, Captain, I hate to break up the party, and the tricks, but I think it's time to sniff out some of that rum and hit the hammock. I'm not fully recovered yet, and tomorrow we reach Eandor Vid."

The old man's words seemed to draw the first mate back

to reality. He turned quick on his toes for such a large man. "Aye, Captain, I'm in need of yer orders for tomorrow. Most of the crew will be loath to leave *The Maiden* at present, and after tonight, we want to use more caution in Eandor Vid. How would ye like to proceed?"

Dain ran both hands over the top of his head. "Eandor Vid will be a provision stop exclusively. There is no need for more than a small party to head into port." He turned to Toff. "Sailor, do you think you'll be fit enough to accompany me tomorrow?"

"Aye, Captain." Toff pulled his spectacles off, wiping them on his tunic. "After a good night's rest, mind you."

"Are ye sure that's wise?" Mo's low tone betrayed concern. "Wouldn't it be safer if I were to go ashore in yer stead, or at least accompany ye?"

"One of us must stay behind. *The Maiden* can't be without a captain right now. Our crew needs that stability. And I'll give my father one thing—he made sure I was trained in all things trade. The loose ends and unavoidable business concerns have been left unattended for too long. I'll be needed in Eandor Vid in person." Dain pointed at Old Toff. "He knows exactly what to watch for, and I'll take Casper and Dev to port with us as well. Casp is the best swordsman we have, and you can trust Dev to secure the provisions. We'll hire a few port hands to assist in loading the boats before we row back. I'll make sure our party departs before sunset to avoid"—Dain had a hard time voicing the reality of them, but he pushed on—"the stalkers." He paused again, trying to decide how to word his next phrase. "My parents may have believed I possess magic and need protecting, but I've never seen hide nor hair of it in myself. I'm not convinced." Admittedly, he didn't want to be convinced. Actually he just wanted to carry on as a "normal" person. Being an adept, as they were apparently called, didn't figure into his long-term life goals, and despite everything, he was still hanging onto those plans. Obviously they'd have to wait a while longer than he'd hoped, but he couldn't give them up just yet.

Mo didn't argue further. The ever-obedient sailor simply tipped his chin in consent.

"One last order, for obvious reasons." Dain glanced at each of them individually. "All talk of magic remains between the four of us, unless and until I say otherwise."

Everyone nodded as though it were a given. Then Toff stood, raised his toque chivalrously toward Sable, and limped for the door.

Mo followed him, but turned in the jamb. His enormous form filled the frame. "Captain, I forgot to tell ye. Before we take to port tomorrow, the crew would like to hold a vigil at dawn for those lost in Tallooj. They are hoping ye'll join us."

"Of course. I'll be there."

After the sailors left, Dain glanced across the room at Sable. Her face was now dry, and she held her chin high, meeting his gaze. He looked away quickly, massaging the back of his neck. His hair had come completely loose from its leather bonds again, and the tangles caught his fingers. "Perhaps a truce is in order?"

Sable laughed, the sound laced with only a hint of mockery. "Indeed, Captain?"

Disengaging his fingers, Dain cleared his throat and turned to look at her seriously. "After everything I've learned this evening, a new ally is far more appealing to me than another enemy."

Sable's shoulders relaxed, and her chin lowered to a more natural level. "I agree, sir. Shall we start over then? Wipe the slate clean?"

"As clean as you cleared the table tonight."

Sable laughed again, and this time all trace of mockery was gone. "Yes, that will do."

Chapter 11

The sun's piercing gaze slowly peeked over the horizon. The sea reflected the blaze in a shimmering path of light that trailed off just before it reached *The Maiden*. Perched on the bowsprit, Dain squinted at the dazzling display. His body swayed naturally in time with the ship as it rose and fell on the waves. He'd arrived an hour before dawn, and he knew that the silent wooden princess had listened carefully while he shared the details of the past few days. However, their hour of privacy now faded as the crew started to gather quietly up on deck. Dain climbed down from his roost, and headed for the railing behind the foremast.

Mo strode across the deck toward him. The man took the steps up to the prow two at a time to stand by Dain in stoic silence.

The majority of the crew gathered in a semi-circle around the mainmast. The able-bodied supported the injured, and

Dain could see that every face was filled with its own particular sorrow.

Dev entered, flute in hand. He was followed by Trait, and then Sable.

Dain was surprised to see the girl in the center of them all. Trait gently clasped Sable by the waist, and effortlessly lifted her up to stand high on the crate beside the mainmast.

A single, solemn note from the flute peeled through the morning air. The wind buffeted the sails, and Dain's spine prickled. It was Sable's voice that rang out next—a pure, steady soprano. Trait's baritone followed close behind, mingling low with Sable's melody.

The two singers seamlessly interwove as Dev accompanied them through the mournful ballad, "Orthane's Call."

Of coin and luck that ever were had
I joined with ye in company
If wrong I done for lack of thought
I take the blame on only me
Remembrance be it all I ask
So fill yer cup and raise the flask
As Orthane calls her bonny home
Goodbye, goodbye, return we loam

Of my companions there stood by
Now joined in sorrow's fray

Of all the loves I ever made sigh
They may resound in longing wail
Though ye may live as I do pass
Raise again the parting glass
Find me far in yonder home
Goodbye, goodbye, return we loam

As life serves out mortality
Seek the key and shed yer shells
Rise, new fearless frames to be
Orthane calls with welcome song
Do not deny, do not prolong
Yer might and glory's coming home
Goodbye, goodbye, return we loam
Goodbye, goodbye, return we loam

Dev lowered his flute, Trait's voice lulled off, and Sable sang out the final stanza one last time, unaccompanied. Not a dry eye remained on *The Maiden* as she concluded. Dain even wiped tears from his own eyes—perhaps mourning all this loss would not be as debilitating as he'd first thought. An enormous sense of peace had accompanied his silent weeping.

While Trait led them into "Cords of Life," Mo rested a giant arm across Dain's shoulders, speaking quietly. "Dying may be the way of all things flesh, but living is too. Never let death shroud life with fear. Live beyond it, lad. Only then can the memory of those ye've loved and lost be rightly honored."

* * *

Eandor Vid crawled from the bay all the way up the side of Vid Mountain. Row upon row of streets, stairs, lifts, manors, houses, and huts climbed toward the rough stone peak. Near the top, carved directly from the mountain face itself, was a palace of imposing proportions. Its rock spires shot like raised swords into the salmon skies. This unquestionably intimidating city was the home of Ernham's monarchy. Yet, the capital made up for its unwelcoming facade by functioning as the largest trading center in all the four kingdoms. It was ideally situated at the heart of every major trade route—anything and everything you might desire could be found in Eandor Vid.

The Maiden had taken port there countless times these past eight years. And it was here that Dain's father had, more oft than not, allowed him leave. Dain now wondered if it had been something to do with the city's sheer size. Was it easier to hide, easier to lose someone in perhaps? Looking out toward the sprawling metropolis once again, Dain felt more at ease knowing that, for whatever reason, his father had felt the most comfortable in Vid. Fastening the leather money belt over his shoulder and around his waist, Dain listened while Mo finished debriefing Dev on the provisions.

"Edvine's Loft is the foremost granary in Vid. Find Ed, and tell him Morgan Crouse sent ye. He'll be sure to give ye nothing but the best."

Dev acknowledged Mo with a formal nod before making

for the rope ladder. Casper and Toff already awaited them in the rowboats.

Dain couldn't help grinning at the first mate before he followed. "It may be under terrible circumstances, and only a day trip, but it's been a long while since I've had leave. I look forward to standing on dry ground again."

"Aye, Captain, ye be deserving of it, but mind ye stay alert."

Tipping his brow, Dain gave a small wave before he headed for the ladder. Just as he reached the edge, a gentle tug on his tunic urged him to turn.

Sable stood behind him, extending a small, blue, stoppered bottle in her right palm. A smirk played across her lips. "Hair conditioner. Just in case you need to . . . look presentable, sir."

He was surprised to see it—Dain had assumed the potion lost in the Tallooj attack. Smiling, he accepted the bottle. "Appreciated, Sable." Her eyes widened slightly, and Dain realized it was the first time he'd called her by her name. The girl quickly looked down. After a moment, she held up her hand in a stopping motion and began rummaging purposefully in her low apron pockets. Dain watched her pendant fall forward out of the top of her frock as she searched. He was still curious about the symbol, but he hadn't revisited his mother's journal since yesterday. Now his curiosity would have to wait until tomorrow.

The girl finally stood upright, and held out a small packet wrapped in waxed parchment. "This is for Toff—an oat cake baked with powdered willow bark. Tell him it'll ease his pains far better than any rum, and with no *unnecessary* side effects. Half now, and half mid-day."

Dain raised a single eyebrow. "Hidden talents? Well, our party thanks you for this. You've spared us suffering his complaints all day."

Sable dipped her chin with a smile. "Happy to oblige, sir." The girl turned to go, but then briefly looked back. "Captain—"

Dain looked up as he pocketed the items.

"Be careful."

* * *

Finding an opening to moor the rowboats proved harder than expected. Eandor Vid was always bustling, but today was particularly busy. They endured a long line up at the port registrars before being permitted up the pier. When they finally made it past, Dev set out with orders to meet back at the docks prior to sunset. Toff and Casper were assigned to guard and assist their captain. Dain could tell Toff's nose was already in the air.

As they walked, the ground undulated beneath Dain's feet. He knew it wasn't actually moving, but after so many months at sea, the sensation would persist for a while. The movement was further amplified by the cramped streets lined with rows of colorful tents. Vendors from all four kingdoms haggled, conversed, bought, and sold. Spice, smoke, sweat, and perfume filled the air. Despite all that had happened lately, Dain smiled to himself. It was good to be back in civilization again, if only for a day.

Casper swaggered ahead, his sword swaying on his hip. The sailor was devilishly handsome, and Dain could tell he knew it. Multiple heads swung in Casper's direction as they passed, all of them taking in the man's thick onyx hair, tall muscular build, and dashing smile. And the sailor smiled a lot, his white teeth brilliant against the deep bronze of his skin as he flirted openly with both women and men alike. While Dain appreciated having the sailor's skill at hand, the man wasn't the most inconspicuous of companions.

Toff seemed to appear and disappear, sometimes ahead of them, sometimes behind. His eyes were always flitting about, ears perked like a canine. Dain guessed, though he fervently hoped he was wrong, that the old man may have already successfully picked a dozen pockets by now. And doubtless he had also listened in, unobserved, on countless conversations. The old sailor would be a wealth of gossip and tidbits by the time they reached the guild. How a man his age moved with such quick secrecy was magic in and of itself. Toff certainly lived up to his old nickname. The Ghost of Aalta, indeed. After watching him for over an hour, Dain decided that stealth just might be a skill he'd like to spend some time acquiring himself. He'd need to ask Toff for some lessons.

Casper fell back. "The guild's another half-hour of walking yet, Captain, and it's nigh on noon. We may be wanting to grab some chow before we head on out of the market streets. Ciebald's Inn serves a decent fare." Casper pointed to the right of the street ahead.

After the previous night's meal, Dain was tempted to tease Casper about his taste in food, but he refrained, chuckling instead as he indicated for the sailor to lead the way.

Toff appeared again suddenly, following along nonchalantly.

The tavern was nearly as busy as the streets, but Casper somehow managed to sweet-talk the innkeeper and obtain a table at the back of the large common room. It was up against the wall near the rear door, well suited for keeping an eye on everything, and exiting fast if necessary.

Toff snorted in approval as Casper dramatically offered each of them a chair.

It was some time before the young serving girl made her rounds, but when she finally arrived, Dain could have sworn she went red to her toes at Casper's flashy grin. Her face flushed a deeper shade yet as he leaned out toward her. "Tell me, beautiful, is there any chance ye can rustle up our grub quickly? We've a great deal to accomplish today." He followed up the question with a wink that seemed full of secret promises. The girl's breath hitched, and she bobbed her head with a small giggle. Dain watched in awe as the handsome sailor took further advantage by brushing his fingers against hers for a brief moment as he ordered the food. As a result, the meal came faster than anyone else's, which led to numerous sidelong glances from the other patrons. Dain had to admit that while Casper was not the most low-profile companion, there were perks to having him around.

As Dain consumed the simple fare of mutton chops, potatoes, and rye, he gave thanks for the fact that it wasn't fish. Time seemed to ebb away while they ate, and Dain thought that perhaps getting out of the city before dark was going to prove more difficult than he'd planned. As if to validate his last thought, someone suddenly called out his name from across the common room.

"Dain Alloway?"

Dain looked up to spy a well-dressed figure weaving his way toward them through the throng. It took him a few moments to recognize the man, but when he did, he stood. "Captain Thornwalsh?"

The older gentleman smiled broadly when he reached Dain's side. "It's been years, lad. My, my, how you've grown. I barely recognized you, my boy."

Dain grinned back. "Indeed, Captain, it has been a very long time." He motioned for the newcomer to sit as Casper swiped an empty chair close by. "Please join us. I'd like to introduce you to part of my crew." Dain indicated his companions. "This is Casper LeVince and Toff Parley."

Thornwalsh looked confused, but he shook hands with each man amiably enough before turning back to Dain. "Captain Alloway here with you, son?"

Toff was eating like it was his first meal in months. After Casper and Dev's cooking, Dain couldn't blame him, but he was surprised when the old man mumbled fast through a mouthful of potatoes, "Captain Alloway recently passed, sir."

Thornwalsh looked at Toff in shock, then quickly back to Dain. Sincere sorrow etched his brow. "I'm so very sorry, my boy."

Casper remained unusually silent, but Toff cut in fast after taking a loud gulp of water. He pointed a crooked finger firmly at Dain. "*Captain*, sir. Not boy. The new Captain Alloway."

The man gave Toff another surprised glance, and then offered Dain an awkward nod. "Right. My apologies."

To soften Old Toff's response, Dain smiled warmly at Thornwalsh. The man was a long-time family acquaintance, and he'd been a faithful employee of the Alloway Trading Company for years. At present, Thornwalsh captained the

Dorie Main. It was a newly acquired galleon in the company fleet. The man wouldn't have heard of the death of his father yet, since Dain had planned to send out missives once he'd reached Eandor's Vid's trade guild this afternoon. He knew that as a result of his father's death, Thornwalsh was now an employee. Considering Dain's youth, the arrangement might be difficult for Thornwalsh to accept. He decided to play it carefully, honeying his words and adding a solemn aristocratic air. "Thank you for your condolences, sir. My father's death was a considerable loss to all of us." Then he lowered his head and paused for a respectable moment of silence.

Captain Thornwalsh nodded in sympathy as he patted Dain's arm. "Truly, he will be missed."

It wasn't all an act—Dain did appreciate the man's condolences. Dougal Thornwalsh was a decent fellow, a lower-rung member of the Zaal gentry, but a man who possessed a lifetime of trade experience. A sudden inspiration struck Dain. "It is, however, an auspicious and pleasant surprise to see you, Captain. It brings me cheer. In fact, I am in need of a man like you. Can I tempt you with a promotional offer?"

The older captain sat up straighter, his eyes squinted. "A promotion—Captain?" His voice was tight around Dain's title.

"Indeed, sir. I want to solicit your services. With my father's passing, I am in need of a company master. A lead man, with experience, to manage the Alloway trading affairs on the ground from Aalta. You've been with us a long time, Captain, and I know you've sailed most of it. I thought you might appreciate the salary raise, and the opportunity to settle at home."

Thornwalsh's face relaxed, breaking into a wide grin as he extended his hand to Dain. "Well, I—my wife and I have been recently blessed with our first grandchild. Being on the ground again, being at home, would please my family infinitely. Thank you. I gladly accept the position, sir."

Dain shook the man's hand firmly. Thornwalsh had spent most of his life sailing away from Aalta, and Dain had hoped the offer would appeal. He also felt relieved that the company would be in safe hands. It was the first thing that had gone right in days.

Standing, Dain clapped the older man on the shoulder in Morgan Crouse fashion. "Wonderful, Captain. *The Maiden* sails for Aalta at dawn. Consider following when your ship is prepared. We can sort out all the details together once you arrive. At that point, I'd also be gratified to hear your suggestions for a new captain to pilot the *Dorie Main* once you're promoted. My apologies though, I have much else to attend to today, and I need to be about my business. I can look forward to seeing you soon?"

Dougal Thornwalsh stood, now smiling even wider. "Of course, sir. I am honored by the offer and by your confidence.

Farewell for now."

Dain paid the tab and then strode purposefully out of the tavern. Toff and Casper followed fast on his heel.

Once they were in the street, Casper leaned in from behind, whispering like a playful conspirator. "Ye played that fellow near as well as I played the serving wench. Impressive, Captain."

Dain laughed out loud, then turned to wink theatrically at the man. "And I did it all without your debonaire smile."

Chapter 12

The day in Eandor Vid passed quickly, but Dain did manage all his affairs, including an additional post to Lydia with the news of his father's passing and their impending arrival. His former nurse had been head-housekeeper at Alloway Manor for the past three years now, a promotion she took very seriously. Dain knew she'd have everything in order when they arrived. He'd only been back to Aalta a handful of times over the years, and, despite the circumstances, it would be very good to see her again.

Sadly, Dain had been unable to procure a ship's healer, and time was running too short to keep looking. Though Toff had sniffed out nothing concerning stalkers, Dain still intended to be back at the ship before sundown.

Grabbing some cold food from a street vendor, the three sailors ate as they walked. The lanes were starting to clear, and people were packing up their tents and goods to head home for the night.

As Dain swiped the crumbs of a greasy meat pie from his hands, he silently wished he had a couple more days in Vid, and not just to nose around more. Today had been a good change, and a welcome distraction. Leaving civilization again for more months at sea suddenly felt ominous. The urge to run resurfaced, but instead of giving in to the impulse, Dain distracted himself by watching Casper casually strike up a conversation with a young vendor. Observing the exchange, Dain envied Casper's ease with people. When he turned back to comment to Toff, he wasn't surprised to find the Ghost was gone. Where did the old man hide?

Taking a deep, steadying breath, Dain stopped walking. The instant he stood still, the air around him became heavy, almost like the moisture and heat were pressing him for something. This seemed to have become a more common sensation while he was outdoors lately. His forehead started to sweat, but the wind picked up in the same moment as well, and the breeze swirled soothingly. Dain shoved some of his long, blond strands from his face as he shifted his eyes toward the view. The road widened broadly up ahead. Enormous black walnut trees lined both sides, their limbs twisting artfully into the sky. The breeze seemed to give up on Dain, hurling itself instead at the trees. It was mesmerizing to watch the ochre leaves sway playfully, one by one, to the ground. And it was a long moment before he tore his eyes away to look at the port beyond. The harbor was still teeming with people and ships, and the coral skies above cast an ever-dimming glow.

Evening had arrived. It was time to get back.

Dain took only one step forward before a strong hand grasped his right shoulder.

"Seriously, Toff, you must stop—" Dain halted mid-sentence when he spun to see three large strangers hovering menacingly behind him. The central figure still had a firm grasp on his shoulder.

Casper was by his side in seconds, rapier drawn, his handsome face twisted into a threatening scowl. "I'll only warn ye once—leave yer hands off my captain."

The man holding Dain's shoulder shifted his pale, bulgy gaze to Casper. "Back off, pretty boy. I need a few words with your *captain*."

Casper did no such thing, advancing on the men.

Assessing the situation quickly, Dain decided the brawling odds were not in their favor. Toff remained at large, and these men looked like the kind who took their job seriously. He raised an arm to halt Casper's advance. Then he stepped back firmly to release his shoulder, swiping at the imaginary dust where the hand had been. Dain assumed his best aristocratic stance. "Have we met, sir?"

The bulgy-eyed man spit on the ground in front of him.

His voice had a high-pitched wheeze. "I heard that Captain Alloway was in town, but it appears only his brat is here." The man leaned forward into Dain's face, his breath putrid. "Your father stole something from me, boy. I want it back."

Still keeping Casper at bay with his arm, Dain leaned away and tried to imagine what, if anything, his father could have stolen from a man like this. The thug was middle-aged, balding. A round, tell-tale grog gut hung over his trousers, and though his clothing belied some form of income, he appeared far from wealthy. His two companions were slightly younger, looking even less prosperous than their leader. They leered at him with dim, lopsided expressions, and Dain guessed they were nothing but hired lackeys.

He allowed his father's voice to fall freely from his lips. Apparently, the tone did come in handy at times. "I would be careful whom you accuse of theft, sir. My father was a well-respected businessman within the Four Kingdom's Merchant Guild. He was an honorable member of the gentry of Aalta, son of the late Councilman Alloway of Zaal. I suggest you choose your next words wisely, or you may soon find yourself standing before the Aaltain court, indicted for public slander. Whose word do you suppose they'll take more seriously— yours or mine?"

His words seemed to fall on deaf ears, and the street was clearing out more quickly now. Perhaps this man had the kind of reputation that scattered crowds? Dain rolled his eyes internally. His father seemed to have left him a legacy of trouble everywhere he turned.

The accuser's face turned uglier. "You're a bit far from Aalta right now, boy. Vid has a different kind of justice system. I think I'm safe to accuse whatever I like, and I intend to get what I came for." He cracked his knuckles coldly, looking pleased with himself. The two cronies continued staring, faces stern and eyes blank.

The threat had been worth a try. Avoiding an altercation would have been the preferred route, but now it seemed inevitable. Lowering his arm to give Casper leave to move when necessary, Dain subtly fingered the hilt of his dagger as he screwed his expression into a distasteful sneer. "I may be far from Aalta, but do not underestimate my reach, sir. My father was incapable of theft, and what could you possibly own that anyone would consider valuable?"

This time, Dain's words had the desired effect. The man's anger made him fumble as he reached for the blade at his belt. Casper was between them all in seconds, but not a single blade clashed, because the gang leader gave an unexpected bark of surprise.

Dain's eyes darted to the man's face. A knife was now positioned firmly at the thug's throat. Toff stood behind him, one dagger at his neck and one pressed at his back against his kidney. The old sailor had simply appeared out of thin air.

Toff's raspy voice filled the air. "Tell your boys to stand down, leech. Or both knives find their mark before you have a chance to blink."

The other two men glanced back in shock. Their leader darted his pleading eyes between them. The lackeys barely wasted a moment before they turned and ran.

Toff laughed roughly. "Faithful sidekicks you have there, leech."

Gathering his wits, Dain sauntered forward. He tried to look even further down his nose as he lifted the man's chin with his own dagger. "Who are you?"

The brute glared defiantly, and Dain thought for a moment that the man might consider fighting back, but when Toff's dagger nudged him harder, he capitulated. "Oswart Dulge."

"*Sir.* Oswart Dulge, *sir,*" Toff prompted him with another nudge.

The man gritted his teeth. "Oswart Dulge, *sir.*"

"Well, Mr. Dulge, not only have you wrongly accused my dearly departed father of theft, you have also accosted me in public, and waylaid my journey. We may need to apprehend you." Dain was surprised by his own tenacity. "How does a trip to Aalta in my brig sound to you?"

The man's brows raised in concern. "Sir, my apologies for

how this played out. Honestly, I never meant you, or your companions, a lick of harm. I was only hoping to gain back what I'd lost. You see, I'm just a poor working fellow, and I lost one of my best wenches to your father. She made off with him months back. It was a terrible loss of income for me. I'm sure you can understand why I was so vexed?" Oswart's bulgy eyes were full of feigned innocence.

Dain paced in front of the man as though considering his pleas. Oswart Dulge had wenches? It wasn't hard to guess what kind of "hardworking fellow" this man truly was. Hiram Alloway would have never taken with a prostitute. Perhaps the girl had been like Sable, an adept? But then she would have been on the run. Maybe she got trapped—Ernhamian law did not permit slavery, but it did allow indentured servitude. This was a backward policy to Dain's Zaalish sensibilities, but it was a plausible theory in Vid. Hopefully he could end this altercation peaceably after all. "Mr. Dulge, you mentioned that your wench *made off* with my father?"

Oswart nodded, barely moving to keep Toff's dagger from digging in further. "That's right, sir. She snuck right off in secret with him."

"I would assume your establishment takes—precautions against members sneaking away, am I right?" He waited for Dulge to blink in agreement. "You are saying that she left secretly with my father, without your knowledge. If that were the case, then how could you know who she had run off with at all?"

"Well—I—"

Dain looked at the man pointedly. "Now, I'm certain my father never visited brothels, Mr. Dulge. And I warn, if you insinuate this again, I will retaliate." He heard Casper growl in agreement as Toff pulled the dagger tighter into the man's neck. Red droplets bloomed from the dirty skin.

"No sir, of course not, sir." Dulge spoke fast now. "He sent a card for me to meet him at Ciebald's tavern. You can ask around there. I'm sure the innkeeper'd remember the meeting—it was less than a year ago. Alloway told me that Anira needed to leave Vid; he said that it was for her own safety. He—"

Dain was right, and thankfully this thug had little spine, and even less of a mind. "Yes, Mr. Dulge?"

Dulge's bulgy eyes watered with his admission. "When I met with him, he offered to pay—"

Dain clucked his tongue. "He paid, Mr. Dulge? Let me guess, he paid the girl's indenture?"

The man had probably meant to make up some story about Hiram Alloway trying to buy the girl for himself, but once Dain guessed the indenture, Dulge seemed to know he was defeated. Dain latched onto his victory. "What you are telling me then is that the girl was freed? She was not actually *stolen* from you?"

Dulge said nothing.

"In fact, you have not been robbed at all. Quite the contrary, you actually turned a profit. My father was a thorough businessman, Mr. Dulge. He kept impeccable records. I'm certain the remitted indenture was legally documented, and notarized by the appropriate authorities. So I say again, in further detail now: you have delayed my ship for a crime that was never committed, physically accosted me in public, and insulted my family name over the loss of a prostitute you no longer have legal claim to. I am not sure I can leave these charges unmet." Dain clenched his fist hard around his dagger, waving it back and forth in the man's face.

The brute looked genuinely afraid now. *Good.*

Dain walked a few paces away. The sky had grown quite dim, and Dev would be waiting at the pier. He shifted his tone to a drawl, turning back to Dulge like a bored aristocrat. "However, my time is precious, and wasting more of it on you doesn't seem worth the effort." He waved his free hand flippantly. "Release him, sailor."

Toff slowly backed off as Dain continued. "You can go free, *this time*. And I *never* wish to see your face again." He emphasized this by launching his dagger, with perfect accuracy that surprised even him, into the toe of Oswart Dulge's right boot.

The man reeled forward as a high-pitched squeal of pain escaped his lungs. He grabbed frantically at the dagger, pulling it out and clutching his foot.

"Is that understood, Dulge?"

Standing as upright as he could manage, Oswart Dulge grimaced and nodded. Then he turned, dragging his right foot behind him as he escaped up the street.

Dain retrieved his blood-tipped dagger off the ground.

Breaking into a wide grin, Casper advanced to slap Dain and Toff simultaneously on the shoulders. "Well played, mates. Now, let's be off before he changes his nappy, and limps back here with more cronies." The sailor waved an arm toward the pier. "After ye, Captain."

Starting down the street alongside Toff, Dain let Casper take up the rear guard. He was pleased everything had ended in their favor, but a nagging suspicion remained. Perhaps he'd been too hasty in letting Oswart Dulge go . . .

Toff interrupted his thoughts. "You handled yourself well back there, Captain. It's too late to second guess your decisions. Let it go. It'll plague you otherwise."

Dain bowed his head respectfully at the old sailor. "Grateful Toff. Thank you, for everything back there. I owe you."

"It's my duty, Captain. You owe me nothing." The old man chuckled as he wiped his blades on a kerchief pulled from his pocket. Then he offered to take Dain's dagger to do the same. "I gotta tell you, Captain—you've got the same clever fierceness as your mother. She would have been proud of you back there."

Old Toff's words were singing straight to Dain's heart when he heard Casper cry out a warning from behind them. He barely caught a glimpse of the fast-advancing figures before everything went dark.

Chapter 13

Muffled whispers carried from somewhere around him. Trying to pry his eyes open through the searing pain, Dain only managed to crack the right one a sliver. The room tilted nauseatingly. Groaning, he struggled to prop himself up on one elbow. He hoped that a more upright position would stop the whirl.

The whispering ceased. Gentle hands touched his shoulders. "No, Captain, don't move. Lie down." The same hands prodded him back into a reclined position, readjusted the blankets, and then placed a warm cloth on his forehead. After a moment, the spinning ceased, the warmth easing the pain. When he tried to open his eyes again, he was barely able.

A blurry Sable stood beside the four-poster bed, stirring something into a teacup as she hummed soothingly. Her face cleared as she leaned closer. She positioned the cup at his lips, urging him to sip. Dain made a couple attempts to drink, but in the end, the effort made him swoon.

* * *

The porthole of his sleeping quarters bobbed with a night sky full of stars. Dain noted Sable sleeping awkwardly in a wooden chair by his bedside. He wondered how long she had been there. The slightest shift caused his head to pound furiously, and a wash of dizziness and nausea followed. Frustrated, he braced against the agony, trying to rise.

Sable must have heard his shuffling, because she was on her feet a moment after. She lit the hanging oil lantern above the bedside table and leaned over him. "Captain, you're awake. Don't rise—you'll never make it far, and we can't have you splitting your head open more. What do you need?"

Dain weakly lifted his arm to indicate the chamberpot in the corner.

Without batting an eye, Sable was up, carrying the pot to his bedside. "Now I can help you with this, or I can place it here. Do you think you can manage?"

Face hot, Dain waved his hand to indicate he would try alone. The girl looked skeptical, but she set it on the bed anyway and left the room.

It wasn't easy. He reeled through the pain, his foggy thoughts flitting from wondering what had happened to guessing who had undressed him.

After a reasonable time, Sable returned. She went about

the necessary cleanup without so much as a blink. Eventually, the girl resumed her place by his bedside with another cup of tea in hand. "Drink this, sir. You must have a monstrous headache. It will ease the pain, and speed the healing."

Dain shakily accepted the cup. It was cold, but he sipped the bitter liquid gingerly. After a few mouthfuls, he tried his voice, and it cracked with disuse. "What—happened? Was anyone else hurt?"

Taking the cup from his unsteady hands, Sable set it on the table beside the bed. "I think I'll leave the full story for Toff and Casper, but no one else was harmed. All you need to know is that they managed to save that messy blond head of yours."

Dain was going to insist she tell him the whole story, but the pain distracted him. Carefully reaching toward the top of his skull, he found it wrapped in a swath of bandages. The area was so tender he couldn't even bring himself to touch it. Somehow, he managed to chuckle hoarsely. "I wish they'd managed to keep it a little more intact."

"Let's just be grateful it's still on your shoulders." She placed her hands on her seated hips. "I thought I told you to be careful?"

Dain tried to adjust himself slightly. "I thought I was— how long have I been out?"

Standing, Sable helped to rearrange the pillows behind

him. "This is the third night—speaking of which, do you feel like you can eat?"

Three days—three whole days gone. He must be seriously injured indeed. He thought again about asking her to tell him everything, but when he looked up to see her inquiring expression, he realized that he had not fully registered her last question. "Pardon me?"

"Food. Do you think you can take some? You've not eaten in days, and I've gotten only the bare minimum of liquids into you."

Dain felt the effects of Sable's tea begin working through his system. The liquid seemed to ease his nerves as well as his pain. "Yes, I think I could manage."

Moving around to the end of the bed, the girl lifted a satchel and drew out some rye bread and dried fish. "It's the middle of the night. Nothing will be prepared in the galley, and this is not exactly captain's fare, but it'll have do at this hour."

The sight of the fish made Dain's stomach lurch instantly. "No fish. I hate fish. Just the bread is fine."

Sable returned the fish to the satchel with a shrug.

Even though the bread was soft, Dain found nibbling was all he could handle. The full force of chewing caused such an uproar in his skull that even Sable's pain reliever couldn't ease it.

The girl sat by his bedside, urging him to sip more cold

tea between nibbles.

Dain studied her out of the corner of his eye while he ate. She looked pale—dark, half-mooned rings wrapped heavily underneath her large hazel eyes, and the freckles bridging her nose looked faded too. When he could bear no more chewing, he asked, "Have you been here nursing me the whole time? Did you . . ." His eyes trailed down the covers to his toes.

Sable studied his expression, and then smirked. "Did I change your clothes? Is that what you were going ask, Captain?" Though he tried to maintain an impassive expression, Dain knew his face was still slightly flushed.

She laughed, playfully crossing her arms over her chest. "No, sir, I did not change your clothes. Mr. Crouse took care of that. I offered to help, but he insisted that you'd never forgive him. I can't imagine why."

He'd heard her laugh only a couple of times, but this time he noticed that the lilt of her giggle was lovely—contagious, even. The corners of his mouth turned up at the sound. Then he recalled their first meeting. "Well, I suppose if you had, we would have been even." He regretted the jest the minute it was out. What was he thinking, teasing such a thing? He must have hit his head really hard.

At first, it looked like she might not respond, but then she leaned toward him slowly. She smelled of herbs and rosewater. "To answer your first question, Captain, I *have* been here nursing you every day through your delirium." Then she smiled slyly. "And I've seen more than enough to make us even."

Dain felt his face get hot. How was it that he could hold his own with the likes of Thornwalsh and Dulge, but now, faced with this softer, teasing version of Sable, he fell to pieces? It was the same problem he'd had around the princess. It'd been much easier when he and Sable had been cantankerous with one another. No doubt Casper would have delivered the perfect comeback, something that would have made every bit of color return to Sable's pale cheeks, but all he could manage was a fumbling change of subject. "Are you sure you don't want to tell me what exactly happened in Vid?"

"No, I promised Toff I'd leave it to him. He said there was important information involved." She rolled her eyes as though she thought she would have been a worthy conduit for said information.

Dain decided not to argue the point further, but he still felt the awkward tension of her last statement hanging between them, so he grasped for another diverting question. "Are you a healer? That is—you seem to have some knowledge of herbs?"

Sable stood, swiped at her skirts, and began tidying what remained of his food. "No, I'm not. I only have a limited knowledge of herbs. I learned them from my brother—he's the healer." Her voice fumbled at the mention of Tars. "I do what

I can."

Relieved that the subject had changed, Dain thought of the other injured crew members. "Are you able to help the others as well? I ran out of time to find a healer in Vid. Can you help them?"

"Yes, Captain. I have done just that. Well, as much as Trait will let me. He seems set on being the designated nurse." The girl giggled. "Although, I think he just likes the unmonitored access to the rum. But for your peace of mind, the crew is recovering nicely."

With a grateful smile, Dain thanked her. "You mentioned your brother was a healer. Is that one of his talents? Or just a skill he's obtained?"

Sable resumed her seat by his bedside. "It is one of his talents. That, and alchemy. Although he has never been fully trained in either. My mother had the same talents as Tars; he learned what he could from her limited knowledge before she—"

Dain could see the distress in her face, but he couldn't stop himself from asking. "Will you tell me about your family?"

The girl dragged both hands over her face. She rubbed deeply at her tired eyes while she spoke. "My brother is ten years my senior. He basically raised me. We traveled constantly, never staying in one place too long. Tars is musical—he writes songs, and plays masterfully on the lute. We panhandled to survive, him playing while I sang. Sometimes on the street, sometimes at an inn for supper and a warm bed." The girl was scrubbing at her face so hard now that it was beginning to gain color again. "Our life wasn't all bad. We had each other, but in the past two years, the pressure increased. The signs were everywhere. It didn't matter where we went, because the stalkers followed. Eventually we headed to sea, hoping that being off the mainland might make it harder for them to track us. We were right; they never followed onto water. We figured there must be something to that, so we stayed aboard as long as our one-way ticket allowed, but we were not sailors. Eventually, the ship dumped us in Tallooj. That was three months ago."

"You survived in Tallooj for three months?" After all the accounts he'd heard of the stalkers so far, Dain was impressed.

"Tars is good at hiding, and the stalkers didn't sniff us out right away. We were safe for a time. Perhaps they had difficulty getting to the island . . ." The girl shrugged. "We tried to scrape together enough money to sail again, but Tallooj is a rough port. People there take little interest in music. We couldn't save a penny—in fact, we nearly starved."

He saw the memory of struggle pool in her eyes, and Dain wondered just how much she had suffered through the years. Maybe one day she'd be able to share it with him, but it felt too pressing to ask now.

"Tars practiced his healing talent sparingly. I don't know if you know yet, but our talents draw *their* eyes even more. The stalkers can sense us even when we don't use magic, but the lure becomes ten-fold when we do. However, we were starving in Tallooj, and it wasn't within us to resort to stealing, so my brother risked it to feed us. The sick are everywhere, no matter where you live, and the tables turned once word got around that a healer was in town. Folk were offering us food, and warm beds lay around every corner. Tars was careful—no one ever knew what was involved. He stuck to mostly herbal remedies, although the occasional concoction required a touch of magic to make it effective. Apparently, even that trickle was enough to draw *them* to the island. It wasn't long after that your ship arrived, and you know the rest."

"Your parents? What happened to them?" Dain felt bad for asking, but he was too curious.

"It happened when I was seven. It was ten years ago when they were both attacked . . ." Pulling out the pendant from around her neck, she gazed at it intently. "This is all I have left of them. I hardly remember their faces."

Dain watched the pendant sway back and forth from her fingers. "Sable?"

The girl's heavily lashed gaze moved wearily from the pendant to his face. He was surprised that there were no tears in her eyes—perhaps time did heal most things.

"In the top right drawer of my desk is a small key tied with a ribbon of green and gold. Would you fetch it for me?"

The girl obeyed, returning moments later with the key. He explained where the chest was hidden, and Sable dug down through the linens. She heaved out the smaller case, and set it heavily on the end of the bed. Then she looked at him questioningly.

"Open it. There's a book in there I'd like to show you."

Upon lifting the lid, the girl took a moment to admire the portrait of his mother, then delicately placed it aside with the other items until she reached the tome wrapped in plum velveteen. Climbing to the head of the bed, Sable gently sat crossed-legged beside him, where she unwrapped the book. In silence, she read the title scrawled across the cover. "This belonged to your mother?"

"Yes, it's a compilation of her studies on magic. Although I think it's only the beginning, from when she first began collecting and recording."

The girl's eyes went wide with wonder.

"There must be more, because it seems this was written when I was only four. She had four more years after that to continue her work, but it must be hidden away somewhere in Aalta. I'd do the honors of opening it for you, but . . ."

"Of course." The girl turned to the first page with a reverent flip.

Dain shifted carefully, signaling for her to look to the back of the volume. When she reached the replica of her pendant symbol, he asked if she was able to read the annotation underneath.

Sable nodded. "It says: The immortal Selteez wore the *Dernamn* in honor of Orthane. It symbolized the purity of the dove, the power of the three creators, and the unity of the four kingdoms."

Dain glanced at the symbol again: a bird above a line of three triangles, with four intertwining circles below. He could reconcile the meaning of the dove and the circles, but the three triangles in the center—*three* creators? As far as he knew, there was only one creator, the goddess Orthane. While Dain had read vague references to other possible deities in the more unrefined realms of Iandior, Orthane was the only one generally accepted in the four kingdoms, and her followers ranged from casual to devote. Dain continued to listen.

"Sent as guardians into the lands Orthane had created, the Selteez came to love those within. They integrated and married. It is from these guardians that magic was birthed into the races. The first born were nearly as powerful as the Selteez themselves, imbued with a portion of the divine. Yet, over time, the intensity of power decreased. Centuries of offspring continued to be born gifted. However, instead of an all-encompassing power, it was narrowed down. Each child came to possess one to three specific talents—on rare occasion, a child would be born with four, but never more. Those born with talents were called Selts. Over time, the gifts were categorized, studied, and recorded by Selt historians and scholars." Sable stopped reading and looked at Dain. "Is this true? The religious parts, I mean?"

Dain shrugged, regretting the movement immediately as pain shot through his skull. "I'm not sure. My parents never professed to be believers. That is—I was not raised in it, but the talents must have originated somewhere. If it wasn't divine, then perhaps the Selts were just an anomaly? A portion of the races that just happened to be born different? They may have simply wanted an explanation, and religion provided an answer. As you are aware, all of this is new to me, and I have only read a third of that journal, and not in its entirety. However, I thought you might appreciate a glance through it also. Religious or not, there are answers in there for us. It could be very useful."

Sable looked as though she might devour the book whole. She hugged the volume to her chest. "Thank you—thank you for sharing this with me."

Dain smiled, then yawned painfully. "How did you learn to read?"

Letting the book lie in her lap again, Sable ran her fingers over the Selteez symbol again. "My mother started my education, and Tars was faithful to continue it as best he could. I cannot read Zaalish though, nor the other pictorial language featured here, but I can read Ernhamian, and manage the common tongue fairly well." Sable started turning the pages of the tome back toward the beginning. Dain's eyes drooped.

Suddenly remembering her patient, the girl looked down at him with concern. "You should rest, Captain. Sleep is your best chance for a faster recovery. The concussion will make you feel tired either way, and you lost a lot of blood. Plus, now that you are cognizant, visitors will come knocking." She smiled. "You'll need your strength to receive them and hear their gallant tale of rescue."

Dain didn't argue, his lids heavy as he wondered again what had actually happened in Vid. Then his mind sleepily flitted from thoughts of Mo, to the wooden princess, to the prospect of being in Aalta soon. Lastly, they landed on the fuzzy fact that he had not dreamed in three days. He always dreamed—

Sleep came, and as though they'd been beckoned, the dreams swarmed to claim him.

* * *

Bloodstained skies hid behind densely knit clouds, lightning flashing from their depths at furious intervals.

The ensuing clamor was deafening.

Dain fought to maintain his balance while the storm

157

thrummed through his soul. His heart beat with the thunder, his veins raced with the rain, and his mind sailed on the winds. He and the tempest were one.

Chapter 14

The light of dawn peeked through the porthole. Instinctively stretching under the blankets, Dain winced as the movement caused the top of his head to throb voraciously, as though it hungered to consume him in pain. Squinting, he turned to see Sable sitting beside him on the bed. She was right where he'd left her the night before. Her knees were up, her nose still buried in his mother's book.

"Good morning."

The girl jerked, then smiled down at him. Her eyes were now ringed all the way around—she obviously hadn't slept at all. "Good morning, sir. How is your head?"

Dain grimaced. "Still very painfully attached."

Sable set the book aside, climbed off the bed, and left the room. When she returned with more of her cold tea concoction, Dain drank it down gratefully. The beverage helped him manage his morning routine, and once he was resettled, Sable brought out several oatcakes, an apple, and some fresh milk. He was curious how she'd procured the items, since she'd obviously not left his side all night. Perhaps she'd used her magic? Either way, his appetite had returned, and Dain tried not to get too frustrated about how his chewing motions seemed to tear apart his skull. The process was slow and painful.

Sable tidied while he nibbled, and as she worked, she talked. "It seems your mother's journal is broken down into three sections. The first is a summary of what she managed to collect about Selt and Selteez history, the second section is a catalog with minor descriptions of the commonly known talents, and the third delves more into her own abilities as an alchemist. She even includes recipes and instructions for some of her own potions and spells . . ."

The girl carried on for half the morning. And when she finished cleaning, she took her place again in the chair by his bedside. Her face was earnest while she related more about her discoveries. Dain listened with sincere interest, all the while wondering how she managed so much enthusiasm on such little sleep. It was evident that, like his late mother, the girl had a scholarly penchant.

"I also came across a note about you in the journal, sir."

Dain felt himself go rigid. "Ah yes, a reference to some talents my mother thought I might possess. I'm sorry to disappoint you, but like I said before, I'm quite sure I have none."

"Your mother writes that talents can surface at different ages for different people. Your talents may not have developed yet, or maybe they have natural tendencies that make them less noticeable. Like . . . something that feels like a normal occurrence, but isn't. I haven't gotten into the journal in depth, and as I said, I cannot read Zaalish—" She suddenly looked at him more earnestly. "When you are a bit stronger, perhaps we can read it together, and try to determine what your talents are?"

Though Dain still felt averse the possibility of any magical powers within him, he couldn't find a polite way to refuse. "I am, at present, your captive audience."

The girl laughed, and Dain marveled again at the loveliness of the sound.

* * *

Old Toff was actually the first to arrive. He walked in close to noon, grumbling about his ribs as he demanded Sable give him something to ease the pain. While she was dispensing a remedy, Mo also arrived.

Dain struggled not to jump into questioning the events in Vid. Had it been a stalker attack? Had Dulge returned? He desperately wanted to know, but everyone else seemed so relaxed about it that he allowed them to get settled first.

Perhaps it was the long length of sea now between *The Maiden* and Vid that made things feel less urgent.

Morgan Crouse reached the bed in three large strides. "The Lion of the Sea awakes." His broad smile beamed with sincerity. "Gratified to see ye recovering, lad."

Sable peeked out from behind Mo. "The Lion of the Sea?"

The first mate looked under his arm and chuckled. "Well, he has a lion's mane if ever I've seen one. Does he not, lass?"

Her glinting eyes captured Dain's own. "True, but what will we call him if he cuts it off? Cub?"

"Now—" Dain didn't get very far, because the others were laughing too loudly to hear him. The chuckles only increased when Casper sauntered into the crowded little room, demanding to be let in on the joke.

Dain couldn't help smiling too—eventually.

Once the merriment subsided, Mo assumed command of the room. He ordered Sable to her quarters for a bit of shut-eye. Then he sent Casper to fetch extra chairs, and gave Toff a reprimanding swat for rummaging through Sable's satchel at the end of the bed.

The chairs arrived, and Dain sat on his bed surrounded by the three sailors. Mo spoke first. "How's yer head, Captain?"

"It's been better, but as Sable pointed out, it's still attached to my shoulders, thanks to these two." Dain looked between the sailors. "Thankful to you both. Truly, I am."

Toff and Casper dipped their brows simultaneously.

Dain finally felt like he had the opportunity to inquire about what he most wanted to hear, but he tried to keep his phrasing light. "I'm anxious to hear about my, uh, heroic rescue. The last thing I remember is Casper calling out a warning, am I right?"

Shifting in his seat and pushing up his glasses, Toff gave Casper a side-eyed glance. "Casper did call out a warning—a *belated* warning, mind you."

The other sailor simply crossed his muscular arms, and raised one perfect eyebrow at Toff.

The old man grunted. "I should never have let my guard down after the leech turned tail. The cronies that ran off at the start decided to circle round, hiding up ahead to ambush us. I'm guessing they figured to catch us by surprise, and snag you. Apparently they had more backbone than we gave them credit for. The surprise part worked, but the capture was obviously thwarted."

Casper interrupted. His copper eyes were gleaming. "Ye never seen such clumsy antics, sir. Waving their blades hither and yon. It was only moments before I had them both out cold."

Old Toff adjusted his tunic in disgust. "You pretentious knob! You did no such thing. I handled one lad, and you handled the other. Stop filling that vain head of yours full of glorified nonsense."

Refusing to back down, the handsome sailor leaned one elbow forward on his thigh. "Yer an old fool if ye think that's the truth. That thug had ye cuckolded. Ye never would've made it back to *The Maiden* without me."

Toff sucked in a hard breath.

Dain expected a spew of obscenities to follow, but Mo cut the banter off. "That's enough, sailors. We've more important things to do than sit by, listening to the likes of ye. The captain'll be needing his rest. Now, fill him in on the parts he needs to hear, and then ye can both get back to work."

Casper managed to obey better than Toff. The old man's voice grated like the hinges of a barred brig door. "Well, Mr. Crouse, as you know, *I'm* always on alert. The lad who hit the captain over the head, he made a comment amidst the tumult. I heard him mumble about hunters and a reward. I can't be certain, but I think Dulge and his boys are mixed up in something more than simply running a brothel." Toff peered at Dain over his spectacles. "Those second thoughts you had after we let the leech go, perhaps they might have been well founded, sir."

The news gave Dain an inward jolt. Was it possible that Dulge had been working for, or with the stalkers? The theory would better explain why the man was so intent on getting what he came for. Dain had not been able to reconcile the loss of one prostitute to the intensity with which Dulge had accosted him. Perhaps this girl, Anira, was now worth more to him than she had been before. Hopefully, his father had stowed her securely away in his haven. If this theory were true, if stalkers hired regular thugs to help them hunt, then an adept was not safe by day either . . .

Toff's voice broke into his thoughts. "We reported the thugs to the port authorities. We didn't go into the full details, just told them we'd been mugged, and how to find the unconscious thieves. Vid has a lax justice system, mind you, so I doubt much will be done. We just couldn't risk more time investigating with you so severely injured, and Dulge at large likely gathering forces. We had to get you back to the ship."

Resisting the urge to drag his fingers through his hair, he looked between the two sailors again. "I understand. You've done me a great service, both of you. I assume Dev grabbed all the provisions, and helped you get everything, including me, onboard? Will you please convey my appreciation to him until I'm well enough to thank him myself?"

Both men nodded.

Mo's low voice rumbled—it was the kind of tone that reminded men to mind, not because they were forced, but because they respected those stationed above them. "Dismissed, sailors."

The shipmates immediately resumed their quarrel, giving

165

each other a few shoves on the way out.

The first mate sat down at the end of the bed. The heavy movement sent a peal of pain through Dain's head. He winced inwardly, but tried hard to keep it from his face. It was time for more of Sable's tea.

Mo's long dreadlocks fell forward on his shoulders as he leaned to cup one enormous hand over Dain's forearm. "Ye had me worried, lad. For all my talk of living life without fear, I admit that I was fearful for ye." The first mate lowered his gaze. "I've never said before how much like a son ye are to me. It felt wrong to tell ye such things when the captain—your father was around. Now, with him gone, I hope it's less improper to say so."

Dain's throat caught, and as his eyes searched Mo's lowered expression, it struck him that truer words had never been spoken. Morgan Crouse had always been more of a father to him than Hiram Alloway ever was. Why had he never put it that way to himself before? Dain found it hard to speak, but he forced the words out anyway. "Mo—I have learned a great many things about my father recently. And as far as I can tell, he appears to have done some honorable, even noble, things, but he was never a real father to me."

Mo looked up in surprise.

Dain stared him straight in the eye. "Don't misunderstand—my father did supply for all my physical needs. He provided for my education, and it appears he even took to the sea to try to protect me. For that, I am beginning to respect him." The baby portrait came to Dain's mind. "I believe, in his way, he loved me—and I do intend to honor his memory, along with my mother's. However, you are right, Mo. When I was afraid, you comforted me. When I was hurt, you bandaged me. And when I was unruly, you took me in hand. You taught me how to sail, how to laugh, how to defend myself, how to lead. You made me a man. From the moment I stepped on this ship, you raised me, Morgan Crouse." It was Dain's turn to lower his gaze. "I have never appreciated you properly for it. I am sorry."

When Dain finally looked up again, he saw tears glistening in the giant's eyes, but they quickly dissipated as the man's charcoal gaze took on a mischievous glow. "So, yer a man now, are ye?"

Dain burst out laughing. It made his skull feel like it might splinter, but he didn't care. "That's all you took from my heartfelt speech?"

The first mate's pearly smile spread wide, and his deep, velvet laugh bounced off every corner of the room.

Chapter 15

His head wasn't going to heal fast, but Dain had only resigned himself to this fact after attempting to reach the chamberpot on his own one morning. Apparently, head wounds and swaying ships did not mix. The escapade ended poorly, and he received a wild tongue lashing as Sable tried to reseal the wound with tighter bandages. She changed the wrappings daily, applying herbal salves to speed the healing process. During one of these nursing sessions, the girl admitted that she had no skill with stitching flesh. She told him the lack of sutures might leave a scar, but she was relieved it would be hidden in his hair.

Dain had made an offhand joke about a facial scar being much more manly. Sable had disagreed. Mild quarreling had ensued.

Eventually, he conceded to her feminine sensibilities. These small disagreements entertained him while he lay idly in bed. It would be a full two months' journey back to Aalta, and being bedridden was not something any young man would take lightly. Dain was already restless, but he kept his word to Sable, and once he could sit upright more comfortably, they began to study his mother's journal together. The tome felt exhaustive, and it made Dain wonder how much more might await them in his mother's belongings back home.

Sable absorbed the knowledge with fervor. Her memory was infallible, matched only by her enthusiasm. Today, cheeks bright with enthusiasm, she said, "Look here, did you know that even though our talents are dependent on our physical limitations, we can still increase their endurance? Just like exercise amplifies the body's capacity to function at higher levels, practicing magic, on a regular basis, does the same." Sable's voice pitched higher as she read. "Talents are spectral as well. It says here that from what she could ascertain from interviews with other migrant adept, two people might be born with exactly the same talent, but the extent to which they can wield it varies." The girl tapped her lips thoughtfully. "I guess that means some adept are just born naturally stronger than others."

Dain listened attentively, interjecting his thoughts and occasionally reading the Zaalish excerpts. Neither of them could decipher the Selt hieroglyphs, and Dain wondered why his mother even bothered to use the ancient language, let alone several languages. Perhaps she wanted it to be readable to more people? Or at least sections of it readable to more? It didn't make a whole lot of sense. He kind of wished he could ask her.

One Zaalish passage read that Sable's particular conjuring talent was labeled adjuration. It was described as the power, or will, to command an animate or inanimate object from one space to another. There were no explanations as to how this talent was achieved, but the notations did expand upon the potential for such conjuration. Apparently, a more powerful adjurationist was capable of commanding themselves, and even accompanying companions, across great distances. There was an impressive reference to a Selt who'd moved an entire castle, along with all its inhabitants, from one kingdom to another.

Throughout their studies, Sable made it her personal mission to try to discover Dain's hidden talents. He politely humored her interest. Magic had begun to intrigue him more, but he still wasn't sure he was ready to become something other than, or more than, he already was. Nonetheless, he was grateful that the studying helped to pass the hours.

One afternoon, a week into his injury, Sable flipped more carefully through the third section of the journal. "Captain, do you recall the day you first saw my pendant? You stood at the prow, leaned over the edge and said to yourself, 'I remember her.' Who was it that you remembered?"

Dain's hands fumbled with the teacup she'd just passed his way. He had hoped she'd forgotten. He was not afraid to speak of his mother, but he didn't have permission to speak of the princess.

The girl didn't seem to notice his hesitancy. She had taken to habitually sitting at the head of the bed, right alongside him, close enough for her scent to play on his senses. She was humming contentedly, waiting for his response.

"Well—it was my mother."

Sable stopped humming and poked her nose out of the book. "You forgot your mother?"

Dain was thankful at least that she didn't ask *who* he'd been talking to. "I didn't forget her, only specific details and moments about her. It was like the memories were—trapped. I always assumed it was because I rarely saw her, but after I read the journal, I remembered it all. It was odd—like a flood of memories while I slept, and by morning everything was restored. Well, as much as a child would typically recall."

Flipping herself around on the bed to face him, journal grasped in hand, Sable eyed him earnestly. "You remembered after you read the journal? And all the memories came back to you in your dreams?"

He gave her a wry grin. "Yes, I believe that is what I just said."

She ignored his poke as she flipped furiously through the

journal, to the section dedicated most to his mother's own talent of alchemy. "Listen to this. 'As my talent grows, so does my capacity to create spells of my own. I recently created a series of incantations for the suppression of memory, and a trigger release which can be applied at a later date. If the subject were to happen upon, or be directed to the trigger, they would recall all the memory suppression. However, the incantation requires an immense amount of focused power to work. I fear I would only use it under the most dire circumstances.'" Sable sprang off the bed, rubbing her face frantically. "Maybe she used this spell on you? Maybe the trigger to get your memories back was the journal?" Looking back at Dain, skin red, she continued. "Perhaps she utilized the spell right before she led the stalkers away the day she died."

"Why, in all the kingdoms, would she have done that?" After Dain asked the question, he remembered considering some kind of magic being involved in his memory loss the day everything had returned in his dreams. It had been so sudden, so timed with the journal. Maybe Sable was onto something. A cold feeling entered his gut. He didn't want to be magical—he didn't want to be one of the hunted . . .

"To protect you."

Dain tried to keep his tone even. "If that were the case, why would she not have placed the spell on my father as well?"

"She wouldn't have to. He didn't have magic, so the

173

stalkers wouldn't have come looking for him. Maybe you *do* have a talent, and your mother suppressed it?"

"I see where your theory is going, but I—"

Sable jumped back on the bed before he could continue. Her enthusiasm was palpable as she flipped to a central section of the journal. "Here, let me read this as well: 'For centuries, visionary prophets ruled the Selt ranks. Their dreams, oracular revelations, and guidance led the Selts to a period of great peace and renaissance.'"

Dain knew his face was blank while he stared at Sable.

"Don't you see? *Dreams*, Dain." It was the first time she'd ever called him by his name. He watched her eyes go wide once she realized her slip. "Apologies, sir—Captain."

Dain was surprised at how pleased he was to hear her use his name. "I prefer it to Captain, actually." Then he added quickly, "Maybe not in the company of the others, but here— just us—it's good, it's fine." Clearing his throat roughly, he pointed to the journal. "So, you're saying my talent is dreams?"

Sable's large hazel eyes burned bright. "It makes perfect sense. How often do you dream? Has there ever been an instance where something from your dream has come to pass?"

The only thing that came to Dain's mind was the princess's story of Elden being turned to stone. He'd dreamed of a man made of stone right before she showed up. It was probably just a coincidence, though. "I do dream frequently–"

Sable squealed in joy as she bounced up and down on her knees in front of Dain. "I knew it."

He raised a hand to motion politely for Sable to cease.

She stopped, and quickly cupped his hand with hers as she pushed the teacup toward his lips. "By the kingdoms, I am so sorry. Here, drink your tea."

He'd forgotten he was holding the drink. Her hands were warm under his, her touch gentle. A fierce tingle shot through his frame. Confused and embarrassed, Dain quickly shifted out of her grasp. "Yes, right, time for more tea." After taking a few large mouthfuls, he recovered himself. "Well, this is an interesting theory, Sable, something I suppose you'll *force* me to explore in the coming days?"

She laughed in response, but the merriment drained as quickly as it had come. "Dain, what if—"

He dipped his chin, and peered at her over the cup. "What if, what?"

"Well, if dreaming is one of your talents—then you would have no control over when the magic was being used. There would be no way to suppress it while you slept. It's possible that if your mother applied a spell, she may have done more than simply subdue your memories. Perhaps she suppressed your talents as well? The stalkers—if you were on land—" Sable looked shaken now.

"If I were on land, I'd never be able to hide. Thankfully,

as you and Tars discovered, stalkers don't seem to follow on the sea." Dain shrugged, trying to lighten the mood for Sable. However, his own mind continued to whir. If this far-fetched idea was true, if prophetic dreams were something he did possess, then they could have been the very reason his mother had been discovered in the first place. The thoughts were sobering. He set his teacup aside. "Maybe we've done enough studying for today."

Sable only nodded.

* * *

Another week passed, and Dain was beginning to get his feet under him. The head wound was still dizzyingly painful at times, but at least he was becoming more mobile. With assistance, he could shuffle around his quarters without any serious incident.

Mo visited daily. He kept Dain informed, but never stayed for long. *The Maiden,* and its crew, were solely dependent on their first mate until Dain recovered.

Occasionally, Old Toff popped in as well. Sometimes he'd stay for only a moment, and others he'd stay for hours to play Rack. They never played for real coin, but Toff always made sure he snatched a bag of spiced nuts from the galley as leverage. Today, the nut competition was fierce.

"That was a terrible bluff, Captain. I could see it plain as day on your face."

Dain shrugged gently, and noted that his shoulder movements were getting easier. "Don't underestimate me, Mr. Parley." He furrowed his brow. "You know what happens to those who do."

Toff cackled loudly. "Dulge had that dagger coming to him, sir."

Sable's head perked up from where she knelt mixing herbs. Dain was always curious where she got the ingredients from. The scent of comfrey and calendula wafted from the corner as she crushed them firmly into the mortar. "Dulge?" she asked. "Is that the man who attacked you in Eandor Vid?"

Toff leaned around the bedpost to better see Sable's face. "Indeed, him and his thugs. Our captain here may have given that fellow a permanent limp."

Dain's heart skipped a beat. He couldn't quite explain it, but he suddenly worried that Sable's opinion of him might be lowered by this violent act somehow. He rushed to explain. "It was an impulse decision. I just pitched the dagger without really thinking it through, and—I was trying to make a point—"

Sable cut him off with a grin. "I'm sure you did exactly what needed to be done, Captain."

For some reason, her approval brought him intense relief. He wasn't sure why her opinion of him was so important to him now. Was it because of their growing friendship—or was there more to it?

Later that evening, after Toff had stalked off, bitter from losing numerous rounds of Rack, Sable checked Dain's head wound again before she settled into the chair by his bed.

He watched her pull a blanket up to her chin. "You know, I'm sure I could manage fine on my own now—that is, if you'd prefer to sleep in a bed again?"

The girl peeked her nose above the covers. "And have you undo everything I've worked so hard to heal in the past couple of weeks? I know men, Dain Alloway, and you'll be doing all sorts of things you're not supposed to while I'm gone. I'll have twice the work afterward. I'm good right here."

Dain didn't admit it out loud, but he was relieved she didn't go. Slipping her arm out, Sable reached above the bedside table and extinguished the hanging oil lamp.

He could hear her trying to get comfortable in the chair. "Sable?"

"Hmmm?"

"Where do you get all the herbs from? It seems you have an endless supply."

Her voice was sleepy. "From the mountains of Ernham. I shift them here."

Dain raised his brows in the dark. "That's a long way to conjure something."

"Mmhmm . . ."

She didn't seem to want to expand on it further, so Dain left off on more questions, but he fell asleep wondering how strong her talent really was.

Chapter 16

He noticed the rocking right before Sable's sleeping form pitched out of the chair, slamming hard against him on the bed.

The girl woke with a gasp.

Skull throbbing, Dain grappled for the edge of the headboard with one hand, and secured Sable with the other as the ship quickly plummeted again in the opposite direction.

Thunder rattled *The Maiden's* frame.

"Storm." Sable's croak was barely audible as the next violent lunge tore Dain's grip loose. The pair launched over the bedside, landing hard against the far wall. The following tumult rolled them towards the bed again, and they scrambled to throw their arms around the large bedpost.

Weakened muscles straining, Dain felt something wet run down his left temple as he bore through the relentless plunges. He didn't loose his grasp to test it, but he was certain it was blood. Sable would be furious that the wound had reopened.

Besides the intermittent flash of lightning through the porthole, the room was black, and Dain only caught glimmers of Sable through the flickers. Her eyes were tightly clenched as she held firm to the post. To his relief, she appeared unharmed. He wanted to ask if she was alright, but the tempest raged so loudly that conversation was near impossible.

Time crawled on.

Dain's head pounded, and his arms began to tremble. Obviously, his body had atrophied from disuse. He honestly wasn't sure how much longer he could keep his grip, and this led him to grow increasingly concerned for the crew, who must be facing life and death up on deck. Were they all still safe? And when would this blasted storm end? Storms were always a moderate risk during the fall season, and *The Maiden* had weathered them before, but none had ever seemed so savage as this. Dain was drawn from his thoughts when he glimpsed a waver of warm light cutting through the darkness in the adjoining room.

He knew the door into the quarters had been locked.

Yet extended at the end of an arm, a lantern rounded the edge of the curtained doorway. It filled his sleeping quarters with a swaying glow.

Sable's eyes remained sealed, her face screwed in focus, but Dain watched the figure as it half-crawled, half-dragged itself toward them.

"Ileana."

Her name was drowned in thunder, but the princess still looked up. The next tumult sent her sprawling onto her belly, sliding fast across the floor toward them.

Releasing one arm, Dain snatched her before she hit the wall, and dragged her toward the post. How had she managed to keep hold of the lantern?

Breathless and soaked, the princess crushed herself in between them.

Sable's eyes flew wide. Her pupils dilated in the lantern light as she focused on the stranger. Then her gaze flitted to Dain and the blood still cascading down his temple. Her brow creased, and she instinctively reached out toward him. This was a mistake, as the next forceful shift immediately knocked her loose.

Dain tried to reach for her, but Ileana caught the girl first. Sable smiled in confusion as the newcomer pulled her back.

The princess had to scream to be heard above the storm. "Sable, take the lantern."

It was obvious that the girl was at a loss as to who the mysterious new woman was and how she knew her name, but Sable didn't argue. Carefully shuffling, so as not to slip again, she managed to wrangle the lantern from Ileana's grasp.

The princess yelled again. "Dain, bring your head close."

He couldn't even guess the reasoning behind her request, but against the pain and the force of the next inundation, he obeyed.

Reaching her right hand around the pillar, Ileana placed it atop Dain's bandaged skull. He saw Sable's eyes grow as a pleasurable warmth radiated from Ileana's hand through the bandages and directly onto his wound. It was followed by a searing stab of pain, which ripped viciously through his body. Then it was gone. In fact, everything was gone. The throbbing, the weakness, and even the dizziness. Despite the torrent outside, and the turbulence within the cabin, Dain's mind felt entirely clear for the first time in weeks. He turned in surprise to face Ileana, their noses only inches apart, and before he could say anything, she mouthed the word, *Go*.

Dain knew what she meant. He had to get up on deck. Perhaps the crew needed him, or perhaps they just needed their lucky charm—either way, there was no time to consider the implications of his healing. Dain disengaged. The moment he released the post, he was thrown with full force toward the curtained doorway. Scrambling, he managed to spin his arms and legs to cushion the impact against the jamb. Despite his renewed strength, Dain realized that reaching the deck was going to be a slow, arduous belly crawl. How had the princess managed to get down here in a huge gown, the lantern remaining lit in her hand?

* * *

Unprepared for the onslaught that faced him when he finally surfaced on deck, Dain's mouth was full of seawater before he could barely pull himself out into the air. He gagged, choking as he rolled from starboard to port with every pitch. He could see nothing, and hear even less. None of the crew were visible, and the next furious wave sent him peeling high across the deck, landing with brutal force against the rail. Thankful that he hadn't flown overboard, Dain groaned as he grasped tight to a spindle. The constant, pressurized sensation he'd recently felt while outside was intensified a hundred times tonight. It was like the air around him was closing in, and an insistent swell threatened beneath his skin. The wind swirled furiously, pushing him harder against the rail as black sheets of rain pelted down.

The cold seeped through his skin, slicing its way to his bones. Shivers wracked his body, and Dain despaired as the frozen ocean rose toward him again. They were going to capsize, and there was nothing he could do about it. His mind grew darker than the storm. He'd felt useless in bed these past weeks, but this—the pressure inside of him snapped. Like a whip cracked within his soul, Dain's inner mind aligned with the tempest. He—he could feel the elements.

Magic.

Dain instantly recalled his recent dream, the dream where

185

he had stood amidst a raging storm and felt one with the gale. Had he foreseen this? Had he dreamed about his own talent? His mind raged against the possibility. This wasn't what he wanted, but it was becoming increasingly clear that life didn't seem to care about what he wanted. Life drove its course with no consideration for those involved; it simply dragged unsuspecting victims from one uncertain outcome to another. Drawing a ragged breath, Dain realized that if there was ever a moment to accept the possibility of a power dwelling within him, it was now. He knew nothing of wielding talents, but Sable had said hers was driven by instinct. Dain would just have to trust his gut. He shivered again, but this time it wasn't from the cold.

The wind buffeted against him as he turned his gaze inward. Trying to follow his instincts, Dain visualized himself driving a carriage drawn by god-sized beasts, each creature symbolizing an element within the storm—the wind, the rain, the lightning. In his mind's eye, he gave an internal yank to one tether.

The imaginary lightning beast roared, yanking ferociously against his leashing.

Pain seared through Dain's frame. It was so intense that his hold on the rail slipped. Grasping to reconfigure himself, Dain released the inner rein. Power, magic, talents—this was crazy, but it was also their only hope. *The Maiden* wasn't going to survive this storm without a miracle. And if this feeling was real, if it worked and he could save his crew, it was worth the risk.

Before Dain even had the chance to try again, the ship dove hard to the port side. It plunged, and a quarter of the hull submerged deep into the ocean's murky depths. Dain thought he saw another figure fly past him as he frantically clung to the rail post, but he couldn't be sure. His arms stretched to painful limits as his legs dangled helplessly in the rain.

The wind shoved at him from beneath.

Seconds later, the vessel flew back out of the water, and Dain crashed back as the ship leveled again on the sea. He thought he heard several sailors cry out. Breathing hard, Dain quickly forced his frayed mind back to the metaphorical carriage. Focusing firmly on each individual tether, he threw his whole being into the fight. This time, he began with the wind, and to his surprise, it jumped at his command. The other two elements were not so responsive. Despite the accompanying pain, and the mental anguish, Dain pulled tighter and tighter. The internal battle intensified, and dimly, he could sense the external storm reflecting it. His thoughts flitted to Sable, then to Mo, and Ileana and Toff, and the rest of the crew. He couldn't fail them.

His body trembled as he imagined his own form growing substantially larger than the elemental creatures. He no longer rode in the chariot, he towered over it. The wind swirled submissively at his feet. And eventually, the other feral elements capitulated. In surly acceptance of their new master, their great imaginary heads slowly bowed. Without hesitation, Dain seized upon his victory. He used the force of his will, body, and mind to stifle the storm completely. Pain wracked his frame, and Dain was convinced he was about to die.

Then the pain stopped.

The Maiden settled into a low, rocking sway.

Somehow, he had quelled the storm—he couldn't explain exactly what had happened, but he'd forced it to dissipate. The rain turned to drizzle, the lightning winked out, and the wind caressed his face gently. He was sweating despite the cold. And his eyes had been shut so tight that they twinged when he released them. He was alive. The world was still black, but the light of the three moons was fighting to be loosed from behind the clouds. Gathering strength to stand, Dain heard Mo's voice bellow a roll call from the helm. Thank Orthane, the first mate was safe.

Groaning could be heard throughout the ship as each name was called. Dain remained desperately silent until Mo was through—every call was heeded, though some did sound wounded.

The lanterns would be lit soon, and while Dain wanted to be there to help, he wasn't ready to explain himself, or his miraculous healing. On wobbly legs, he made his way back to his quarters through the wet darkness.

* * *

Ileana sat on the edge of the bed, wrapped in a large white blanket. The coverlet had no doubt been drawn from the linen chest. Her heavily embroidered gown dripped rhythmically from a peg on the bedpost.

Sable was seated opposite her on the chair. She was listening intently as the princess summarized her personal history.

Neither of them looked harmed, and Dain sighed in relief. Remaining hidden a few moments longer, he quietly eased himself down to the floor and leaned wearily against the door frame. Despite his exhaustion, Dain's thoughts galloped. An adept—he was an adept. He'd doubted it all this time, from the moment he'd read the excerpt in his mother's journal. He'd resisted, but now there was no escaping the truth. The storm had subsided because of him.

An indwelling power, one that words failed to express, beat fiercely beneath the surface of Dain's consciousness. It was undeniable. And when he focused inward, he could feel the magic thrumming naturally along with his heart. The sensation was astonishing, but it made him slouch forward in dismay. Hanging his head in his hands, Dain groaned inwardly. He didn't want this. And like so much that befallen him lately, it thwarted all his plans for the future. Yet—Sable had probably never wanted this either, or her brother, or Ileana, or any other gifted child whose life had been pillaged by the stalkers for generations. They were all in the same boat.

Dain straightened. Life might enjoy flinging its fated chaos around with thoughtless abandon, but Dain had never been one to back down easily. Mo sometimes called him stubborn. Dain preferred to think of it as purpose-driven. He was used to making resolutions. And unless he planned to live the remainder of his life aboard *The Maiden*, he'd need to continue fighting for the life he wanted. And, the waves willing, he'd help turn the tides for everyone else like him. The wooden princess already knew where to begin. Her mission was now his own. It was time to find the safe haven.

Clearing his throat to alert the women of his presence, Dain rose. His internal strength had been renewed, but his external frame still suffered miserably. As he rounded the curtained doorway, his knees gave a threatening wobble.

Sable flew to her feet, a mix of anxiety and relief in her expression. "Captain, are you alright?"

Dain buckled. Sable lunged to grab him around his middle.

After he managed to get his legs back underneath his shaking torso, he became awkwardly aware of her supportive embrace. Face flushed, he gently disengaged himself to lean supported against the wall. The exhausted edge in his voice betrayed him. "Sable, I'm fine."

The girl backed away with one eyebrow cocked. "You are notoriously bad at seeing the obvious." Before he could respond, she ran to the chest and yanked out another blanket. Then she headed to the cupboard to grab a change of clothes, and pushed the items into his arms. "Into the other room with you. Get yourself out of those drenched nightclothes, and warm up before you catch your death. I'll procure some dry things for the princess. Once she's proper, I'll call you back."

Dain smiled. He was quickly learning that this girl lived life with her fists permanently planted on her hips. The moment a crisis abated, she stood tall again, flinging orders to set the world right. He couldn't help admiring her.

Chapter 17

Moonslight beamed calmly through the diamond-paned windows. Dain gazed out at the now-calm skies in wonder. He'd done that. He'd tethered the elements. Apparently he was more than just a lucky charm . . .

All the times the wind had buffeted the sails in his presence—all the instances when the weather had settled when one sailor or another dragged him up on deck. Everything now pointed to this new, but not-so-new power within him. The thought made him chuckle, and then cringe. The revelation was going to take some time to get comfortable with. Laying his dripping nightclothes over the back of the desk chair, Dain wrapped the blanket tightly over his shoulders. His knees wobbled again as Sable called from the adjoining room.

The princess was dressed in one of the girl's modest gray frocks, a leather belt secured snugly at her waist. Somehow, the lady managed to make even the simple garment look regal.

Dain dipped his brow to her respectfully. "Princess, it's good to see you again."

Tall enough to look him directly in the eye, Ileana advanced. She took his free hand in her own. "I believe we already had this discussion. You were to call me Ileana, no? Perhaps, now that you bear a title yourself, you shall want me to call you Captain?" Her smile was radiant and teasing, but she quickly sobered. "Dain, I am sorry for the loss of your father and so many of the crew."

Dain's stomach flipped—how could anyone not be affected by such beauty? Grasping his blanket more tightly, he gently squeezed the hand she offered, and smiled back. "Thank you for your condolences. And yes, first names will do, Ileana. You have obviously had the pleasure of meeting Sable." Dain turned to his ever-present companion of the past weeks, but he was surprised to see that his friend's expression was hard as granite.

"You're introduction comes late, Captain. Weeks late, in fact. You failed to mention *The Lost Princess*…"

Dain released Ileana's hand, and stepped back on wavering legs. "It never came up."

"Never came up?" Sable crossed her arms over her chest, and stalked closer. "I beg to differ, *sir*. I think you had the perfect opportunity to share, but you conveniently omitted the detail. Now I know exactly who you were talking to that morning on the prow."

Before Dain could retort, and tell her that it hadn't been his tale to tell, a loud knock rang out from the adjoining office. The trio looked at each other in surprise.

Sable was the first to spring into action. "Stay here, stay quiet. They are probably just checking in." She looked at Ileana briefly. "Hopefully no one has leaned over the prow and noticed the missing figurehead."

Ileana grimaced slightly. "It's still dark, and the crew will be fully occupied for a time. I've risked this before, and we can always turn it into a ghost tale later if needed."

Sable nodded, grabbed the lantern, and then headed purposefully through the curtained doorway.

Dain peeked around the frame to see Sable stop to hide his wet nightclothes underneath the desk before she opened the chamber door in a wide welcome.

Casper stood on the threshold. He was soaked to the bone, but the sodden look somehow only served to make him look more attractive. It seemed almost a kind of magic in its right. "Evening, lass. The first mate sent me to check in with ye. We want to be sure the captain ain't injured further, or in need of aid?"

Sable replied easily. "All is well, Casper. Thank you. The Captain is resting now, and we are happy it's over. Is everyone alright? Can I help?"

"Nay, lass, some lads are pretty badly bruised, but for the most part everyone was tied secure. We just have a crew load of water-logged sailors, but——" Casper leaned in toward Sable and whispered something inaudible in her ear.

She giggled, and gave him a playful shove.

Casper bowed. A rakish grin spread wide across his face as he backed out the door.

An unexpected pang of jealousy tore through Dain's chest. It simmered for a while until he finally shook his head, internally reprimanding himself for the absurd feeling. Casper flirted with everyone, and Dain had no grounds for jealousy. There was nothing romantic between Sable and himself—the girl was free to flirt with whomever she pleased. Dain backed away from the curtained door, trying to distract himself by giving thanks that no one had been lost. The figure he'd thought he saw tossed through the rain must have been an apparition.

When she returned, Sable's disapproving gaze fell fast on him again.

He tried to ignore her, but it was like trying to ignore the glare of the sun.

Ileana stepped between the pair. "Thank you for handling that, Sable. I am indebted to you for keeping my secret. Which is exactly what Dain was doing when he didn't reveal me to you."

Sable's head snapped up, and then her expression turned contrite. Ileana didn't let the girl say anything, but simply took her by the hand and led her to the edge of the bed. "Now, my dear friends, please sit. We have much to discuss." The princess indicated the bed as she took the chair.

They both obeyed, but Sable sat further away from Dain than she normally would. He didn't know if it was because she was still angry, or because she felt embarrassed that she hadn't thought of his reason for keeping Ileana's tale to himself. Either way, the positioning made him a bit sad.

Ileana tried to lighten the mood. "So much has passed since our last meeting. Thankfully Sable has related most of the missing details." The princess nodded thanks at the girl before settling her gaze on Dain. "First, before we continue, I believe that you have special news for us, do you not?"

Dain looked at her in feigned confusion.

"The storm—" she urged patiently.

Sable's head whipped toward him.

Dain ignored her. He wasn't ready to discuss the storm, but the princess's eyes overwhelmed him. If this woman ever assumed her rightful place on the throne of Derchar, all would bow to that gaze, he had no doubt.

"Well, the storm." Dain swallowed. "It was—that is—I subdued it."

Slapping the bed hard, Sable seemed to completely forget everything that had just passed. "Elemental conjuration! You *do* have a talent. Maybe even more than one!" Cocking her head knowingly, she reached out to poke his ribs. "I knew it. No wonder you are so tired right now."

Dain couldn't resist a smile. He was thankful she'd moved closer to him again, and he realized she was right—talents did drain the wielder of physical energy. No wonder he felt like he'd run the longest race in history. Obviously, he needed to do a bit more training before he attempted a magical feat like that again. Still, he wasn't ready for this discussion, so he changed the subject. "It seems you also possess a talent yourself, Ileana? This is not something you shared the last time we met."

Ileana beamed. "Ah, Dain, there is much I did not have time to share with you—"

Sable couldn't contain herself. Before the princess could resume, the girl looked at Dain in excitement. "She's a binary healer, Dain. Don't you remember reading about it? It's different from the kind of healing Tars does. He uses his gift to create remedies. His healing talent is related to alchemy, you know—potions, spells and such—but Ileana heals the body directly via her own physical resources. She draws on her physical strength, just like us. It can be extremely useful in emergencies, though entirely consuming, and sometimes dangerous. The journal said that some binary healers have been known to kill themselves attempting to cure others—but I suppose any of us could kill ourselves if we pushed our talent to the limit."

The princess gave Sable a motherly glance. "It appears we have a natural-born scholar in our midst. And we have another healer? Who is this Tars you speak of?"

Dain watched Sable's enthusiasm drain faster than a bottle of rum in Trait's grasp. Her thickly lashed eyes quickly fixed themselves on the floor. The girl had spoken little of her brother since Eandor Vid, and Dain had carefully skirted the subject as well. In the weeks since Sable had become his friend, Dain had tried to think of a way to retrieve him. While in Vid, he could have sent a missive to the trade's guild of Tallooj. He could have suggested they seek out Tars, and offer him a medical position aboard a needy merchant vessel, but that thought had come too late. Returning to Tallooj was not a viable option either—Dain couldn't put his crew in that kind of danger again. He knew Sable understood, but it had plagued him nonetheless. Now, he only hoped that Tars had saved enough coin to secure passage off the isle, or that he had been clever enough to stay safe and hidden.

When Sable finally responded, her voice was low. "Tars is my older brother, Princess. He was left behind in Tallooj . . ." Looking up fast, she amended her words. "No one is at fault.

Circumstances were extreme, as you know. And yes, he is also a healer. A singular healer, and a half-trained alchemist."

Ileana's expression was full of sincere empathy as she reached forward to cup Sable's hands in her own. "You must be terribly concerned for his safety. It may be of little consolation, but I have noted that alchemists are commonly the most proficient at evading stalkers. I am confident that you will be reunited soon." The princess leaned back into her chair again, and shifted the subject for Sable's benefit. "And you, my dear Sable, are absolutely correct. Binary healing is *one* of my talents."

"*Talents?* You have more than one?" Dain over-emphasized his surprise and curiosity, hoping to distract Sable's attention from her missing brother. From the corner of his eye, he watched with satisfaction as the girl's gaze lifted from the floor to the princess.

"Indeed, I have three."

This time, Sable snapped to full attention.

The princess continued. "As you have probably learned, talents tend to appear when we are children, though in some cases they develop later. This was the case with me. And even if my talents had manifested earlier, people were already on the run at that point. There may have been more adept, maybe even remaining Selts, in the four kingdoms during my time period, but I did not know of them. Growing up, I suspected there was something different about me, but a first-born Derchar princess has little time to contemplate anything but learning how to rule one day. What I did know was that I was drawn to the injured, and have always wondered if my magic was what compelled me to Elden's side in the first place—but it wasn't until after my imprisonment that my talents truly surfaced. As you can imagine, I haven't had a great deal of time to practice healing, but over the course of a couple hundred years, I've found the odd opportunity. My other two talents are functional even when I'm wooden, so practicing them is not an issue." The woman wriggled on her chair. "Binary healing was the last of my talents to develop, though. The first was disjunction." She smiled at Sable. "It's in the journal, too."

"You can unravel the magic of others?" Sable's voice pitched from low to high.

"Close." Ileana nodded at her approvingly. "It behaves more like a ... separation, than an unraveling. I think it surfaced first because of my imprisonment. I'm guessing my talent responded to the magical attack on my person, trying to resist. It took nearly twenty years, but one night, during the light of the full moons, I found a weakness. Since then, I have been able to take my true form one night in every month. Sadly, this is the only vulnerability I have yet to discover. I think it's because Rectlor's power functions on an entirely different level than our own. I can only guess at why the moons affect it, but perhaps it has something to do with the divine."

Sable practically bounced with interest now. "Your third talent?"

Ileana smiled. "My third talent is corollary."

This time, the girl's face went blank. Even Dain couldn't recall this talent being mentioned in the journal.

Ileana shrugged—even her shrugs looked royal. "I named it myself because I couldn't find it in the journal, but this talent is what Old Toff would call *a good sniffer*." The princess tapped her nose, and then laughed lightly at her own reference. "I can sense the presence of magic within a certain vicinity, and I can feel it within other people and objects."

"That's why you sent me into the storm. You knew—" Dain's voice stumbled into silence.

"Partially." Ileana reached down to play with the ends of her damp hair. "I knew something was within you, though it was deeply buried. My talent is not precise, and I only guessed the rest—after all, the skies were almost always calm when you were up on deck."

Dain wished he'd noticed it as early as the princess had. "Was this also how you knew about the journal, and why you led me to it?"

"It was. I felt the book years ago when you and your father first came to live upon *The Maiden*. It was imbued with a spell— a strong, potent enchantment." The princess dipped her head in sincerity, lowering her eyes demurely. "You must forgive me for taking liberties with your father's belongings, but I had great purpose for doing so. I read the journal long ago, on nights when I was flesh and the captain was away. It confirmed for me what I had felt within you. I knew the book was charmed. It pulsed with power. I guessed, even back then, that the tome might be significant to you—one day. This is why I stole the key, and left it for you. I promise, I am not normally a thief. I had no way of knowing the full implication of the journal's purpose in the end, but now I'm so glad that I did what I did."

Dain nodded thoughtfully. Ileana's account confirmed many things, but his mind turned back to the present. "Ileana, I've learned much since the last time we met, and now I realize the importance of the safe haven. My father promised it to Sable and her brother in Tallooj, and from what we can tell he's taken others there as well—others like us. You said that finding these people would help us. How do we find them? Are they in the north?"

The princess let go of her hair, and gazed intently between the pair. "Sadly, I do not know where it is. I drew the conclusion that it was in the north because of a conversation I overheard. Years ago, Captain Alloway spoke in hushed tones with a new crew member. He was a young man, clearly imbued with talents. His name was Jord. The captain told the boy that they would sail north to take him to the haven."

Dain remembered Jord, but barely. The young man hadn't lasted long on *The Maiden*. Crew hands were always coming and going. It was the normal ebb and flow of a merchant vessel, but it now made him wonder how many more of those transient sailors had been adept over the years.

Ileana spoke again. "I know it's imperative that we sail to Aalta right now, but perhaps after business is settled there, and the worst of winter has passed, we can sail north?"

Dain nodded in response to her question.

Ileana's brow drew together in concentration. "Your father kept impeccable records, did he not?" She waited for Dain to agree before continuing. "It might be worth retracing his last stops along the way. Maybe with some investigative inquires at each port, we'll find clues or connections to the adept he gathered throughout the years. Someone may know something."

Dain didn't think the princess was entirely convinced of her own plan. It was certainly an arduous route, but still plausible. Another idea struck him as well. "My mother's journal isn't comprehensive. You can tell by reading it that it's not the end of her studies, merely the beginning. If we can find her archives back in Aalta, she may have left some clues. Toff believes that before her death, she charged my father with a mission to protect me—but what if she charged him with more than that? What if she was the one who sent him out to save others?" Dain knew this was all speculation, but they had to start somewhere.

Ileana nodded thoughtfully and echoed his last thought out loud. "It is a place to start." Her gaze turned toward the porthole—sunrise was not far off. She turned back to them. "We must speak of a few more things before my time is up." The princess looked at Sable, her voice pitching an octave lower. "You own an item of immense magical power—I sensed it the minute you boarded this ship."

Sable's eyes widened briefly, looking genuinely confused. "I have no idea what you mean."

It took Dain a moment, but when he realized what Ileana might be referring to, he turned to his friend. "Sable, may we see your pendant?"

The girl stiffened. He knew why she hesitated—revealing something so personal to a stranger had to be difficult. Dain had forced her to do that once before, and he hated to ask it of her again, but he was pretty sure this was what Ileana was sensing. "Please?"

Sable stared at him for a moment longer before reluctantly pulling at the string around her neck. The pendant peeked out from under her blouse, and once it was released, she held it suspended in the air for Ileana to see.

"A *Dernamn?*" The princess reached toward it. "May I?"

Sable nodded as she pulled the cord over her head, handing the necklace to the princess.

Cradling it carefully in her palm, Ileana fingered the design. Then the lady closed her eyes. "Do you know the meaning of this symbol?"

Sable responded. "We know it was supposedly worn by the Selteez. The dove represents purity, the circles below signify the unity of the four kingdoms, and the three triangles represent the three creators. At least, that's what we read in the journal." Then the girl echoed Dain's exact thoughts. "Mind you, I have never heard of *three* creators before. I've only ever heard of Orthane."

Ileana remained silent. Long moments passed before she opened her eyes again. "Magic is not the only thing that has been stolen from our world." She didn't continue with the thought, instead she gently handed the necklace back to Sable. "This pendant is important, Sable. Guard it fiercely."

The girl accepted it back, but her expression was skeptical. "Why—why is it important?"

Ileana took a deep breath. "If I were to share the full scope of that with you, you couldn't fathom it. You, and most of those who dwell within the four kingdoms, were born *not* to fathom it. Although, one day, I hope the veil will be lifted."

Her words were so cryptic that Dain and Sable couldn't resist a confused glance at each other. When they looked back at Ileana, she smiled warmly, as though she were trying the dispel the mysticism of her words. "However, there is one thing I can tell you about the pendant. It is capable of summoning a god."

Sable stared at the necklace again, weighing it in her hand like she wondered how a simple piece of jewelry could be so powerful. Her words were rife with skepticism. "You have the talent to discern magic in people and items. You've proven that to us, so I guess I should believe you when you say that this pendant is magical. However, what I'm struggling to believe—not that I've ever been one to have faith in the divine, but like the annotation in the journal, you speak as though there is more than one god..."

Ileana nodded politely. "As I said before, I hope that one day everything will be revealed—just heed my warning, Sable, and keep the *Dernamn* safe. Now, listen carefully. I have more to share."

Before dawn struck, Ileana went on to describe why the stalkers did not follow on the sea—apparently if seawater touched them, they died, and even stepping on a ship was too great a risk of that. She said that it was the only way they could be destroyed, but on land they were unstoppable—immortal. She reminded them of the spell Toff said his mother used to confuse the stalkers, and suggested they try to find it.

Sable spoke up at that point. "I saw no such spell in the

journal."

Dain rubbed at the back of his neck, tangling his fingers in long, damp strands. "Perhaps it isn't there. It could be back home in Aalta? Either way, we are, none of us, alchemists—the spell would be useless."

Ileana stood, dark auburn hair falling in silken waves, glimmering in the approaching sunlight as she breathed her final words fast. "Indeed, *we* are not alchemists, but Tars *is*." Then the princess fled.

Dain wondered briefly how Ileana would reach the prow without being seen, but shortly after she exited, the green gown laden with gold embroidery dematerialized from the bed post, and Sable's gray frock appeared on the floor. Rectlor's horrible curse seemed to take care of itself.

He turned to see Sable replacing the *Dernamn* around her neck, tucking it back into her blouse carefully. She looked slightly shaken, but when her eyes lifted to meet his own, their hazel depths burned determinedly. He guessed that she might be thinking the same thing he was, but he voiced the thought first.

"We need to save Tars."

Chapter 18

The *Maiden* had been thrown off course during the storm, and the delay would add at least another day to their journey back. At first, Dain felt frustrated by the setback, but soon decided that any extra time might be a blessing.

Sable had re-bandaged his head. For all intents and purposes, they would keep up the appearance of his injury. For now, they would work on a rescue plan for Tars, and they would do so alone. The feigned injury would give them ample time to plan undisturbed. It would also postpone revealing the princess's presence. It would be difficult to explain how he'd been miraculously healed otherwise. Dain knew the first mate had his hands full with *The Maiden,* which after Tallooj ran on a bare-bones crew. Toff had recently been promoted to chief's mate, increasing his duties as well. Dain felt guilty deceiving them, but he reasoned that it was only temporary.

Sable had never explored the extent to which her talent could be pursued. Hiding from stalkers all her life had not afforded such luxuries. The journal had given both of them some insight into her potential; however, it had been Ileana who helped them to see that saving Tars might just be something an adjurationist could do.

Dain already knew Sable was capable of shifting things from great distances from the mountain herbs. She said could only command things from places she'd actually seen before, but Tallooj figured into that equation. The only obstacle was that she'd never shifted a person—not even herself. Nonetheless, Dain offered to be her first test subject. They knew it was risky, but after she successfully managed with a rat they found beneath his bed, Dain pushed the idea. It made him nervous, but he had a resolution to uphold. Plus, he knew how important Tars was to Sable, to them all. If the man could recreate his mother's spells, it would give them a decided advantage over the stalkers. It would also be easier to save others, and give them far more security in seeking out the safe haven.

They began practicing at night, when the chance of discovery was minimal.

"For Orthane's sake, stand still, Dain."

Dain fiddled restlessly by the desk in his office. "It's difficult, Sable. I lie around all day pretending to be injured. I can hardly bear the idleness anymore." They'd grown quite comfortable together, and formal address never applied now when they were alone. Dain enjoyed the casual air, even if it meant she scolded him occasionally. There were even times he found himself admiring her. He often stared at her thick lashes as they fluttered from place to place. He counted the freckles across her nose, and even followed her lips closely when she teased by calling him "Lion Cub." At times, he thought he caught her admiring him in a similar fashion, but he usually reasoned it away.

Sable's voice sliced through his reverie, her tone adding validity to his last thought. "Well, the sooner we figure this out, the sooner you'll have action on all sides. Now, stand still."

Dain smiled, stomped his foot, and stood like a proper soldier at attention. She rolled her eyes at him, but he was pretty sure he caught a wisp of a smile as she began to concentrate again.

In the earliest sessions, he had felt nothing while the girl attempted to shift him. More recently, a slight itching sensation had started to curl its way up his spine as she worked. Tonight, that feeling intensified. Dain watched Sable weave her fingers laboriously through the air as her eyelids clenched tight in concentration. The itch started to grow so insistent that Dain began to feel quite uncomfortable, disoriented even. He stumbled forward, eyes shut against his warping vision.

Then it passed, as quickly as it had come.

Opening his eyes, Dain saw only darkness. Feeling blindly about, he realized that he was inside Sable's cabin, his old quarters. The moment he managed to get his bearings, the insistent itch began again. Dain's head swam, and a second later, he stood back inside the well-lit office once more.

Sable tottered toward him. Reaching out fast, he caught her before she fell.

Exhaustion lined every inch of her frame, and her eyes drooped heavily. "I finally did it, didn't I?"

Dain lifted her easily, though he was still shaken by the transportation. He carried her to the four-poster bed in the adjoining room, laying her gently atop the covers. He pushed a few stray strands of hair from her face as her eyes closed. "Yes, you did. I knew you would." Then he covered her, and patted himself all over as he gave thanks that he was still in one piece.

* * *

As the weeks passed, Dain slowly "healed," and as a consequence, Sable was called upon to resume most of her regular duties on board. The extra labor drained her further, but the practice sessions still advanced. The girl grew stronger—she could shift Dain from cabin to cabin easily now, but shifting both of them still tipped her to the point of exhaustion. He knew she'd need strength enough to carry three people when the time came, so he drove her more. Even when her days on board were long and arduous, he pushed.

It wasn't until a week before they were due to land in Aalta that they decided it was time. Three weeks of training had not made Sable's endurance perfect, but they were hopeful that she could manage well enough. Dain knew the time had come to include Mo and Toff in their plans. If something were to happen, if he and Sable didn't return, it would be unfair to leave their friends with such a terrible mystery.

Dain summoned them all to a meal. Mo was suspicious. Dain could tell by the way his first mate carefully took a seat and shifted his eyes across the table between Sable and himself.

Old Toff seemed none the wiser. The first words out of his mouth as he sat at the captain's table came with a sharp slap to his knee. "Let's hope this meal is better than our last one." Laughing hard at his own joke, the old man proceeded to jabber loudly through the rest of the meal. He graced them all with countless tales from his previous lives as The Ghost of Aalta.

Sable soaked up the stories, her laughter contagiously joining with his.

Dain guessed that she simply wanted to enjoy the calm before the storm. He, however, could not suppress his own thoughts so easily. His mind whirred repeatedly through all the plausible outcomes: what if they failed to find him, what if Tars was already dead, what if they were taken by stalkers?

Mo noticed his distance. And while Toff entertained Sable with yet another escapade, the first mate set his attention on Dain, speaking softly. "Yer quiet this eve, lad. Are ye feeling well?"

Dain took in Mo's familiar features. "I believe I am quite nearly healed now. I plan to resume my regular duties soon."

Mo's pearly white teeth glistened as he smiled. "Har! Ye know that ain't what I mean, lad."

Smiling in spite of himself, Dain decided that there was no point in delaying the inevitable. Raising his voice above Toff's jawing, he interrupted. "Sable and I plan to return to Tallooj—tonight." It was a terrible introduction to the subject, but at least it was out in the open.

All talk ceased. Both Toff and Mo stared at their captain in silent confusion.

Dain heard Sable draw a long breath. "We plan to retrieve my brother. I have learned a great deal about my talent in the past weeks. It has—grown. I believe I am capable of commanding myself, and the captain, to Tallooj. We'll search for Tars and bring him back the same way."

Toff coughed loudly, then leaned forward on the table as he peered at Sable over his spectacles. "That'd be a suicide mission, girl. Using that much power would instantly draw the stalker's eyes. Neither of you would stand a chance."

"That's not entirely true." Dain felt his natural propensity toward leadership returning. He had taken so much time off that it surprised him. His role as captain flowed forth more easily than expected. "We are not as helpless, or as indefensible as you might think. We still have enough Harborage left to cover us both—that should help mask the shift, and us, long enough to get us onto the streets of Tallooj safely. After that, we'll stay carefully hidden as we search. We're clever, and we'll stay on our toes. And when we flash away, they won't be able to follow."

"Alis Alloway was clever too, sir, but remember, she was overtaken by stalkers herself in the end." Toff's jovial demeanor had vanished entirely. "I caution strongly against this, Captain."

"I appreciate your concern, and I acknowledge your warning. However, I have already made my decision in this, and more." Dain faced everyone at the table. Stretching his leanly muscled arms wide, he grasped both corners of the table in front of him. "And I now invite you, Sable included, to become a part of that *more*. For generations, people have been hunted, drained, and murdered for their talents. My father gave his life trying to save them, but I believe that we need to take things a step further." Dain's knuckles tightened white. "This immoral genocide must end, and the only way for that to happen is to fight back. There needs to be no more death, and no more running. This rescue mission is only the beginning."

Turning pointedly from one individual to the next, Dain noted their expressions; Mo looked at him with what could only be described as pride, Sable returned his gaze with fierce loyalty, and Old Toff—well, the Ghost surprised him. The sailor sat wiping large crocodile tears from his wrinkled cheeks. "You are most definitely your mother's son."

Morgan Crouse rose from his chair, and in one giant stride he stood beside Dain. Placing an enormous hand on Dain's shoulder, the man made a pledge. "I am ever in yer service, Captain." Then he turned to look directly at Sable. "Let's retrieve that brother of yers then, shall we?"

Chapter 19

Toff held firm to Dain's coat sleeve as he pulled him through the shadows. Even at night, in the dim light of the street lanterns, Tallooj was a sorry sight. Filth and litter lined the cobblestone streets. The piles of garbage were only half-hidden by a light skiff of snow. The brick buildings looked centuries old, and seemed to be deteriorating into rubble where they stood. Dain cringed inwardly as he imagined Sable living on these streets for months, but it was an image that served to further strengthen his resolve. She deserved freedom.

Toff had convinced them that Sable needed to stay behind on *The Maiden*. He reasoned that she was their ultimate failsafe. If anything were to happen to her, then everyone would be left stranded in Tallooj.

Sable had resisted, but only briefly. She was always quick to see the practical side of a situation. Dain admired her for that.

They had discussed searching for Tars during the day, when the stalkers were less apt to roam, but the problem was that he might be anywhere during the daytime, on the move. At least at night, he'd be still. In the end, they had settled on a search at twilight. Sable had drafted them a map of all the places where her brother might be sheltering. When she had finally shifted the pair of them to Tallooj, she'd placed them right inside the first plausible hideout.

After the disorienting itch dissipated, Dain and Old Toff had found themselves on a rooftop, where six chimneys formed a semi-circle. The stacks provided warmth, and solid camouflage from the streets below. The plan was to return to this location by dawn, right in the middle of the smokestacks— that way, Sable would know exactly where they were. From there, the instant the sun rose, she'd conjure them all back to *The Maiden*. Dain had made the girl promise to rest in between, hoping her strength would be renewed when their critical hour arrived.

Before they left, Dain and Toff had been thoroughly doused in the foul-smelling Harborage potion, and thus far it seemed to be working. Of course, the potion wouldn't last forever, and he was thankful that the old man somehow managed to navigate them invisibly through the streets. Dain tried hard to note Toff's choices. He paid close attention to how the old man's feet fell, and where his eyes scanned. It wasn't a formal lesson in stealth, but Dain absorbed everything he could. All the while, he wondered why he was not afraid—or rather, he worried that he should be.

It was a long night of searching; they had almost reached the twelfth hideout marked on Sable's map when the old sailor made his first sudden stop in the shadows. Toff's nose was high in the air.

To Dain's eye, he resembled a weathered hound. Toff remained still in the comical position for only a moment before he motioned at Dain to resume the trek, shaking his head.

The next three locations were also empty. Stopping by a broken-down shack, the old man pulled Dain into the shadow of a crooked doorframe, whispering close. "I don't think we're going to find him, Captain. Dawn approaches, and we are running out of time. If he's even still alive, he may have found a dozen new hideouts that aren't marked on this map. This is like trying to find a needle in a haystack—a needle that doesn't want to be found."

Dain was having the same thoughts. While Sable's map was extensive, her brother may have already moved well beyond its locations. And because of this, Dain had decided to bring his father's compass. He hadn't told anyone about his theory—in fact, the idea had only occurred to him the night Toff gave his testimony. When Dain heard that his father had referred to the compass while searching for Tars, he wondered if the broken instrument wasn't really broken at all. Perhaps he should have had Ileana test the object for magic before he gambled on it, but she would have no way to communicate what she sensed right now, and either way, it was worth a try. Pulling the compass from his jacket pocket, Dain gazed at the swaying arrow within. It was hard to make out the small, red-tipped pointer under the dim street lamps. It was only a second before the arrow swung into action. First it pointed at Dain, and then it swayed quickly to the northwest.

When Dain finally looked up at Toff, he could see that the old sailor understood. He supposed the man had experienced enough magic in his life to know that this compass might just lead them directly to what they were searching for, in this case Tars. Dain handed the instrument to Toff, and silently indicated that he should lead the way.

The Ghost of Aalta resumed his hunt more swiftly than before.

A lazy drizzle of snow began to fall as they followed the swaying arrow. Miniature flecks of white floated softly through the darkness, alighting upon a graveyard of rubble as the compass pointed onward, through it.

Climbing through the rubble quietly was a struggle even for Toff.

When they reached the heart of the mound, Dain stopped.

Crunch.

Toff halted, staring down at the compass as though it was going to jump from his hands, and then his head snapped to look behind them. Dain swiveled slowly, but before he'd even made a half turn, a dark figure lunged from the shadows. He groped for his dagger, but the attacker angled toward Toff instead.

The old sailor was too fast. Toff slipped easily out of their assailant's path, and let the flying figure slam roughly against the half wall of rock behind him. It was mere seconds before Toff had the attacker secured, on his knees and firmly confined. Casper had definitely over-exaggerated his defensive role in Eandor Vid. Toff was far too good to let himself be taken by surprise. The old man had been, and still was, a true assassin thief.

Stepping carefully toward the pair, Dain leaned down to examine the attacker's features in the dim light.

Small snowflakes landed on thick lashes as large, hazel orbs stared defiantly up at him. The man's resemblance to Sable was uncanny. They had found Tars—or rather, the compass had.

Dain bent down toward the man's ear. "We mean you no harm. Sable sent us."

Tars's eyes went frantic, and he seemed to lose all sense. Writhing against Toff's hold, he screamed, "Where is she? If you have harmed one hair on her head, I will tear you to pieces!"

The old man cinched harder. "Be silent, you fool! Stalkers aren't deaf, and you're making enough noise to call an entire army of them down upon us."

Dain watched as Tars worked to suppress his wrath. The mention of stalkers seemed to help quell his rage, but his body still quivered with the effort. Eventually, Tars managed to still himself, yet the defiance never left his gaze.

Sable had mentioned that her brother was not the trusting sort. It was unlikely that Dain could win him over in the next few minutes, and they had a long trek back to the chimney stacks. Time was short. Dain leaned forward again, but this time he let his voice drift into a fiercely threatening tone. "Listen to me closely, Tars Cortham. If you *ever* want to see your sister alive again, you will follow us quietly and obediently. If you betray us, or make one false move, then I swear to you that Sable will not live to sing another day." Dain punctuated these quiet lies by ripping the man free of Toff's grasp and silently shoving him, arm twisted behind his back, facedown in the rubble. "Is that clear?"

Tars growled audibly, and Dain twisted the arm harder as he squirmed. To his credit, though, the man stayed quiet despite the increased pain, and after a moment, he gave a curt nod of agreement. Dain dragged him to his feet, dagger poised at Tars's back, urging him forward through the ruins.

Toff silently skirted around them to take the lead. The old man waved a barely visible hand, directing them to follow in his footsteps.

When they reached the street, Dain moved forward to stand alongside Sable's brother. Tars refused to look at him. The man kept his chin straight ahead as he focused on Toff's every move. He was near Dain's height, but much broader in the shoulders, and far thicker across the chest. Dain was shocked that, considering his own more leanly muscled frame, he had managed to wrestle this man to the ground.

Up ahead, Toff stopped inside a large shadowed doorway, and waved fast for the two of them to follow.

Dain didn't notice the change in temperature immediately. It wasn't until they reached Toff that he felt it. The chill. It was not the normal cold one expected to feel on a snowy winter's eve. It was more severe, somehow. Like tiny, solid stakes of ice being driven through his flesh. A violent shiver writhed through Dain's entire body, and he noticed the others were shaking as well.

Toff lifted a finger to his lips, encouraging them to stay silent.

Dain suddenly wished that he had brought the Harborage for Sable's brother as well. Shifting closer to the vibrating man, Dain hoped the potion was still in effect, and that his own proximity might help to mask Tars as well. The raw terror only intensified. Dain wondered if his bones might begin to rattle, but it wasn't until something inside suddenly urged him to run that he fully panicked. Shooting a frantic glance at Toff, he barely kept his frame from writhing as the old man lifted a silent hand.

He was telling them to wait. And against every natural instinct known to man, Dain obeyed. Straining through the tremors, he listened desperately for any sign of their pursuers.

Nothing.

His heart raced faster, and Dain couldn't seem to find a natural rhythm in his breath. The ends of his fingers began tingling as a numbing sensation spread up toward his palms. He had never been so afraid, or so cold.

After an incalculable spell, the sensations began to subside. They ebbed ever so slowly away, like a frozen tide returning to the sea. The natural winter air felt unexpectedly warm in comparison. A remnant of dread lingered, but Dain still sagged forward in relief.

Toff made them stay where they were for several moments longer before he slunk out from the door frame to peer down the street.

Dain noticed that he no longer held the dagger poised at Tars. Sheathing the weapon, he decided that, for the sake of his sister, the man would likely them follow without further prompting.

Toff had already moved a short distance up the street. The old sailor was once again swallowed in shadow.

The snow began to fall thickly as Dain and Tars mimicked the old man's moves. They now left large, visible footprints as they traveled, and Dain hoped that the stalker had continued on a long way off. If he remembered correctly, they were still fairly far from the rooftop refuge, and dawn was less than an hour away.

The snowflakes grew larger, giant falling discs that brightly reflected the sparse streetlights. The wind swirled behind the trio, as though trying to sift the snow over their deep footsteps. Dain gave thanks to the element.

Toff picked up the pace, slicing and swerving more quickly through the streets. How could a man his age move so quickly?

After rounding another two corners, the street opened wide and their rooftop destination came into view. One more block, and they'd be safe. Dain heaved a sigh of relief just as the wall of iced terror returned.

There was nowhere to hide. And if the stalker accounts were accurate, it might only be minutes before the demon arrived. Standing to fight would mean death, and running wouldn't get them any farther. They needed cover, and they needed it now. Dain made a quick decision. He knew that using his talent would draw the stalker's gaze more accurately, but while they might sense the magic, it would be useless if they couldn't see their prey. He reached deep inside, and this time, the elements reached eagerly for him in return. Dain wondered if they somehow knew they wouldn't be reined in.

The large, lazy snowflakes turned frantic, and the wind began to whip wildly. Dain urged the elements to peel forth in an ivory fury, and then he snatched for Toff and Tars and dragged the two men along behind him. Tallooj became a freezing blur of white snow.

Tars ran in silence, but Dain heard Toff cursing as they tripped through streets.

Before all visibility was lost, Dain made a quick mental map of how to reach the alleyway access. He only hoped that he could now stay the course blind.

The elements raged on with furious joy. They pounded the buildings around them, and tore at Dain and his companions without restraint. Holding and releasing his breath with each step, Dain navigated them slowly through the curtain of snow. He was constantly afraid that, at any moment, a black figure might materialize before them through the blizzard. When he finally felt certain that they had neared the access, Dain drew on the internal elemental reins. He commanded the storm to dissipate so he could get a visual on their shelter, hoping desperately that the stalkers were disoriented enough to give them a chance.

The wind decreased first, and then the snow lessened as well.

Walking had warded off some of the cold, but now, as he stood still, Dain felt the chilled dread begin to seep back in. The sensation spurred him forward faster, thankful that he had gauged the distance correctly—the alley was only a few paces ahead. Without so much as a glance back through the streets, he dragged the two men behind him into a run. It only took seconds. Dropping his grasp on the others, Dain scrambled for the stacked crates that provided a makeshift ladder up to the first windowsill. He didn't look around, only listened to be sure the others were climbing behind him. Dain's heart beat nearly to bursting as they scaled the building. They needed to get to the roof, out of sight.

The moment Dain pulled himself up over the roof ledge, he saw it—a figure lurking through the lantern-lit streets below. It was dressed in blood-red robes now dusted with snow, and it moved with lethal grace. Plunging flat against the opposite side of the trusses, Dain pressed himself hard into the snowy wooden tiles, and the others immediately followed suit. Slithering hand-over-hand along the peak, Dain slowly worked his way toward the stacks while Toff and Tars followed close behind him. The remnant lure of his magic must be strong, because when Dain risked another glance over the edge, the singular stalker had been joined by two more. His urge to run grew more pressing. Ducking his head down again, Dain tried to shuffle more quickly. His limbs went weak. His grasp slipped. He'd forgotten about the fatigue that came along with using his talent. Scrambling to latch onto the peak, Dain missed the mark entirely as drifts of snow propelled him downward. The wind buffeted beneath him as though trying to shove him back up, but it wasn't the wind that stopped his fall, it was the hand that quickly grasped the edge of his coat sleeve.

Dain looked up to see Tars clinging desperately to the roof edge with one arm as he yanked Dain up with the other. Wriggling carefully, Dain assisted the upward motion as best he could until he was close enough to grasp the peak again. Looking briefly toward Sable's brother, he gave the man a silent nod of thanks. Tars's face was blank. Dain didn't have time to contemplate the expression, as fear pressed them on in a slow, steady belly crawl.

When he finally reached the chimney group, Dain turned to see raw relief in the faces of his companions, and he imagined that it must be equally evident in his own. The warmth of the stacks did little to ease the onslaught of undiluted terror, but at least they were out of sight.

For all the talk about how fast these demons were, Dain only noted a slow, meticulous scan below. Through the crack between the stacks, he watched as the red demons, many of them now, roamed. It appeared as though the stalkers knew an adept was near, and they were quite content to do a calm, thorough search for their cornered prey. And Dain knew it was only a matter of time before they found them. Drawing a deep breath, he uttered the first wordless prayer of his life. He had no idea who he was praying to, perhaps Orthane, perhaps one of the mysterious gods mentioned in his mother's journal, but he begged for one of them to speed the dawn.

Chapter 20

Whether a god answered his prayer or not, Dain would never know, but as the snow continued to fall, a dim glow soon radiated through the dense clouds above. An itch drove itself along Dain's spine. He saw Tars's eyes grow wide, and Toff's shoulders sagged in relief.

She was pulling them back.

Dain peeked again through the stacks. Three crimson hoods swung fast toward the rooftop, sensing the magic. Tearing his gaze away from the empty-faced demons, Dain pressed his back against the brick, and tried to steady his breathing.

The itch grew more insistent.

Hurry, Sable. *Hurry.*

Moments later, Dain and his companions stood in the center of his office, shivering, disoriented, relieved, and drenched from the snow.

Once his head cleared, Dain sought Sable's face. When he found her, the sight made his chest nearly burst with pride. Though she slumped against an attentive Mo, she was still standing. He wanted to shout, he wanted to tell everyone of the incredible feat she had just accomplished. He'd only taken three steps toward her when something fastened hard onto his wet hair and pulled him, with irresistible force, to the floor. A swift, strong pair of hands wrapped themselves firmly around his throat, and Dain's vision blurred as he watched Tars hovering angrily above him. Darkness threatened, but barely a second passed before he could breathe again. Dain sucked at the air furiously as he watched his attacker being easily lifted into the air.

Mo stood just above, his two enormous arms clutched around a writhing Tars. The first mate looked as calm as if he were holding a large doll.

Toff now supported Sable, letting her lean hard against him as she stumbled toward her brother. Reaching out a tired arm to Tars, the girl cupped her sibling's clenched face with one hand.

The man's eyes flew wide, and then he went completely still.

"Shhhh . . ." Sable cooed. "I am safe. You are safe. These are my friends."

Mo slowly released his grasp on the rigid man, and gently set him on his feet.

Tars crumpled, sinking to his knees in front of his sister. With Toff's help, Sable lowered herself down beside her brother. Tars snatched her fast, pulling her into his lap and cradling her like a child.

Sable began to sing a low, soothing lullaby as she ran her fingers through her brother's hair.

Rubbing at his throat and pulling himself to his feet, Dain backed away. Mo and Toff had already left ahead of him. As Dain closed the door, he shot one last glance at the siblings. Tars was rocking Sable like a baby, and all Dain could think was, *No more running, no more hiding.*

* * *

The bucket of water was cold, but after what he'd just experienced in Tallooj, everything felt warm in comparison. For over an hour, Dain had tried to sleep. His old bunk smelled sweetly of herbs and rosewater, but even Sable's scent did little to soothe his nerves. The chilling remnant of stalker-induced fear lingered on. The feeling reminding him of all those nights, so many years ago, when *The Maiden's* ghost stories had haunted him. If stalkers could infest a soul with such thorough terror, then how could someone persist in defying them? He suddenly felt more sympathy for what his crew had endured during the first Tallooj attack. It surprised him that no one had spoken of it, this cutting fear. Perhaps it was too hard to discuss? Or perhaps it was because it made you feel like less of a man? He thought of how the first mate had taught him to set an opponent off guard by upending his emotions. It seemed the stalkers used the same tactic, only it came in the form of potent magic.

Bending naked over the bucket, Dain tried to wash away the frightful unease, but no amount of scrubbing seemed to help. Blindly grappling for the towel, he yelped when he felt a hand pass it into his palm. Swiping the water from his eyes and hastily wrapping the sheet around his waist, Dain recognized Sable's small frame leaning against the nearest wall. A mischievous smile played across her lips. She hadn't used the door.

"Is there no privacy on this ship?" Dain knew his face was flushed with embarrassment.

"Oh come now, Captain, we've shared the same quarters for weeks, and now you complain about privacy?"

"At that time, close quarters were a necessity. And you never helped me bathe."

"I offered."

It was true, she had offered during the worst of his injury. Of course, he'd never accepted. Wrapping the sheet more firmly about his waist, he tried to ignore her last statement. "I hope you don't plan to make these uninvited appearances a habit?"

"And if I do?"

Dain cocked his eyebrow, leaning forward. "Then you'll have to spend the rest of this voyage in the brig."

Sable burst out laughing. "You think you can keep *me* in the brig?"

He had grown to love her laugh. Through the giggles, she said, "I'll be honest, I didn't expect to find you awake, and then it was just so tempting—" Her laugher ceased as her cheeks began to brighten. "Well, what I mean is, it was tempting to give you a start. I suppose considering your undressed state, and last night—this wasn't very proper, or appropriate. I really should have thought—"

Flustered, the girl dug into the pocket of her sage-colored frock, and pulled out a small, folded letter. "I only planned to leave this here while you slept. It's a thank you note. Oh, and I wanted to bring you a change of clothes." She indicated the fresh pile on the bunk. "Tars is finally sleeping. And I should probably join him soon, but we'll be out of your quarters by noon. I'll keep him hidden here, in my cabin, until we reach Aalta."

Accepting the paper, Dain glanced at the clothes, and then back to Sable's lowered lashes. "I couldn't sleep."

Looking up, she fixed her large hazel eyes firmly on his own grays. "It passes, you know."

"What?"

"The cold panic. It passes—eventually."

Dain didn't know how to respond. It only made him wonder how many times she had suffered through the stalker-induced fear herself. The thought made his heart ache, and he shivered again, remembering.

Clearing her throat, Sable changed the subject. "Dain, how did you locate Tars in the end? He told me he wasn't hidden in any of our usual spaces."

Her question sparked a little joy in Dain's frayed demeanor—he knew she was going to love this answer. Setting her note on the crate beside his bunk, he reached for his still-wet jacket, and pulled his father's compass from the folds. Handing the instrument to Sable, he kept quiet while she examined it.

Tilting her head sideways, the girl looked up at him. "It's pretty, but it's broken."

"That's exactly what I thought too, but that's not the case." Dain pointed at the instrument. "Watch the arrow again. Watch where it points exactly."

Sable's brow furrowed as she concentrated on the swaying needle. "It points approximately west, then east, then basically north, and south, then it repeats again. The same pattern over and over."

"Yes." Dain took the compass, and held it up for both of

them to see. "Look, it doesn't just point in those directions. It actually points at you and me, then the wooden princess, and then toward Tars in my quarters."

Sable's eyes went wide. "The compass has been charmed. So that's how your father tracked us down in Tallooj that afternoon." She rubbed her chin thoughtfully. "Your mother must have created it. This will come in handy in the future."

Turning it over again in his palm, Dain envied his late mother's talent a little.

Sable cleared her throat again. "I guess, since you are awake, I really ought to just thank you in person." Dain looked up to see her thick lashes flutter briefly before she lunged. Her arms encircled him fiercely as her head pushed hard into his damp chest. "Thank you, Dain. Thank you for risking yourself to save my brother." Then, just as quickly, she released him and disappeared.

Standing, surprised, compass still in hand, Dain's skin was hot where she had touched him, and he regretted not embracing her back.

* * *

The cool sea breeze played with Dain's long, matted mane. His body rose and fell with the waves as he perched comfortably on the bowsprit. Every stir of wind, every drop of moisture in the air, every current of elemental energy sent sparks off inside of him. His talent thrummed, invisible, beneath his skin. He was growing accustomed to the sensation now, but an occasional surge still surprised him. Releasing the ever-eager wind, Dain sent a hearty gust to fill the sails. It propelled *The Maiden* onward as he leaned casually on his perch. No one noticed; no one even gave him a second glance. He was merely the recently recovered captain, finally enjoying some air up on deck.

Dain spoke to the wooden princess intermittently, keeping his voice low as he gazed toward the horizon. Her silent confidence, coupled with the crisp morning air, worked to soothe his nerves slightly.

He knew that Sable was right. The fear would pass—eventually.

He'd planned to take the helm today, but then thought twice, deciding that the crew needed to see him resume his duties slowly. A rhythm had finally returned to *The Maiden*. Things were relatively settled again after the first Tallooj attack, and Dain didn't want to disrupt the flow, or stir up any suspicious unrest. Sable, Mo, and Toff seemed to have the same idea. He'd seen all three of them up and at their regular duties shortly after lunch.

Dain didn't return to his quarters until mid-afternoon, but when he arrived, he found everything in perfect order. No sign of Tars, or Sable. The space was now his own again, and instead of feeling unburdened, he found himself at a loss. He'd grown used to Sable's constant presence, he wasn't sure he wanted her gone.

Thankfully, the frosty dread had eased itself into a dull haze, so a nap was immediately in order. He lay his head down on the lush pillows of his four-poster bed, and sleep found him quickly this time.

His mother met him on the other side of slumber, where she earnestly offered him an outstretched palm. Dain took her hand willingly in his own. Their twin, storm-filled gazes met, and he noticed her altered age. She had always been youthful in his dreams, the way he'd remembered her as a child, but now she appeared to be the same age as his father before he'd died. They walked, and the fields before them burst with wildflowers, the endless ripples of color flaring to life as beauty trumped adversity. Dain closed his eyes to breathe in the fragrant air, and the last eddy of stalker fear finally disintegrated.

When he opened them again, his mother had vanished. The fields were replaced by leagues of beryl water. Dain walked alone across the waves. Staring out toward the horizon where the salmon skies plunged into the sea, he saw a distant ship hovering there. An urge to reach the vessel overcame him, and he burst into a run, but the more he sprinted, the further the ship faded in the distance. Dain only drew near enough to see that the frame was constructed of pure gold, the sails blowing crimson on the breeze.

* * *

Died low the wind, and sails unstirred
Tears mourning dropped to be
We rose to find a frightful sight
As silence rocked the sea

Over the mast, beyond the world
Amidst the blood-red sky
Hovering so sad, forlorn
The three moons hung on high

Would this be death, would this be life
No way to know, no way to fight
Find the peace in silence still
Behold the merrow's flight

'Twas night and day, and day and night
No motion played, or swayed
Lithe forms swam nigh through beryl waves
Beckoning, they showed the way

It was upon that midnight hour
That men found life, beneath a squall
Of stone-cold waves, and battered shores
Scales glimmered saving one and all

Sable's voice carried high through the chilly evening air, "The Merrow's Ballad" ringing from her chest as though a true siren called it.

Dain had never heard the song like this before. Goosebumps rose on his arms as Trait joined the chorus.

Would this be death, would this be life
No way to know, no way to fight
Find the peace in silence still
Behold the merrow's flight

Seconds after the ballad's last note dropped, a wicked peal shrieked from Dev's flute, and Dain watched Trait lock elbows with Sable. He dragged her in circles as they plunged into a rowdy folk tune. The crew followed suit, stomping their heels, and twirling each other gleefully across the deck as the music escalated. Dain's own foot tapped lightly in response.

The Maiden was only two days out from Aalta, and Dain had no idea what awaited them back on land. As he stood leaning against the foremast, his attention was drawn to the port side. No one would have seen it from the main deck, but from Dain's vantage point, he glimpsed a figure retreating into the shadows. It was Tars. The man had tucked himself safely out of sight, but he was still within earshot of his sister. A silent, hidden sentinel. It would probably be a long time before the man left his sister's side for any extended length of time.

Shifting his gaze to the party below, Dain saw an enormous form making its way through the lantern lights.

Mo leaped up the steps to the prow. Pulling away from

241

the foremast, Dain looked up into the first mate's faintly lit features. The whites of Mo's eyes gleamed against the darkness as Dain greeted him. "Evening Mr. Crouse. Are you ready for some leave?"

"Aye, Captain, a chance for leave is always welcome."

Dain lowered his tone. "I wanted to thank you for watching over Sable last night. Your support was important."

Mo dropped his voice as well. "I did little compared to the likes of ye, but I'm always happy to be of service, lad." He twisted the thick golden hoop in his left ear as he shifted his gaze to the merriment below. "This magic business be perplexing, and I'm not sure I've wrapped my mind around it yet."

Dain followed Mo's gaze, and ended up fixing his eyes on Sable's bright, singing smile. "My mind is most definitely not wrapped around it."

"Yet, ye have some magic yerself, do ye not?"

Dain's head snapped up.

A deep, silken chuckle rose from the first mate's chest. "I glimpsed ye on the night of the storm. I saw ye making yer way back below after the gale settled. And after Toff's account of the sudden storm that blew in and out of Tallooj last night— well, I figured it must be ye. The Lion of the Sea apparently rules the wind and the skies." Mo's arm swung up to take in the full scope of the stars. "So many years with ye here, and I never knew it. I only figured ye were lucky."

Dain wasn't sure how to respond. He hadn't really wanted to tell anyone else. "All those years, and I never knew myself, Mo . . ." Swinging his head to search through the shadows for Tars again, Dain pushed at the errant hairs the wind now playfully shoved in his face. "As you always say, 'Life is what it is.'"

"Do ye quote me often, lad?"

He laughed. "More than you'd know."

Clapping Dain hard on the back, Mo's voice nearly drowned out the music. "Well, I am flattered, lad."

For a time, he and the first mate silently stood in the cool air, enjoying the music and their jovial crew.

Dain eventually located Tars again. Staring intently in the man's direction, he wondered if the healer might actually talk to him now that he knew everyone aboard *The Maiden* was a friend.

Following Dain's gaze, Mo said, "I was wondering—that is, I was thinking about that safe place, the one that the lass mentioned weeks back. Where do ye suppose that is?"

Dain's eyes remained locked on Sable's shadowy brother. "That's a good question, Mo. No amount of searching through my father's records has produced a clue. Perhaps it's up north, but honestly, I don't know. Hopefully, a little investigation back in Aalta will help. We need to find it, there's no question about that. If the location is secure, and the people there do feel safe, then I won't force anyone to leave, but I do hope that some of them will join our cause." Dain tore his gaze away from Tars to look up at Mo. "This slaughter won't end without a fight, and a war like that cannot be won by so few of us."

Mo only gave a grunt of agreement.

Dain's words felt ominous, even to himself. He knew that the stalkers and their hired hands weren't the only thing to contend with—other foes stood in their path as well. If everything Ileana had said was true the first day she'd revealed herself to him, then they might even one day face an emperor.

Chapter 21

Of all the cities in all the kingdoms, none compared with the classical beauty of Zaal's capital. Beyond the harbor, beyond the bustling, carriage-lined streets, the white spires and columned pillars of Aalta rose out of the gray gloom. The dull clutches of winter barely diminished the city's glimmer—it was incomparably reflective, and it welcomed every ship with glowing arms.

The first person to greet Dain on the pier was Dougal Thornwalsh. The new master of the Alloway Trading Company stood patiently by as all the necessary port logistics were put in order—the cargo was unloaded, the remaining crew were compensated and sent on leave, and guards were hired to attend to *The Maiden* in their absence.

Casper, Dev, and Trait said their goodbyes to Dain, inquiring whether or not they might be considered for the new crew that would assemble after the worst of winter had passed.

Dain told them they were welcome to apply, but deep down, he wasn't too sure how they'd feel once they knew the true nature of his upcoming voyages. Clasping each of their hands firmly, Dain thanked them for their faithful service, and wished them a pleasant leave.

Sable and Tars had been ushered off in secrecy. They'd been coated in what remained of the Harborage, and sent to Alloway Manor along with a note for Lydia. He hoped they would be secure enough there until he could get all of the company business out of the way.

Toff and Mo refused to leave Dain's side. They mirrored his every step as they followed Thornwalsh to the company carriage, then headed into the city.

* * *

Floor-to-ceiling windows fixed within towering marble walls boasted a glorious view of Aalta's city center. Leaning back into a luxuriously cushioned chair, Dain wondered how different his life would be if he were to ever return to Aalta permanently. The softness of the opulent armchair was only a slight hint. He leaned back further. Dain had listened for hours to Thornwalsh discussing endless points of business, and felt thankful that the company master was finally wrapping it all up.

Dougal nodded his head in sympathy as he droned. "I am saddened that *The Maiden* suffered such terrible losses in

Tallooj, and then there was that squall you faced shortly after . . ." Shuffling through the final bit of paperwork on his massive walnut desk, Thornwalsh sucked air through his teeth as he spoke. "We were concerned by your delay, but now I am only thankful to hear that no one else was hurt during the foray. As you are aware, sir, the families who lost loved ones have been sent compensation and missives, but I have also taken the liberty of sending extra gifts. Plus, a shipyard crew has been dispatched to examine your vessel. We should make sure *The Maiden* sustained no lasting damage in the storm." The man looked up at Dain, a deeper line of concern marking his brow. "I know you've had the funeral arrangements set for three days hence, but I must ask, despite this difficult time, when do you intend to report the Tallooj murders to the Aaltain authorities?"

Dain had expected this question—there was no way around it. His father's death, the lost crew members, it would all have to be officially investigated. However, the ordinary world knew little or nothing of magic, and Dain understood that the truth wasn't the kind of tale the Aaltain authorities would believe. This city was built on progress; it prided itself on modern innovation, infrastructure, commerce, and liberal-minded philosophies. In Aalta, magic was an archaic notion, long lost in the mythic annals of history. Dain knew Mo had worked hard on the crew these past two months to downplay the nature of the attackers in Tallooj. The first mate had tried to convince the men that the assailants were only specially trained brigands. Dain had no idea how well that ruse had stuck, but for his part, as Aaltain gentry, he'd need to stick with reducing the stalkers to mere men.

He still needed a bit more time to decide the best way to represent the story. He looked Thornwalsh firmly in the eye. "I had hoped that those legalities could be left until after the funeral. I am sure you can understand, Master Thornwalsh?"

The man's lips cinched sideways, and a sympathetic crease etched his brow again. He really was a good man.

Dain changed the subject before more talk of his father's death ensued. "It seems our delay gave you ample time to put all of this business in order before I arrived. I am grateful for your labors. You have done well indeed, Master Thornwalsh. I do not regret promoting you. And I am exceedingly pleased that you are willing to take on so much more responsibility in my upcoming absence."

As expected, Thornwalsh's expression shifted from sorrow to gratitude. "Happy to be of service to you, and to the company, sir. This new position has done a wonder of good for my family. They have asked me to express their great gratitude to you as well."

"Well, that is definitely the kind of good news I needed today. I am happy to hear it all." Dain knew that Mo and Toff would wait as patiently as necessary outside the office, but he didn't want to keep them there much longer, so he pushed onward. "Now, you mentioned that there was one last order of business to discuss before I depart?"

Thornwalsh hummed in agreement, rummaging once more through the papers on his desk. "Yes, right, I've come across something odd—a mysterious record. I found it in the company vault." Donning a pair of reading spectacles, Thornwalsh lifted a worn, yellowing paper. "It seems we have an additional ship in our merchant fleet, but it's not on any other official business records."

Dain bent forward in his chair. "Is that so?"

"Yes, and barely anything is logged here. It simply states that it's a carnival vessel. As you know, carnival ships would seem an exceedingly low form of business for your father to engage in, but one never can say." Clearing his throat and removing his spectacles, the company master looked up. "According to this schedule, it's due to take port here in a fortnight. Honestly, sir, in all my searching I haven't been able to determine why we own it, nor the nature of its contribution to the company."

Dain stood, took the paper, and perused the Zaalish text. It contained nothing more than what Thornwalsh had relayed. "Do you think that the records could have been misplaced or stolen?"

The older gentleman shook his head doubtfully. "I suppose that's possible, sir. However, merchant records are of little monetary value to a common thief. Future port dates might be of use to a pirate, but other than that—" Thornwalsh rubbed at his chin, and then shrugged his shoulders.

Dain folded the sheet of paper. "Well, I suppose we'll find out exactly where this phantom ship fits into the company scheme when, and if, it arrives." He lowered his voice. "In the meantime, let's keep this between you and I."

Thornwalsh nodded in agreeable obedience.

* * *

The horse's hooves clicked on the cobbles as the leafless oak-lined lane broke wide and Alloway Manor came into view. Like most of the architecture in the city, the mansion was constructed of solid white marble, and somehow the stone still managed to gleam in the cold, foggy drizzle of winter. The classical peak and extensively pillared veranda may have looked imposing to some, but the sight was warmly inviting to Dain.

For the entire carriage ride, he had listened impatiently while Toff complained. The old man whined about the ruts in the road, and he cursed the horses for being so poorly trained. Accustomed to the smooth sway of the sea, any sailor would find the hard thump of a carriage—inconvenient. However, Dain thought that if anyone should be complaining, it was Mo. The first mate had not jammed his hulking form into this conveyance easily, but once inside, the man had suffered the journey in silence.

For the most part, Dain joined Mo in his silence. It was good to be back on land, but so much weighed upon this visit. Dain couldn't help asking if Toff had noted anything unusual in the city. The old man had not, but he said that he planned to head back in as soon as possible to connect with old contacts.

The carriage dropped them at the expansive front steps, and as Dain made his way up to the veranda, Lydia burst forth from the giant manor doors. Her short but ample frame ran from the mansion straight toward him. Bracing himself for the onslaught of affection, Dain smiled as his former nurse hugged him fiercely. "You're back. At long last. By Orthane, how I've missed you." Pulling her wet face away, Lydia looked up at him with concern. "I am so very sorry for the loss of your father, my dear."

Dain reached down to embrace her back, and Lydia leaned into him again. This woman had been hired on as his nurse just before she turned fifteen years old, younger than Dain was now. Her father had also died tragically, and being the oldest of five in a low-income family, Lydia had taken on the responsibility of supporting her mother and younger siblings. When he was born, Alloway Manor became Lydia's place of employment and her home, and it had remained so for seventeen years. She was a permanent fixture here, one that Dain always looked forward to seeing, despite her incessant hugs. Looking down into her cobalt eyes, Dain flipped an orange curl from her wet cheek and smiled. "All is well. I've dealt with a lot already, but it eases everything to be back here with you."

Pulling out of his embrace, she stood back to look him up and down appraisingly. "My, how you've grown. I imagine you're nearly a man, am I right?"

Dain heard Mo give a small chuckle behind him.

The sound made Lydia turn. She wiped what remained of her tears on the sleeve of her blouse, and promptly placed a fist on each of her generous hips. "Well, it's been years since I've seen the likes of these two scoundrels."

Only a grunt escaped Toff's lips, but Mo walked up the remainder of the veranda steps to stand politely in front of Lydia. His enormous frame towered over her as he gave a slight bow. "We offer the worthy mistress of this home great gratitude for taking in such wayward sailors."

The head housekeeper of Alloway Manor waved a hand at Mo. "Pish, posh. I'm the mistress of nothing, and you are welcome here because my master wills it. Come on then, let's get you all settled." Taking Dain's arm, Lydia led the way inside.

Chapter 22

His old apartments had been refurbished, but Lydia had made sure that certain childhood elements remained. Reminiscing, Dain wandered the rooms, marveling at how his memories were so much more intact than the last time he'd been here. It was like his previous visits to the manor had only been a dream, though he knew they hadn't. The nostalgia was bittersweet, but he tried hard to focus on the sweet. Spotting an old set of hand-carved animals from Iandior, he could recall that they had been a gift from his mother on his seventh name day. It was a rare kind of gift to receive, and he now realized that his mother must have been a forward thinker indeed. Deep, racist veins ran through most of the other three kingdoms toward this southernmost realm. Iandior was regarded as a savage, uncivilized nation, its people barely welcome outside their own borders. Zaal had more liberal views than most, but there were still a great many rifts between the neighboring kingdoms. Everyone knew about the animals in Iandior though, and as a child, he'd been obsessed with them. It was as if every known creature had been mixed up together in exotic variations just for fun. Dain picked up one of the miniatures. Fingering the slightly worn details on the beautiful half-peacock, half-catlike critter, he wondered if he'd ever get the opportunity to see any of these animals in real life.

Setting the toy back, Dain wandered back into the bedroom and looked over the clothing spread across his bed. Everyone had retired to their apartments to refresh and dress for dinner. Lydia kept to the same household customs that his father had once enforced. Dinner was always a formal affair— it required full jackets and proper evening gowns.

It had been a very long time since Dain had dressed for supper. He'd refused the butler's services, but the servant had still supplied him with an ample assortment of his father's best suits. After sifting through a few choices, Dain eventually donned a forest green frock coat, a pinstriped charcoal vest, and a rich, rust-colored cravat. He felt fairly comfortable with those items, but when he added the shiny, black, knee-high boots over matching pants he started to wonder if he looked precocious. After a glance in the free-standing mirror, he decided that the overall effect wasn't too garish, but his hair— it was a riotous mess.

A light knock sounded at the sitting-room door. Dain exited the bedroom and headed through the apartment.

Standing on the threshold was Lydia. His former nurse stood an entire head shorter than himself. Her tangerine curls had been pinned on the top of her head in an attractive pile, and she was dressed in a modest silk gown of silver-gray. The corseted framework of the gown accentuated her generous curves pleasantly. The woman smiled broadly up at him. "There now, you finally look like a gentleman again, but I was right in figuring you'd need a hand with that lion's mane of yours." Striding purposefully into the room, she pointed to the seat by the fireplace. "Sit just there, and I'll fetch what's needed."

Dain knew there was no point in arguing. She would have her way no matter what he said, he'd learned that years ago. The fire crackled softly as he took a seat on the ottoman. The warmth seeped in while he gave silent thanks for the time he had here, however long or short it may be.

Lydia bustled back into the sitting room, her arms loaded with hair tonics and tools.

Dain wondered if he should be afraid.

"I'll not be surprised if this hurts. Brace yourself, my dear." Then Lydia doused his hair in some kind of smoothing tonic, and began ripping into his tangles.

* * *

Alloway Manor was three stories of solid marble. It boasted over twenty family apartments, two ballrooms, three dining rooms, two parlors, a library, and extensive kitchens. The servants' quarters housed a variety of maids, retainers, butlers, gardeners, and stable hands. Besides Lydia and Glory, the upstairs maid, most of the present-day staff were new. Dain didn't know any of them, but they, of course, knew exactly who he was. The staff bowed, greeting him in the halls as "Master Alloway." As Lydia led him through the corridors to dinner, Dain inquired after each servant he met. He asked them about their families, and thanked them for their service. His father had always been above chatting with the help, but after years of laboring at sea, Dain probably felt more kinship with the men and women who worked the manor than he would with any of the Aaltain gentry.

Dain and Lydia were the first to arrive in the family dining room. It was the smallest of the three, reserved for more intimate parties, but the long, elegant table still seated sixteen comfortably.

The head housekeeper had gone to great lengths this evening. The three golden candelabras lining the center of the table were interspersed with floral arrangements, and the Alloway family china was polished and fully dressed.

Dain took Lydia's hand in his own. "You have made me feel so welcome."

"And I even managed to tame that shocking hair of yours." Lydia laughed warmly, then gave him a motherly grin. "It is the greatest of all pleasures to have you home again, my boy."

Removing her hand from his grasp, she dabbed at her eyes quickly. "Now, I should be checking in on the kitchens. I'll be back to join you shortly."

It wasn't long before Morgan Crouse entered. He'd been led by one of the upstairs maids, and it appeared as though Lydia had done her best to find a large enough suit jacket to fit him, but Mo still looked uncomfortably stuffed. The coat was so tight, in fact, that if the giant man moved too quickly the seams would probably burst. Apparently, there had been no suitable pants either, because Mo still wore a pair of his regular breeches. Nonetheless, the first mate cut an impressive clean-shaven figure. The dark gold necktie, chartreuse vest, and black jacket complemented his enormously muscled frame. As usual, his dreadlocks were neatly tied back, and the thick golden hoop still glinted in his ear.

Striding over to Dain, Mo clapped him on the shoulder, the lift of his arm impeded slightly by the coat. "Ye look mighty dapper, lad, but how, in all the four kingdoms, did ye get yer hair tied so right?"

Dain laughed. "I had help."

Toff arrived moments later. His beard was brushed out,

but his red toque remained firmly in place. He was yanking at the blue cravat around his neck. "How the hell do you genteel folk wear these things on a regular basis?"

Both Dain and Mo laughed. Dain couldn't resist teasing. "What do you mean, Toff? I think aristocracy suits you."

The old man adjusted his spectacles with a gruff grunt, then yanked at his collar again. Just as Toff managed to get the tie loosened, a young, bashful maid led Tars into the dining room. The man barely nodded his thanks as she exited. Taking a seat at the farthest end of the table, Tars acknowledged them with a brief glance before turning to stare into the fireplace.

Old Toff muttered something about manners as Dain carefully studied the newcomer. Tars was truly the spitting image of his sister: identical chestnut hair just grazing the top of his shoulders, the same long, thick lashes, and a twin spray of freckles that whipped across his cheeks and nose. The only real difference in his facial features was his handsomely sculpted jaw, and the extra dash of green in his hazel eyes. He cut quite a figure in a suit, though the sudden shift from months of hardship on the streets of Tallooj to now being a guest at Alloway Manor had to have been difficult for the man to grasp. That might account for a portion of his sullen behavior, but Dain thought that, despite the rescue, it was going to take time before Sable's brother trusted any of them. He wondered how long it had taken her to even convince her brother to join them tonight.

Tars suddenly stood, and his expression softened as he turned toward the entryway.

Dain followed his gaze, and then his knees went weak.

Sable's entrance commanded every eye in the room. The hunted songbird turned sailor girl now stood before them as a full-fledged lady. Her hair had grown in the past couple months aboard *The Maiden,* just long enough now to be swept up in a delicate twist, with tiny, ivy-style leaves woven into the top knot. She wore long pearl earrings that directed the eye down to her collarbone, where the *Dernamn* had been fastened on a shorter matching chain. The medallion gleamed brightly above her décolletage. It was the first time Dain had seen her wear the pendant so openly. The front portion of her masterfully crafted gown was embroidered in a subtle pattern of varied leaves that stopped at her tiny waist and grew into a larger, more visible design on the lower portion of the garb. Despite the glory of her burgundy couture, Dain's eyes quickly returned to her face. Her thick lashes remained demurely lowered as she accepted Tars's offered arm. Color bloomed on her cheeks, and her lips glistened with a slight red gloss.

When she looked up, she caught Dain's gaze from across the dining room, and he forgot everything. He forgot the hardship and loss, he forgot the mission--even the ever-present thrum of elemental power faded away. It all disappeared before her. They had barely spoken a dozen phrases to one other since Tars had been rescued, and until now, Dain had not realized how much he missed her.

Lydia returned at that moment, and when she spotted Sable, she clucked loudly. "By Orthane, child, you are liken to the goddess herself."

Sable blushed. "I doubt a goddess was ever a street rat, or a cabin girl on a merchant ship. And I doubt even more that she would have chosen to be splayed with such freckles." The girl wrinkled her nose distastefully.

Dain's throat bobbed. He remembered how he'd counted those freckles so many times before, and he wanted to tell her they were worthy of any goddess, but it felt inappropriate given their relationship as friends. Staring again at Sable, he finally admitted to himself that he wanted them to be more than that, and it was not just because she looked so beautiful tonight. He'd grown to admire everything about her: her laugh, her kindness and empathy, her strength in the face of adversity, her practical get-it-done nature, her love of music and learning . . . He wanted to say something to her as she stood before him now, but everything that came to mind seemed inappropriate in present company—and Mo beat him to the punch.

The first mate slid smoothly forward between the women. "Ye be correct, Miss Lydia. Sable is the goddess incarnate this eve, and ye are belle of the ball. " Lydia was no blushing maid.

She simply winked at Mo, and playfully accepted his giant arm as he led her to a chair.

Remaining silently broody, Tars directed his sister to a chair further down the table, away from the others. He was stopped in his tracks by Lydia's polite, yet firm request. "I suggest you guide that lady nearer to us. I'll not be yelling up and down the table during dinner."

Dain thought he heard a disgruntled groan escape Tars. Honestly, it was probably the worst sound the man could make in Lydia Romailo's presence. Dain knew because such groans had nearly always ended in discipline when he was a child.

The fiery redhead's chin snapped up fast, a mother's terse, commanding timbre replacing her formerly polite tone. "You'll do as I say, or you'll spend midnight til dawn mucking out the stables." Lydia's words were not rude, but neither were they arguable.

Tars was only Lydia's junior by a handful of years, but her voice seemed to command his obedience. He moved back up the table toward the rest of the party, and placed Sable and himself in the seats directly beside Dain's former nurse.

Lydia nodded in approval, and then clucked at everyone else to take a seat.

Dain made his way to the head of the table. He glanced briefly at Sable again, and she met his gaze with a grin and an arched brow. He knew the look meant that she liked Lydia.

* * *

Directly after dinner, Toff made off to the city on horseback. They tried to convince him to wait until morning, but the old man wouldn't hear of it. The ever-diligent hound was led away by his nose.

The rest of the party retired to the second parlor after Toff left. It was a lush, high-ceilinged marble apartment with an enormous fire crackling in the central hearth. To the right of the fireplace stood an ivory grand. The piano had been in Dain's family for generations, a gift from his great-great-grandfather to his first wife. Dain couldn't remember her name, but the woman had apparently been an accomplished pianist. Sadly, only a few short months after their nuptials, she'd died. Dain's family history mentioned little about her after that, and the piano remained her only legacy within the Alloway annals. Surrounding the grand were numerous other stringed instruments, including a harp, a mandolin, and a lute.

Dain noticed the look of obvious desire on Tars's face as the musician entered and spied them. Turning to Sable, Dain raised his voice loud enough for everyone to hear. "I had hoped you would grace us with a song this evening, Sable?"

Lydia perked up, and moved quickly toward the girl. "Oh, indeed, my dear. It's been a long, dry spell with no music in this house."

Sable suddenly looked shy as she gazed toward her

brother. "Tars, please don't make me do this alone."

Tars hesitated for only a moment before coming to her side. He quickly cradled the lute in his palms, and as the man seated himself on the piano bench, his sullenness seemed to dissolve, his face relaxing while he plucked the strings to test the tune.

Dain watched Sable stare at her brother. He could only interpret her expression as one of relief. Then he realized that the girl, quick as always, had probably feigned shyness to entice Tars to play. Perhaps she hoped music could help to heal the healer's soul.

Long after Sable had sung two arias, three ballads, and a final, more lively folk tune, Tars continued to play. He was not any average musician—his hands flew over the lute strings in fast, fluid strokes. His head swayed, and his eyes stayed tightly shut as he focused every ounce of energy into the instrument.

Dain had never heard anything like it. This man could have played for kings.

Sable left her brother's side breathless. And as she passed by, Lydia pulled the girl into an appreciative hug before letting her take a seat.

Dain offered Sable some tea.

Gratefully accepting the cup, the girl glanced over at Tars as he continued to perform. "After I went missing, people started to treat him suspiciously. The attack, the dead lying in the streets, turned everyone wary. They began to refuse his aid as a healer. He had no choice but to sell his lute to survive." Sable hung her head. "He suffered a great deal in my absence— cold, hunger, and constant fear. He was always running, and always hiding."

Dain sat down on the small settee beside her, the warmth of the fireplace seeping into his back. "It's not your fault, you know."

Sable's eyes glistened with tears when she tipped up her chin to look at him. She had beautiful eyes, even when she was sad. "Isn't it? I left him behind."

Dain reached for her hand. "You did not leave him behind willingly, and he knows it. He understands the difference. *Choice* is the difference, and you had none. Mo dragged you aboard *The Maiden*."

Sable's throat bobbed as a large drop ran quickly from the corner of her eye. "I should have insisted. I should have forced you to turn back and get him, but I was a coward. I was afraid."

Dain chuckled, and saw Sable's eyes widen slighty. "I doubt you could have convinced me to do anything at that point, and you know my crew would have never supported that." Dain couldn't resist reaching out to brush away the tear that had now reached her chin. "Mo always says, 'What's done is done. Start where yer at, and do what ye can with what ye have left. Regret never moves a man forward.'"

Sable smiled. "You're terrible at accents, you know."

Mo's laughter pealed out from across the room where he stood by Lydia. "Did I hear ye quoting me again, lad? Ye always have permission to do so, but at least have the decency to get my voice right."

Tars paused in his playing as Dain called back, "I'll work on that, Mo, as long as you promise to have the decency to refrain from eavesdropping on other people's conversations."

Then all four of them started to laugh, and Dain thought he even caught a hint of a smile on Tars's lips before the man resumed his song.

Chapter 23

Whatever joy may have played on Tars's lips the night before had entirely vanished by morning.

Dain had enlisted the siblings to help him search his mother's apartments. While there were other rooms in the house that could be combed, they were all public spaces, and Dain concluded that if any archives still existed in this house, they'd probably be found in her locked rooms. The quarters had been sealed tight since her death, his father permitting no one entrance, not even for cleaning. Perhaps Hiram Alloway had done so out of grief, or perhaps he had done so to keep Alis Alloway's secrets safe. Dain had obtained the keys earlier that morning from a reluctant Lydia. He'd offered his former nurse little by way of explanation, other than hinting that he'd like to know his late mother better. The excuse wasn't entirely untrue.

As they reached the sizeable ivory doors, Sable gently

touched his arm. "Are you prepared to do this today? Do you need more time?"

Sable's thoughtful concern moved Dain, and her touch made his stomach flip, but when he glimpsed Tars's wary, protective glare, he quickly shifted out of the girl's touch. Dain fixed his eyes on the doors instead. "It's been a long time since my mother died, and I was never allowed in her apartments, so I should be fine. And, I honestly don't know how much time we have. We are on land, and who knows when *they* will find us. We need that stalker confusion spell, and if we could find a recipe for concocting more Harborage, that would be useful too. Not only will these spells protect us now, I also hope they'll grant us more ease as we search for clues to the safe haven."

Sable only nodded, but Tars rolled his eyes with a skeptical groan.

Dain knew that the healer didn't believe in the haven, and that the man expected to find nothing, but when Dain glanced at him again, he wondered if Tars possibly *hoped* they'd find nothing. Being only a half-trained alchemist made the weight of learning new spells an enormous responsibility—Dain admitted that even he would find it daunting.

It took some wriggling to get the key inserted, and the doors creaked loudly on the dry hinges when they finally swung into the massive, ivory sitting room. The air in the room was cold and stale, but a rare winter sun burst through the large, filmy windows. Dain's first steps caused the dust on the floor to swirl. The bright, sparkling filaments floated through the beams of sunlight as he gazed around the apartment. A doorframe to the left led into what looked like a study, and on the right, a wide marble archway framed the entrance to an expansive bedroom and bath. The sparse furnishings had been carefully covered with protective sheets, their white fabric now powdered in thick gray. Dain wasn't sure what he'd expected, but the apartment was an empty-looking shell. It did not remind him of his mother at all.

Dain turned toward the study first. If any books on alchemy still remained, they would most likely be in there. He began a slow, silent search through the dusty desk while Sable and Tars checked in the office cabinets. It didn't take long to realize nothing was there. The cabinets were bare, the desk drawers vacant. Nothing.

Dain scoured the sitting room while Sable and Tars combed the adjoining bedroom and bath. Every drawer in his mother's chambers had been cleaned out. Her closets were empty, her cupboards too.

Sable emerged from the bedroom with only a small piece of folded paper in her hand. It was the single item she'd found in the entire room. Shaking her head, she handed the slip to Dain. "I'm sorry, there's just nothing else here."

Dain heard Tars scoff as he came up behind his sister. Sable turned to give him a scolding glare. Dain unfolded the paper to read two words hastily scrawled across the center.

Sable drew up beside him. "What does it say? What does it mean?"

Dain blinked. "I have no idea."

She placed her fists on her hips. "You're not sure what it says, or you're not sure what it means?"

He gave her a blank stare. "It says, 'The Wildflower.'"

* * *

Toff was set to check in that evening at dinner, but the hour came and went, and when the old sailor still hadn't appeared, Dain began to worry. Excusing himself from the parlor, he made his way to the front entrance, where he hoped some fresh air might ease his nerves. As he reached the foyer, he saw the butler open the front doors, and Toff appeared on the threshold with two brawny, heavily armed companions.

The old sailor skipped any formal greeting, pushing into the room. He commanded the butler to bolt the doors after him, and told the two large men to remain outside on guard.

Dain's palms began to sweat. "Toff?"

The old sailor was nearly breathless. "Dulge. Oswart Dulge. He's in Aalta."

* * *

"You mean the thug that accosted you in Eandor Vid?"

Sable asked the question that Dain knew was on Mo's lips as well.

"Yes, girl. He's just landed in the harbor, and he has a small army of brigands with him. It'll be short work for him to find Alloway Manor. This family is far too well known in these parts. I only managed to snaffle a couple hires when I was in town. They'll watch the entrance, alert us of any incomers, but they will do minimal damage when the leech shows up with his entourage."

Pulling his fingers through his hair, Dain cursed himself for setting Dulge free in Vid, but he'd never imagined the thug would follow him all the way to Aalta. Obviously, the villain *was* working with the stalkers.

Surprisingly, it was Tars who spoke up next. "Then, we hide."

Everyone turned to the healer in shock. The man hadn't spoken a word to them since they'd arrived, and now he even continued. "If we are all as exposed as your sailor says we are, then we need to hide. I've spent a decade hiding from unearthly beings—staying out of sight of humans will be simple."

"Unearthly . . ." Lydia's question trailed off.

Dain gave her a sympathetic nod. "We'll explain everything." Then he turned back to the others. "He is right— hiding *is* our best option." Settling his gaze on Tars, he noticed the man's eyebrows raise; perhaps he hadn't expected anyone to agree with him so easily, especially Dain. "I assume your next suggestion will be that we split the trail?"

Tars only nodded.

"Alright then. It's time to plan."

* * *

Though he held the journal reverently, Tars still refused. "I can't do it, I just don't have the training. And even if I could, this amount of power would lead every single stalker within a thousand spans directly to us."

Toff cut in gruffly. "The lad's right, Captain. It's too great a risk."

Dain straightened his back. He was trying to mimic Ileana's posture, trying to use his body language to further convey his authority. "This house contains thirty-five souls in total, and we cannot evacuate them all in time. Even if we did, where would they go? Most of them are women, and the men that are here are not fighters. This is their home—it *must* be protected. If Dulge is here, and if he is a stalker henchman, then the demons will know where we are shortly after he does. Eventually they will come, magic or no." Dain's voice shifted into an even more fervent tone as he looked Tars in the eye. "You are claiming defeat before you've even tried. You're the only alchemist we have, and the only one who can hide us all safely with magic. Our kind has spent generations running, hiding, and suppressing our talents out of fear of being found.

We only outwitted the stalkers in Tallooj because I *used* my power. Perhaps instead of suppressing our talents, we need to apply them to fighting back."

Dain knew all of this was easy for him to say, and he could see the fear behind Tars's eyes. This man had faced stalkers more often than Dain had forced himself to eat fish. He knew his own life trials paled in comparison to what this healer must have suffered, but Dain couldn't consider that right now. There were too many lives at stake. Old Toff's hired men had been sent back into the city to alert the Aaltain authorities of the impending attack, and to spread a rumor in every tavern, from the east end to the west, that Captain Alloway had headed on vacation to his seaside abode. It was Dain's version of splitting the trail. Dulge would likely leave no stone unturned, and while Dain still expected the brigands to show up at the manor, he hoped that at least a portion of them, however small, might be sent scouting south. Still, it wasn't enough. Tars was their main hope now, and every minute they delayed, the enemy drew nearer.

Tars narrowed his brow, and shook his head again. "You're crazy, you know that?"

Dain didn't respond, only turned to a patiently waiting Sable. "Find a place where Tars can concentrate, help him gather everything he needs, and use your talent if necessary. *Hurry.*" The girl nodded as she took Tars's arm and led the reluctant alchemist out of the parlor.

Dain turned to see Mo sitting in the corner, talking with Lydia. Her expressions rose and fell dramatically, and she made occasional superstitious signs with her hands. And yet, through it all, Dain could still see that Lydia liked Mo. She let her hand linger on his arm longer than necessary, and when her face relaxed, she looked on him with a soft gaze. Perhaps Dain's matchmaking skills were not as far off as he thought. Despite what loomed before him, Dain smiled. No one was impervious to Morgan Crouse's charm. His first mate could probably lead the four kingdom's roughest band of brigands, and every single miscreant would honor and respect him. Lydia never stood a chance. Dain watched the giant finish up with a sympathetic shoulder shrug as he gently patted the housekeeper's arm.

Drawing close to the pair, Dain now took Lydia's hand in his own. "This is a lot to believe, I know, but you need to trust me now. This house needs you. You must get all of our staff to return to their quarters. Tell them to stay silent and locked in. No matter what they see or hear, they need to stay put. Do you understand?"

The redhead squared her shoulders. "I understand."

Mo added, "Keep an eye on them, lass. See to it that they obey."

Lydia gave Mo a firm nod. "My staff obeys my every word, Mr. Crouse."

Dain believed her. Now, it was time to wait. For Tars, and for Dulge.

Chapter 24

Midnight chimed on the grandfather clock in the hall as Dain took in Sable's apartment. Tinctures, herbs, and all manner of instruments and ingredients lay sprawled around a prostrate Tars. Sable was kneeling over her brother in concern, and in one raised hand she held a small, glowing bottle.

Dain moved into the room without knocking. "He did it?"

Looking up, Sable raised the shining vial. "He believes so, but he can't say for sure. It's not something he's ever done before. As you can see, he doesn't have the stamina for such an expenditure of magic. He pushed beyond his limits, for all of us."

"To be honest, I'm surprised he didn't scrap the plan altogether, and force you to run away with him."

Sable looked at the vial. "I think after what you did in Tallooj, and what you said this evening, he saw some spark of hope. He's been running for a long time, Dain. Perhaps, like me, he's grown weary of it."

Dain didn't respond. He wasn't so sure he'd inspired Tars to do anything. If the healer had done it for anyone, he'd done it for Sable. He reached for Tars. "I think it might be best if we pull him underneath the sofa. Hopefully, if this works, he'll be fine, but just in case, I think we should hide him."

After Sable stashed the journal and quickly tidied the carpet, she helped Dain drag Tars underneath the long couch. Once the healer was sufficiently hidden, Dain pointed to the bottle. "We need to activate that spell before it's too late. Did Tars tell you how?"

Sable held the vial out to Dain. "It's simple, really. It's set to activate when applied to the entrance of the house." An unspoken concern edged her words. "It will be a huge burst of magic."

"I know."

"You're not afraid?"

"I'll quote Mo again, this time without an accent: 'It's fear, and fear alone that binds a man from living.'"

Sable tilted her head, the way she always did when she was about to reprimand him. "That doesn't answer my question at all, Dain Alloway."

Running his fingers through his hair, Dain swallowed. "I'm not sure I'll stop being afraid until *all* of this is over. Until everyone is free."

* * *

There was no way of knowing if it had worked. When the potion was applied to the front doors, a small sliver of light twisted through the frame edges, and then it was gone. Everything felt the same. There was no blast of power, no gleaming burst. Theoretically, at the moment it was applied, the magic should have concealed every person and their effects currently within the manor walls. It should have rendered them all invisible to anyone entering after. It was only a visual illusion though—they could still be heard and felt, but it was a form of hiding in plain sight. To further the mirage, every fire had been doused, every lantern and candle snuffed out, and every piece of furniture in the main rooms covered with dust jackets. The manor needed to look abandoned, like its master had truly gone on an extended vacation. Dain sent up a quick, fervent prayer, to whatever god was listening, that Tars had concocted the potion correctly. Then the waiting began again.

In the darkness, Toff remained on the top floor, eagle eyes trained through the upstairs windows. Mo stood watch at the front entrance, and Dain and Sable stood just inside the back garden door. Lydia remained hidden within the servant's quarters.

As another hour passed slowly by, the manor began to properly chill.

Dain stood only a couple steps from Sable. It was the first time in weeks that Tars had been absent for longer than a few minutes. Plucking up his courage, Dain leaned over Sable. "I wanted to tell you that you looked very lovely last night."

He could barely make out Sable's expression in the dark. "Are you implying that I didn't look lovely tonight?"

Dain's felt his face grow hot. "No—I mean—of course, you look just as lovely tonight also."

Sable giggled softly in the darkness. "Thank you, Dain. Truly." Her voice got quieter yet. "You looked very handsome as well. It has been fun to—to play dress up for a little while."

As her voice trailed off, Dain guessed at the true meaning behind her words. The illusion of safety, enjoying a "home"— it had been good while it lasted. In all his future life plans, Dain had never considered returning to Alloway Manor. It had always been his father's home, not his, but the last couple of days, being here with Sable and the others—

His train of thought was lost when Toff appeared out of nowhere.

Dain and Sable jumped fast toward each other, and Dain couldn't hold his tongue. "Dammit, Toff!" The old man didn't need a glamour spell to hide himself from the outside world— it seemed he could be invisible whenever he chose.

Toff ignored the reprimand. "They're approaching, about half a mile off, lanterns leading their way. I'd hoped the authorities would arrive first, but no such luck. I already alerted Mr. Crouse, and he's in position." Toff turned to Sable. "Here's hoping the spell your sourpuss brother concocted is actually the real deal." With that, the old man dissolved in the shadows.

Dain and Sable had nearly embraced in their surprise when Toff had popped out of the darkness. Dain liked the closer proximity, and he bent down to her ear. "If you were to pray for any one thing, just for yourself, right now, what would you pray for?"

Sable leaned toward him. "If I had any faith, and it was just for myself, I suppose I'd pray for a chance at a normal life."

Her breath was warm on his skin, and he bent closer yet. "That's all? Nothing else?"

Dain could hear a quaver in her voice. "You don't think that's enough?"

His reply was soft. "You deserve that, and so much more." Then Dain quietly snuck off to his next position.

* * *

SMASH.

One of the large entryway windows gave way, and countless shards of glass showered onto the foyer floor as lantern light poured in through the gaping hole. It wasn't a surprise—Dain had figured Dulge wouldn't be subtle. He watched as a man climbed through the opening, snapped the locks, and pulled the enormous doors wide for his companions. Numerous lanterns cast an ominous glow throughout the room. Dain remained stock still while his eyes adjusted to the light. He'd volunteered to test the glamour by placing himself in the most vulnerable position of all: the center of the foyer. His friends had argued vehemently against this plan, but he'd reasoned that Dulge was searching for him in particular. And if the illusion failed, and Dain was taken first, then hopefully the henchman would have gotten what he came for, and everyone else could remain hidden in safety. He was willing to sacrifice himself for the others. He'd brought them all here after all.

Holding his breath against the onslaught of light, Dain focused and quickly counted three dozen men or more. Then he heard the man who'd entered first speak. "The place is deserted, Dulge. Those rumors we heard in town must have been true. I think your bird has flown the coop."

It worked. Tars had done it. Dain was invisible to the crowd of brigands directly before him. Letting out a silent breath of relief, he tip-toed back toward the hall that led to the far parlor. Before rounding the corner, he caught a quick glimpse of Oswart Dulge. The man limped slightly as he strode forward into the manor foyer. His squeaky voice rose above the clamor of his men. "Search everywhere, boys. Leave nothing unturned, and take whatever treasure you want."

The others were supposed to meet Dain in the first parlor, the farthest back in the house. But when Dain entered, the light was so dim that he couldn't see a soul. He kept his voice low. "It worked. We're good to move onto the next phase."

Toff materialized beside him. "My lads should have gotten to the authorities by now. Let's hope it's not too long before the Aaltain soldiers arrive."

"Yes, let's hope."

Dain heard Sable reach his side. The girl sought out his hand, giving it a tight squeeze. A few seconds later, Mo was by his side as well. Dain lowered his voice further. "Give the brigands time to spread out and separate. It'll be easier that way. Remember, you are invisible, but they can still hear you and feel you. Use sound only when necessary. And knock them out, but do not kill anyone unless you have to. We need them alive. Everyone have enough gags and rope?" Dain heard Mo and Toff hum in response, and Sable squeezed his hand again.

He knew the girl by his side was more than capable of taking care of herself—she'd been living on the streets her entire life—but Dain still felt protective. And he wanted her by his side. "Sable can take out at least three by shifting them into the closet we have locked, but after that, she'll need rest. I'll keep her with me. I know this manor inside and out, so I can get her somewhere safe if she's exhausted. See you when it's all over. Be careful, my friends."

No one said another word. The small, invisible guerrilla band dissipated out into the extensive marble halls.

* * *

Holding fast to Sable's hand, Dain wove them silently along the corridors and through the darkness. Thanks to a childhood of playing and prowling through these great halls, he knew them like the back of his hand, and he planned to head to the library first. Of all the rooms in the house, the library was the most precious to him, and surprisingly, he'd not set foot there yet since arriving.

The grand marble room was dim, but Dain could still see the floor-to-ceiling shelves lined with row upon row of books. He wasn't even sure the public library in Aalta compared to the collection of volumes stored in Alloway Manor. Dain had spent a large portion of his childhood surrounded by these tomes; he was used to the grandeur, but when he heard Sable draw a deep breath of admiration by his side, he realized how impressive it truly was. Though it had never seemed probable, maybe one day he'd get the opportunity to appreciate this space, and its contents, as an adult.

It wasn't a long wait. They'd only been in the library for minutes before a pair of noisy brigands could be heard barreling down the hallway. Despite the glamour, both he and Sable instinctively ducked behind one of the desks.

A blast of the lantern light rounded the entrance, and Dain's eyes strained to adjust. When he could finally see clearly, he looked at Sable, and made a stopping motion with his hand. He wanted her to wait to use her talent; there was no need to throw more magic lures out into Aalta unless it was absolutely necessary.

"It's only books," one of the thugs complained as they entered the enormous space.

The second man marched up to one of the shelves and started pitching tomes to the floor. "Books can be valuable. Besides, they remind me of home."

"Home? You're an idiot. I highly doubt you had a library in that hovel you grew up in."

The second man kept pitching books. "We had some books. My mother could read, you know. She was educated."

The first thug snorted. "And look where that got her."

Both spoke in Ernhamian. Dain gave thanks that he had paid attention to his language lessons as he moved toward the entryway.

The first man, the one holding the lantern, stalked up behind his partner. "So, you're telling me that you know exactly which ones are valuable, huh? Maybe your mother could read, but you can't. I say we move on and find smaller treasures, ones we can pocket. Books are too large—and heavy."

The second brigand ignored his companion, and

continued pitching.

The lantern bearer growled loudly in frustration and headed back toward the entrance. It was exactly what Dain had hoped for. As the rogue rounded the doorway Dain silently smashed his dagger, hilt first, into the back of the man's head. The man fell fast, and so did the lantern. It crashed loudly to the marble floor, and surprisingly didn't go out.

The book fiend turned fast. "Whaa—you've gone and tripped yourself? Stupid bastard." The man sauntered toward his prostrate companion, and Dain's invisible dagger hilt struck home again. This time, only a low thump sounded as the second man hit the ground. Being invisible definitely had its advantages.

Sable was by his side moments later, rope and gags in hand.

After the men were secured, Dain dragged them to the back of the library, and shoved them out of sight between the furthest bookshelves.

Two down, dozens more to go.

Chapter 25

As Dain grasped Sable's hand more firmly, two lanterns bobbed in the darkness ahead. He couldn't quite make out whether the band consisted of three or four men, but he knew they were headed for the kitchens. And the kitchens would inevitably lead to the servant's quarters. He couldn't let them get there.

Clenching his free fist, Dain wondered why the Aaltain soldiers hadn't arrived yet. This was the third set of rogues he and Sable had set upon. The second set had been nearly as simple as the first, but too much time had passed, and Dain was beginning to worry that Toff's trusted hires had not fulfilled their assignment.

The kitchen entrances came into view, and the lanterns divided. One group headed to the right, the other to the left. Though the kitchens were connected internally, Dain still gave thanks that they'd split up. He and Sable quickly caught up to the right door and peeked around the open frame. Three men rummaged loudly through the drawers and cabinets. From the way they clattered about, Dain could tell they were entirely convinced the manor was deserted. Releasing Sable's hand, he quietly slipped into the room. Before he reached the men, he noticed a shadow advancing from the far corner. When the figure was in line with the lantern light, Dain clenched his teeth.

No, Lydia. Go back to the servant's quarters.

Of course, Lydia heard none of his internal warnings. She continued to advance, enormous iron frying pan in hand, toward the closest thug. This was not going to be subtle, and Dain would need to move fast against the other two once she'd struck.

SLAM.

The sound reverberated through the room as Lydia's pan hit with unyielding force. The man simply crumpled. She raised it again, moving fast toward the next fellow, who stood staring in shock at his fallen comrade.

Dain got to him first. In seconds, the gawking brigand slumped to the floor. Turning toward the third, Dain spied Sable. She was breathing hard, large marble rolling pin in hand, the last brigand already lying at her feet. In the general commotion, Dain hadn't even heard her do it.

The riotous rummaging in the second kitchen stopped. Dain used hand signals to motion Lydia and Sable with him to either side of the internal archway. He held his breath as the next man entered.

"Roland? Shorty? Everything all—"

The man didn't have a chance to finish before Lydia's iron pan smashed loudly into the center of his face.

The next thug carelessly rushed in after, and Dain dispatched him quickly as well.

Five. That was five of them down, in less than a minute. Maybe they had a chance after all.

Lydia set her weapon of choice on a nearby workbench, and then smacked her hands together as though dusting them. "Well, that took care of that lot." Sable had already begun tying and gagging.

The head housekeeper stalked toward the back of the kitchen. "I'll get the cellar door up. We'll stash them down there with the others."

Dain's voice cracked. "Others?"

"Yes, I took down three of them earlier on."

Looking down, Dain saw Sable smirking up at him from where she labored. "She's fierce, that one."

"Indeed." It was the only response he could think of.

Dain begged Lydia to return to the servants' quarters, but she would hear none of it. The head housekeeper was intent on guarding the kitchens. She would let nothing, and no one, reach her household staff. He gave up arguing after witnessing the three men already in the cellar. All of them were bloodied and bruised, from forehead to chin. That pan must have hurt. And they'd been neatly dragged down, unbreakably secured, and positioned in an unconscious row against the cold mortar wall. Dain actually pitied anyone else who might turn up.

After the next five were stowed alongside their cellared comrades, the hatch was locked tight, and Lydia was left on guard duty once more.

* * *

Loud voices, crashing piano keys, and breaking glass sounded out from the main parlor. Dain and Sable crept quietly along the walls as they followed the noise.

Nearly a dozen men were inside, their gathered treasure mounting in a heap, filling the far corner of the room. It was obvious that they'd discovered the wine cellar, because empty bottles lay scattered everywhere while they celebrated riotously in the lantern light.

Dulge stood, a smug smile plastered across his ugly face, right in the center of it all.

There were too many of them here—he and Sable wouldn't be able to take down a group this size. It was time to move on.

Suddenly, a single brigand burst through the door past Dain's invisible shoulder. It was the same man who'd broken the window when the miniature army had arrived. The man yelled to be heard above the ruckus. "Dulge, the men are going missing."

A few scoffs and cynical snorts sounded from the others as Dulge turned his pale, bulgy eyes toward the newcomer. "What are you talking about, Serge?"

"Men are missing, sir. I've been searching high and low for Roland and Shorty, but they're nowhere to be found. The halls and rooms have grown quiet—it's like the house is swallowing them up."

Dain's brow furrowed. If the Aaltain soldiers didn't arrive soon, then everything would be foiled. Scrubbing his fingers silently through his hair, he glanced at Sable. The girl met his gaze with mirrored concern.

"So you're saying there are ghosts in the house, Serge?" Dulge laughed. It was the kind of laugh that grated the nerves. "You are a superstitious idiot." The brigand leader swung one long arm toward a pair of men in the corner. "Card. Taniz. Head out and locate our missing comrades. I bet they've found a stash of whiskey and are holed up somewhere they don't have to share."

Before the two men had a chance to follow Oswart's orders, a chill, deeper and far more penetrating than any normal draft, swept mercilessly into the room. Fear followed fast on its heel. Dain watched every face in the room go hollow, the grown men frozen with dread, even Oswart Dulge.

They were here.

Sable snatched for Dain's hand, her eyes wide with terror.

His own heart began racing as he squeezed her fingers in return. It was little comfort. Dain knew he couldn't risk backing out, in case the stalkers were headed down the hall. Instead, he pulled at Sable's arm and edged further into the parlor. He wanted to run, and it took every ounce of will to move slow and silent. The room had a secret entrance, the sort you always find in storybook mansions. In fact, there were several others of its kind throughout the house. The portals had been created by his father, to ensure the staff was not intrusive while serving his guests. The servant's entrance led to a narrow hall which, at the end, placed you back near the kitchens. Dain's palm began sweating in Sable's hold. They needed to reach the entrance fast. They needed to get to Tars before it was too late.

Dain tried to keep his eyes trained on the hidden doorway. He worked to quell the terror and ignore the rising panic as he and Sable tiptoed invisibly around furniture. They'd made it halfway in when the cold intensified to insufferable heights. There was nothing else he could do. Dain froze, shivering, and Sable stopped beside him. Glancing sideways, he saw two tall silhouettes round the door frame. Faceless under their hoods, the figures seemed to float instead of walk, and darkness shrouded the demons as though the light of the lanterns couldn't touch them.

Throat tight, Dain gazed warily at the stalkers, but they never glanced his way. A trickle of relief worked to ease his petrified state. The illusion seemed to hold even before these monsters—or perhaps the overwhelming swarm of the glamour masked their own personal magic?

Oswart Dulge somehow managed to straighten himself before the newcomers. His features were contorted into a mask of outrage as he made weak, squeaky demands. "What are *you* doing here? This is not your business, or your mission. I was hired for this job, not you. Get out."

It was like a flash of lightning, only without light or warmth. One moment the stalker stood in the entry, and the next, in a whirl of crimson, it stood directly in front of Dulge. Its arm was poised to strike. The long, unyielding claws at the end of its black fingers hovered near his neck.

The brigand leader paled perceptibly.

The stalker's voice sliced through the air like ice-coated steel. "You useless worm."

Dain shivered violently, and Sable grasped his hand harder.

From some unknown source, Dulge seemed to pluck up his courage again. His face was still pale, and he gave a sideways glance at the stalker's raised claws, but he managed to make his voice firmer. "You wouldn't dare. The master would have you thrown into the sea if you so much as laid a hand on me." The man's pale, bulgy eyes turned to look up into the cavernous scarlet hood. "And you know it."

A frightful hiss of frustration emanated from under the hood. The demon lowered its claws.

Dain breathed in slowly. Dulge wasn't directly working with the stalkers? The news was surprising, but even more surprising was that somehow Dulge had gained the upper hand.

Oswart's ugly face regained some color, and a smidgen of his greasy swagger returned. "Now, I suggest you leave. There is nothing for you here. The house is abandoned."

The stalker's voice cut through the air again, and Dain saw several men wince. "Stupid, insolent human. I cannot be bothered to explain the obvious. We will only leave after we have searched."

Dulge tried to straighten under the force of the creature's voice, but his own voice squeaked in betrayal. "Then the master will hear of your interference."

The stalker whipped its claws forward again, and this time the points hooked directly underneath Oswart's jowls. "I am willing to take my chances, worm. We can even make it a game. I wager that the first of us to retrieve this prey, and return it, will have the master's ear." The stalker's hood nearly engulfed Dulge's face as it bent over. "Let's race."

Then, in a red blur, both demons were gone. Dain's feet loosed. With less caution than before, he dragged Sable toward the servant's entrance.

As he ran, Dain heard Oswart's men erupt into a confused tirade. Their loud questions and indignant shouts flooded the parlor. He hoped they were distracted enough to miss the hidden door swing slightly open and shut tight.

Inside the miniature hallway, Dain heard Sable gasp for air as he pulled her through the dark. Where was the city guard? Racing through the shadows, Dain took every short cut he could remember to reach the second floor as fast as possible. The cold fear followed, haunting them as they ran.

It appeared Toff and Mo had had the very same thought, because when he and Sable entered the apartment, Dain could just make out the two sailors quietly trying to rouse the unconscious Tars.

Dain barred the doors while Sable ran to a cabinet beside the sofa. Pulling out a small vial, she lifted the stopper, stuffing the bottle under her brother's nose. Tars weakly opened his eyes, sputtering. Seconds later, his gaze flew wide, and he tried to stand. "They're here."

Sable shushed her brother as she tried to keep him from falling. Dain shifted close to the group. "Tars, how long will the glamour last?"

The man was barely able to stand. "It should last until

dawn, if not longer."

Dain quickly told everyone his theory about the larger spell masking their own magic. He questioned Tars again. "How long do you think that aspect might last?"

"I doubt much remains. After the initial blast, it should have slowly ebbed away—they won't feel it forever. But this is all speculation." Tars hung his head in his hands.

Dain talked faster now. "Then they might sense us soon?"

The healer was too tired to respond. He leaned nearly all his weight onto Sable as he gave a weary nod in response.

Turning to Toff, Dain heard his voice pitch higher. "Where are the soldiers? Where are your men?"

He could barely see Old Toff's shrug in response. "Likely in a tavern at the bottom of a barrel. I shouldn't have given them the coin until after the work was done."

Mo swore under his breath.

Mind and heart racing, Dain clenched his fists tight. He needed to get better at backup plans. What was he going to do now?

They all jumped when a frightful steel-on-stone voice cut through the door frame. "We know you're here. We followed the residue to this house, and this particular source spot, but now we *feel* you."

Cold terror oozed under the doors as the ivory-washed oaks started to shake furiously.

How strong were these monsters?

Dain knew they couldn't get past the stalkers, even with the glamour. Turning fast toward Sable, he relieved her as Tars's support, and lifted his voice over the battered doors. "Shift the stalkers to the sea. *Kill* them." Even in the barely lit room, Dain could see Sable's face contort. He had no time to consider her expression. "Sable, send them to the sea."

Sable remained immobile as the doors strained loudly on their hinges. Her voice quavered. "I think—"

Dain cut her off. "Now!" It was the first time he had yelled at her since they'd met.

She shook visibly.

He instantly regretted his tone.

The doors burst.

Sable's gaze swept to the advancing stalkers, and she raised her vibrating hands.

Chapter 26

The room warped, and Dain lost his balance as his spine started itching.

No.

He heard the waves first, then felt a wintry sea breeze against his cheek. The open air caused the steady pulse of power beneath his skin to leap. It took several minutes for Dain to regain his sight, but he knew exactly where he was. He was still supporting Tars's full weight as he searched through the moonslight. Sable stood just to his left, leaning heavily against the rail of *The Maiden's* main deck. Exhaustion lined every inch of her frame. Obviously, shifting three people was still difficult for her, but Dain could only think of those left behind. Letting Tars slump to the deck, he raced toward the girl. He tried not to panic, but his voice seemed to rise of its own accord. "What have you done? You've left everyone in the hands of those monsters back at the manor!"

Sable's breath was visible in the night air. "I could not—"

"You *could not* do what?" He knew he should stop yelling, but he was frantic. The residual sensation from the stalkers was also working to escalate his fears. What about Mo and Toff, what about Lydia and the staff?

"I—"

Her knees buckled. Dain instinctively reached out, but Tars beat him to it. The healer had managed to drag himself toward his sister. She eased down beside him, leaning heavily into her brother. She was too weary to even lift her head. Tars held her close as he looked up grimly up at Dain. "She couldn't follow your orders—she could not kill them—because any of those stalkers could be one of our parents."

Dain stumbled a few steps backward. He'd assumed they were dead. Then he realized that Sable had never told him the full story.

A commanding voice from the prow interrupted his thoughts. "Even if that had not been the case, and Sable had chosen to kill, it only would have only served to make this genocide darker still."

Dain turned to see a gold-and-green hemline descend the staircase to the main deck. Had it already been a month? Looking to the skies, Dain saw that the moons were indeed full.

Ileana drew up in front of him. Her presence seemed to

quell some of his fear, but he couldn't meet her gaze. Instead, he lowered his eyes to her hemline again. She was right—killing stalkers probably wasn't the answer. Those demons had once been human, and if possible, they needed to be saved along with everyone else. Worse than that, he'd thoughtlessly ordered Sable to kill, and he'd failed to listen when she tried to offer an alternative solution. A solution he still didn't quite understand—and was now too ashamed to ask about.

The princess walked away.

When he finally looked up again, Dain watched Ileana reach for Sable and Tars. Surprisingly, Tars did not resist. Perhaps Sable had told him about the princess? A spark of white flame flashed beneath the princess's palms. Both brother and sister arched their backs momentarily, and then hunched over in gratified relief. Dain remembered that feeling.

Before he had a chance to think through anything else, a loud question rang out behind him. "Who—what in all the four kingdoms was that, Captain?"

Dain flipped his head over his right shoulder to see Casper standing, half-naked, and probably half-hungover, just behind him. As usual, the underdressed, disheveled look did nothing to dull Casper's charms. But what was the sailor even doing aboard *The Maiden*?

The princess strode elegantly toward Casper, the tall woman looking him directly in the eye as she offered her hand.

"I am Ileana. It is a pleasure to meet you in person, brave Casper."

It seemed Ileana's presence was capable of tongue-tying even the most flirtatious sailor in all the four kingdoms. Casper simply accepted her hand, and stared back at her in awe.

Ileana gently pulled away. "Casper, I am thankful you are here. We have need of you."

The sailor gave a glassy-eyed nod. Then he seemed to recover himself as he broke into a rakish grin. "Aye, milady, whatever ye be needing." His smile grew wider, but only for the briefest moment before he continued. "As long as it doesn't require me being in the city for long. I need to lie low for a bit, if ye know what I mean?"

Dain's surprise mounted. He hadn't thought there was any situation that Casper couldn't talk his way out of.

With one eyebrow cocked, Ileana looked the sailor over. "Indeed." She turned, the long train of her gown swaying behind her as she moved. "You will not be required to go into the city for long, but it will be necessary for a short time. There's obviously been an attack on Alloway Manor. The first mate, the chief's mate, and a household of staff must still be there. It's not safe for the captain, or the others, to return." She turned back to Casper. "However, we are going to send you to fetch help—"

Dain cut in. "I will go for help."

Ileana's head snapped toward him. Her tone was forceful but not unkind. "That would be unwise, and I strongly advise against it. We'll quickly hear Sable out, and then decide. She made some kind of decision outside of your authority, and I'm guessing she had good reason."

Sable was standing again now, her brow knit as she glared at Dain. "I shifted us all."

"All?" Dain was a little afraid Sable might tear him limb from limb for asking, but he needed to understand. And he didn't blame her for being angry; he deserved anything he had coming to him. He'd treated Sable very poorly, and his panicked fear was no excuse for the disrespect he'd shown her.

Sable's words were clipped as she responded to his second question. "I did try to shift the stalkers like you asked, but not to the sea—into the Ernham mountains. Something prevented me—a barrier of some kind. I've never encountered anything like it." Sable shook her head and shifted her eyes away from Dain. "So, I made a quick decision. I knew Dulge and his cronies were convinced that the manor was abandoned, and after the stalkers showed up, I guessed that the brigands wouldn't stick around for long. The race was on, and Dulge probably believed that heading south sooner than later would give him a jump on the hunters. I knew if I could get *us* to the sea, away from the manor, the stalkers wouldn't linger. Of course, I'd never leave Mo and Toff stranded, invisible as they

303

are, so I shifted them into the kitchens with Lydia first. Then, I commanded the three of us here. Once all trace of our presence is gone, the stalkers will leave. They've no interest in people without magic, especially people they cannot see." She raised her chin defiantly, and looked back at Dain. "It was a risk, but it was the best I could think of under the circumstances."

Dain gaped. *Five.* Sable had risked herself, her very life, to shift all *five* of them. His stomach tightened hard, and he felt his face grow hot in the chill air. There were no words.

Sable obviously took his silence poorly. After a few moments, she sniffed and stalked away toward the prow.

Tars simply followed.

The princess turned to a dumbfounded Casper. "Apologies Casper, everything will soon be clear. Please, dress quickly, obtain your effects, and meet us at the prow."

In uncharacteristic silence, Casper obeyed.

Before Ileana joined the siblings, she settled her dazzling, azure eyes on Dain. "You can make your own choice, but with stalkers afoot, I suggest you remain on *The Maiden.*" Then she sighed, and her voice softened. "Life is a constant series of lessons, Dain Alloway, and they are often wrought through failure. Inevitably, leaders *will* have the lion's share of it—I, above all, should know. The most important thing is not how you feel about those failures, but what you *do* with them afterward. Failure has a way of preparing us for victory."

Dain remained dumb as he watched the princess walk back through the moonslight toward the prow. He repeated her last words silently to himself. *Failure has a way of preparing us for victory.* After how horribly he'd just failed everyone, he hoped her sentiment was true.

* * *

Dain sat in his office onboard *The Maiden* amidst piles of paperwork. He tried to focus on the task at hand, but his mind kept wandering to the events of the past two weeks. Sable had bargained well. Everything she'd projected came to pass. Dulge and his entourage had exited the manor shortly after the stalkers appeared, and due to their haste, they took less away with them than expected. Toff said the thugs had only done a brief search for their lost companions, but the effort had been minimal, and most of the captured men had been left behind.

The dark demons themselves had dawdled longer, but had been gone by morning. Thankfully, they'd never ventured near the kitchens, and the household staff was spared their terror.

Casper had hastened the Aaltain soldiers to the manor via Thornwalsh. The captive brigands were seized, and they, as Dain had hoped, were framed for everything, including the attack in Port Tallooj. They were the perfect scapegoat—the main reason Dain had wanted them alive. At least one part of his plan had gone right.

The authorities easily assumed that the culprits had followed *The Maiden* to Aalta, and attempted to finish what they'd begun on the isle. According to the judge, the brigands' main objective had been money. The trial was short, and not a word from the accused about magic or stalkers was taken seriously. Dain had tried to get Toff to pry more information out of the captured brigands in private visits to their cells, but they only confessed to being hired by Dulge, and had seemed to have no connection to Dulge's employer. Dulge was fully implicated by his men, and though he was never caught, at least the allegations would make it much more difficult for Oswart to enter Aalta again in the future.

The trial had delayed his father's funeral further, but he was finally laid to rest in the family cemetery alongside his wife two days after the proceedings ended. The ceremony of remembrance was postponed for a week after that, and instead of being held at Alloway Manor, it was organized within the great halls of the trades guild. All the Aaltain gentry and trade community attended. In the end, the formalities were reasonably touching, but not nearly as moving as the informal vigil the crew had held upon *The Maiden*.

After the funeral, Toff remained inside the city, checking in once a day by missive. He recommended the adept stay away from land unless absolutely necessary, because signs of stalkers persisted.

Morgan Crouse had spent most of the past two weeks assisting Lydia with restoring the manor. The first mate said he felt responsible for some of the damages, and didn't want to abandon Lydia to all the work. Dain figured Mo had other reasons as well, but he kept the questions to himself.

The Aaltain authorities had, for the present, provided a battalion of soldiers to guard the property. Lydia sent word of their progress daily, and mentioned in a recent note that the ladies of the household didn't seem to mind the addition of the uniformed sentries.

Dain, Sable, and Tars had taken Toff's advice and remained at sea. Casper chose to stay as well. The later had taken everything in stride, especially after Sable demonstrated a small amount of her talent. After that, the handsome sailor became an easy believer, and offered to remain on *The Maiden* as an extra sword in case more brigands happened to show. Dain figured that Casper had personal reasons for staying behind as well, but once again, he kept his questions to himself.

Sometimes, like today, Dain wondered if they'd simply gone back into hiding. He was desperate to push on. He wanted to keep fighting, keep searching, but if he'd learned anything from his failures thus far, it was that there were times to fight, times to retreat, and even times to hide as well. Victory died with its soldiers, but as long as they were alive and a forward momentum was maintained, however slow, then hope remained. And, truth be told, the momentum was slow. Dain had asked Lydia to search more of the manor for his mother's belongings, including the library, but she had turned up nothing. This mystery, and the lack of clues regarding the safe haven, were frustrating to say the least, but Dain tried to move on. Revisiting the plan Ileana had suggested, he mapped out all of his father's last port calls. Perhaps some investigative research would uncover a lead. Yet, with winter ravaging the seas, sailing was not something they could embark upon until the spring.

Dain's thoughts drifted back to Sable again. They'd spoken little since the manor attack, and every time he did run into her, which was fairly often aboard the limited surface area of a ship, he simply froze. She seemed happy to maintain her cool demeanor, usually offering him nothing more than a glance over her cold shoulder. He didn't blame her.

Tars, on the other hand, had actually become more approachable. His scowl remained, but the healer now actually sought Dain out on occasion. The man had been reading his mother's journal, and he seemed as insatiable as his sister with regard to learning. Dain felt like he contributed little to the study process, but he always tried to engage when Tars approached.

A knock at the door broke Dain's reverie. "Afternoon, Captain."

Dain looked up to see that it was the man himself who now stood in the open doorway. Tars was determined to call him captain, no matter how often Dain had insisted against it.

"Afternoon, Tars." Dain rearranged a stack the papers on his desk as though he'd been deep within his task. He knew he really should be organizing the ship's log to submit to Thornwalsh, but instead he smiled up at Tars. "I'm glad you're here. You've saved me from drowning in paperwork."

One corner of Tars's mouth twitched up, but only a sliver.

Dain didn't know why the man had begun to warm to him. He'd anticipated the opposite considering the tension with Sable, but he wasn't one to look a gift horse in the mouth. "I have something for you, Tars." Heading into the cupboard to his left, Dain pulled out a leather casement. Setting it onto his desk, he flipped the latches, and watched as the healer's brows rose.

Inside the case was a lute, the very lute that Tars had played at the manor. Dain had asked Toff to bring it back to *The Maiden* on his last trip out. Thankfully, it hadn't been harmed or stolen.

Gently lifting the instrument from the case, Dain handed it toward Tars. "As far as lutes go, I haven't the faintest idea whether this one is well crafted or not. My father had good taste, and high standards, but none of my family were musical. Mind you, I was forced to take some piano lessons as a boy, but they were short-lived. My instructor was quite plain about my lack of *an ear,* as he called it, so this instrument will find more use in your hands than sitting in the manor, gathering dust." Dain knew he talked too much when Tars was near. Perhaps it was because the healer was a man of so few words.

Tars reached toward the lute, his eyes flicking hesitantly between Dain and the instrument.

Dain urged the instrument forward again. "It belongs to you now, no strings attached." He gave Tars a quick wink. "And no pun intended. Honestly, I require nothing in return, except perhaps the occasional tune for my crew."

Tars's hands wrapped around the lute, and he drew it close to his chest as he slid into the chair on the opposite side of the desk. The musician traced his fingers along the length of the strings, and then strummed lightly as he adjusted the tune.

Dain sat again, listening to the strumming with satisfaction. He admitted to himself that the gift hadn't been entirely free of selfish motives. While his teacher had been brutally honest about his own musical ineptitude, Dain still had an immense love for song. He couldn't play, or sing, but he could listen. And after all, what is music without the people who appreciate it?

Tars stopped strumming.

Dain looked up.

The healer eyed him seriously—his tone held no anger,

but perhaps there was a hint of exasperation. "I think it's time you apologized."

* * *

Why is it that pride often overrides every other emotion? At first, Dain thought he'd frozen up in front of Sable because he was embarrassed, or nervous, but honestly, it was just because of his pride. And a verbal apology would make this admission all the more real. Nonetheless, Tars was right. It couldn't go on like this. Sable was his friend, his ally, his— either way, the quarrel had obviously grown tiresome for everyone, including Tars. And the time had come.

After a restless, dreamless sleep, Dain rose, and sent Casper to fetch Sable to his quarters. When a firm knock sounded on the door of his office, Dain started, then took a steadying breath. "Enter."

Sable stalked into the room, and slammed the door loudly behind her. Before she even spoke, Dain realized his error in sending Casper to fetch her. His apology was definitely starting out on the wrong foot. He winced.

She waved her arms through the air. "You couldn't even come find me yourself?"

He winced again.

The girl's hands flew to her hips. She glared in his direction, but did not fully meet his gaze while she waited for his reply.

Dain said the only thing he could manage. "I'm sorry."

It was like a flood gate. Sable started to pace, scrubbing furiously at her face. "You know what, Dain Alloway? You are not the only person involved in all of this. You are not alone. You may think you need to make all the plans, all the decisions, but you don't. You *are* a natural-born leader, and you *are* clever, but regardless of that, a good leader doesn't do *everything* by himself. Your problem is that you don't give anyone else a chance to help you see the bigger picture. If you truly want to bring freedom, if you really want to fight this war, then you need real supporters. You don't need mindless soldiers who do as you say. As much as it's a leader's job to plan, give orders, and delegate tasks, it's also their job to serve, and to listen. If you don't do that, then you *will* fail."

Dain ran his fingers through his ever-tangled mat of hair. "You are right."

Her thick lashes fluttered rapidly in his direction. "You are so blind sometimes."

He couldn't meet her gaze, so he lowered his eyes to the floor. "I've been a fool, Sable. A selfish, stupid fool. I've always felt alone—always felt like I didn't belong, like I needed to do everything by myself, but I hear you. I understand. I need others. While I cannot promise you that I won't make the same kind of mistake again, from here on in, if you choose to see this through, I'll try harder to own up to it when I do." He still couldn't look up at her. "I hope you can forgive me?"

"You hurt me."

"Yes, my actions were inexcusable, and I should have listened to you."

Sable's right hand grasped his left. Somehow, she'd moved silently to his side while he spoke.

"I am sorry too. I should have told you more about my parents. It was just—hard to talk about." She squeezed his hand gently. "That said, both of our apologies mean little without eye contact."

Dain looked up fast. Her thick lashes were lined with silver, and her hazel gaze swallowed him whole. He tried to clear his throat. "I am so sorry. For everything. You handled yourself brilliantly at the manor. You were—you are, extraordinary."

Sable raised her free hand to cup his cheek.

Dain closed his eyes and leaned into her palm. He didn't know if looping his free arm around her was by choice or by instinct, but he grasped her tiny waist and firmly lifted her off her toes. As he leaned his forehead gently against her own, his insides fluttered. Part of him expected her to resist the embrace, but she didn't. Instead, she looped her arm around his neck, and firmly planted her lips against his own.

The kiss sent a wave of heat through Dain's frame, a sensation that made him feel inadequate and brazen all at the same time. He'd never kissed anyone before, but Sable didn't seem mind. She tasted like she smelled, the sweet herbs and rosewater railing against his senses, and his entire frame filled with longing. It was hard for him to let her go, but she eventually leaned away, and he set her back on the floor. He couldn't, however, bring himself to take his hand from her waist. Admiring the flush of her freckled cheeks, he teased, "If every serious argument we have in the future ends like this, then I think I might need to start more."

Sable laughed.

It had been too long since he'd heard her laugh. The buoyant sound shook something inside of him—either that, or the physical contact had been a trigger of release. All the loss, the responsibility, the pain, the terrors, the failures, and the longing surfaced in full force. Dain began to cry. Not a blubbering mess of tears, just small, steady droplets that leaked from his eyes, slowly saturating his face.

It took the merry girl a few moments to notice, but she soon sobered, reaching up to wipe away the tears. "You are not alone, Dain Alloway. *We* are not alone. Since I met you, I have grown, and learned so much. It *is* better that we fight for freedom. It *is* better that we fight for a chance at a normal life. Now, no matter what we face, I would rather try for freedom than regret never having tried at all. You taught me that. And even if the outcome is not what we want, even if we never get to have the life we dream of, we can still make a home right here, right now, for however long we have, with each other."

Dain released his hold on her waist and staggered backward.

Sable grabbed for him. "Dain, are you alright?"

Working to steady himself, Dain clasped her outstretched hand in his own. "Sable, I have been so blind."

The girl smiled wryly. "Didn't I already tell you that?"

Dain's tears continued, but he felt his lips turn up in a smile. "I have spent the last eight years scheming to get off this ship, because all I ever wanted was to start a real life, create a family, and build a home. That plan, that hope, has been everything to me, and in the midst of it all I completely missed that fact that everything I've ever wanted is all right here." Dain pulled her close against himself, and bent into her hair. "You, Sable Cortham, are my family. Mo, Toff, Lydia, Tars, Casper, Dev, and even Trait—they are my family too. I am already home."

Chapter 27

Sable abandoned Dain to attend to the daily food prep in the galley. He'd offered to help but was told, in no uncertain terms, that his cooking skills left much to be desired. The kiss had, of course, left Dain craving more, but even if he wasn't touching her, he just wanted her near. When she continued to shoo him away, he reluctantly decided that starting out as a clingy lover might not be putting his best foot forward.

Despite the dreary pelt of winter rain, Dain made his way up on deck. His hair quickly grew damp as he headed for the prow and climbed to his usual perch on the bowsprit. He wrapped his cloak tighter around him, and the wind tugged at the fabric playfully. The breeze grew more insistent, threatening to whip the fabric from his grasp, but Dain reached for the element and gave it a small, internal reprimand. The air buffeted around him indignantly. This kind of interaction was making Dain start to believe that the elements had personalities of their own. The breeze swept away, distracted by some winter gulls trying to roost on the topmost part of the mainmast. Dain watched the exchange for a few moments before looking down toward the wooden princess.

He hadn't thanked her for being there to pick up the pieces after the manor attack, and she deserved recognition. There was no one nearby to overhear him, but he still spoke his thanks in a low voice. "You were spectacular after the attack. Thank you, Ileana. Now, I know you don't need my affirmation, but you will make a perfect queen one day." He wanted to follow up by promising that it would happen. He wanted to tell her that he'd free them all, even her beloved, Elden Grayspire. Dain wanted to swear that he'd hand her the kingdom of Derchar, but he knew he couldn't promise any of it. Instead, he promised her something else. "You have been so long imprisoned here, and you've had a far lonelier existence than any of us. While I can't promise you that we'll win this war, I can promise that you will not be alone while we try. You will have a real family aboard *The Maiden*. We are a motley crew, and nowhere near noble, but hopefully, as we vie for freedom, this little family will be a decent consolation prize."

Dain didn't know what else to say, so he lifted his gaze toward the city. The spires of Aalta still glowed through the gloom beyond the bay. He stared out at them, wishing he could take Sable there again, wishing he could spend days, weeks, a lifetime by her side, enjoying the beauty that never dimmed. She'd love it here in the warmer months. They could explore the streets, the museums, the theaters. They could attend symphonies and operas, and take holidays in southern Zaal. He would make her laugh—every day. Dain shook his head. Water sprayed from the ends of his now-drenched mane. He was getting way ahead of himself, and getting way ahead of everything they still needed to face. Perhaps being so sedentary the past couple of weeks was getting to him. There was something to be said for the forward motion of the sea, for a destination on the horizon.

Later that afternoon, Dain tried one more time to get Sable to allow him into the galley, but she still flatly refused. Her resistance confused him. Maybe, after their kiss, she just needed time to think?

Dain idly wandered the ship. Casper had taken a quick trip into the city, and Tars was locked up, as per usual, in his cabin with the journal, so neither friend was available to distract him. He considered going back on deck to spend some time practicing his talent. The ever-present thrum just at the edge of his consciousness always longed to be exercised in the open air, but the other boats in the harbor might just wonder at the varying weather patterns circling above *The Maiden*. He knew he needed the open seas to practice undetected.

He could resume working on the stack of papers piled on his desk, but that held no allure whatsoever. In the end, he opted for a nap. No doubt his sleep sent waves of magic echoing through the city—this had been another thing he'd neglected to consider while at Alloway Manor. For whatever reason, his dreams had not drawn the stalkers the first night in Aalta, so maybe it wasn't a talent after all? He'd have to study it further to find out; he figured Sable would probably agree.

* * *

Only a single star shone in the dark maroon skies. Like countless nights before, he watched unblinking, as the sky turned from pink, to crimson, and then to night. A rage rose. It pushed and shoved against his external encasement, but his limbs did not obey. They *never* obeyed. Clouds swept over the lonely star, and lazy flakes of snow began to fall. How many seasons had he seen? All seen, never felt. Not even the frozen depths of winter, nor the blazing furnace of summer could penetrate this body of stone. Why was he not crazy? Why did he not just lose his mind? It would be far easier to bear if he were no longer sane—Ileana, my love . . . Let me out!

* * *

It took only a light shake to his shoulder for Dain to sit bolt upright in his bed. He was breathing hard as he patted his arms and legs. Flesh. He was flesh. Looking up with a gasp of relief, he saw that Sable had woken him, and now stood back, staring at him wide-eyed.

"Are you alright?" Her voice was tender with concern.

Dain noticed he was sweating profusely even in the coolness of his bedchamber. Running his hands through his hair, his voice cracked in reply. "I think so—just a bad dream . . ."

Sable nodded sympathetically. Then she headed over to the cabinet and pulled out a fresh set of clothes. "Perhaps one day we should explore those dreams of yours."

"Perhaps." It was all he could manage.

As she set the clothing at the end of his bed, he noticed that she was wearing one of her best frocks. The cream-colored dress was cinched up tight at the waist with a decorative leather corset, and a plum overskirt was pulled up attractively on one side. Her hair was loose, the dark chestnut waves swaying just below her chin. She even wore the *Dernamn* high upon her neck again. She noticed him staring, and a blush rose to her cheeks. "Now, get cleaned up, and dress. You've slept right through until dinner."

Before she was entirely out of the room, he regained some composure, and called after her. "Are you sure you wouldn't like to stay and help me?"

He heard a small giggle as she rounded the curtain out to his office. "I think you'll manage just fine alone, Lion Cub. Hurry up. Dinner is getting cold."

Dain did as he was told, washing fast in the bucket Sable had obviously placed for that purpose by his bedstand. The nightmare lingered, though. It had been so real . . .

He tried to shake off his unease as he made his way to the dining room. He was looking forward to sharing an intimate meal with Sable after weeks of avoiding each other.

However, the sight that met him in the dining room was anything but intimate.

"Surprise!" The unanimous yell filled the small space to the corners.

Lydia came flying toward Dain, wrapping him in a crushing hug. "Happy name day, my boy."

Mo followed her closely. He slapped Dain hard on the shoulder while Lydia held fast. "Eighteen now, lad. I'd say ye're most certainly a man now."

Dain embraced Lydia back, and his eyes flitted through the other faces in the room. Tars stood leaning in the corner, his expression blank as he gave Dain a small nod of acknowledgment. Toff sat beside a smirking Casper on the opposite side of the table, and his mouth broke into a wide, semi-toothless grin as he tipped his red toque.

Sable stood at the head of the table, grinning ear to ear— she was obviously proud of her deception. She indicated the table. "No fish, I promise."

Dain laughed, looking down to admire the heavy spread.

A large plum cake sat temptingly in the center of all kinds of delicacies. Now he understood why he hadn't been allowed in the galley all day. Sable had done all this, for his name day . . . Dain's throat thickened. "I—my name day—I forgot."

Lydia gave him another squeeze.

Mo still held his shoulder. "Aye, well lad, ye've had a certain amount on yer mind lately." The first mate gently pried Lydia away. He seemed to touch her and speak to her with even more familiarity now. "Let the man sit, lass."

Wiping at her face, Dain's former nurse disengaged, and motioned him toward a chair. "Yes, sit, my boy."

Casper jumped up to drag Dain to the head of the table where Sable stood.

Dain smiled into her glee-filled face. He wanted to memorize every inch of her expression, but Casper didn't give him a chance—he plunked Dain down hard and thrust a goblet in his hand as he called, "Wine all around."

Everyone, except Tars, cheered in loud agreement.

As the cold winter rain pelted ceaselessly outside, as demons haunted Aalta, as evil men scoured the countryside, and as an emperor plotted against the kingdoms, Dain and *his* family celebrated. Amidst the merriment, he couldn't help praying. It was the third prayer of his entire life, and Dain directed it vaguely out again. He gave thanks for *The Maiden*, and for the safe arms of the sea.

* * *

Stumbling into his bedchamber, Dain tugged at his clothes. He'd only drunk three—or maybe it was four goblets of wine. When he'd finally gotten undressed and into his nightshirt, Dain crawled clumsily under the blankets to rest his spinning head.

It was only minutes later that Sable landed, lantern in hand, on the bed beside him.

He squinted painfully into the bright light as the girl stuffed a sprig of herb under his nose. "Here, chew this."

"Where did you come from?"

She gave a low *tsk*. "You did have too much wine." Shoving the sprig at him again, she repeated herself. "Chew it."

Bleary-eyed, Dain accepted the herb. It was dry and woody, exactly like chewing bark. He'd tried bark as a child. As the herb broke down, Dain managed a few swallows, and his head quickly began to clear. Even the spinning started to stop.

"Better?"

Sitting up to lean against his pillows, Dain nodded and kept chewing.

"Good."

The girl went round to set the lantern on the hook above the bedside table, and Dain noticed she only wore a nightdress. While he had already seen her fully naked, the first time they met, this felt entirely new. The garment was thin and loose-

324

fitting, and Dain caught glimpses of her small curves beneath.

She saw him gawking. "Don't get any ideas, Dain Alloway. I may have kissed you once, but that doesn't mean I'm ready for anything more than that. I think I'll just sleep better. With you—in here."

Dain's head swam again, but this time it wasn't from the wine. This was going to be hard, but the alternative would be sleeping without her, and he definitely didn't want that. During his injury, he'd grown accustomed to her in the chair beside him, and he'd missed her everyday since.

Crawling under the blankets beside him, Sable lay down, and leaned her back up against him.

He finished chewing the wooden herb, snuffed out the lantern, and turned on his side to lean his back against hers. The smell of herbs and rosewater wafted toward him as her warmth seeped in. "Sable, am I the first person you ever kissed?"

She let out a small giggle. "No."

Dain couldn't resist probing further. "How many others? When?"

She laughed louder this time. "Only two. They were childhood kisses, snatched behind barns long ago. Nothing serious."

"Was our kiss—serious?"

Sable cuddled further into his back. "I suppose that

remains to be seen."

Dain wasn't too sure what that meant, so he chose to stay silent.

Sable changed the subject with ease. "Did you know that binary healers can heal emotions as well as physical injuries?"

Dain raised his eyebrows in the dark, but before he could reply, Sable continued. She was ever the scholar. "It was fascinating. She eased the stalker fear entirely—it didn't linger this time at all. I believe she did the same for Tars, and perhaps a little more besides."

That would explain Tars's more approachable demeanor. Maybe Ileana had healed some of the man's past suffering as well?

"Dain?"

"Yes?"

"Did you ever find out what that paper meant? The Wildflower?"

He shrugged. "Not yet."

Sable began to hum softly, the vibrations quivering through her back to his. The hum slowly turned into a soft melody. If Dain remembered correctly, it was an ancient Erhamian lullaby, and the music eased every knot in his soul.

"Sable?"

"Hmmm?"

"Thank you for the Name Day celebration. It was—it

was—"

The girl cut him off. "You're welcome, Dain. It was, wasn't it?"

"Yes, it was."

Chapter 28

Mo stumbled down the hallway toward the main deck. The first mate looked a little worse for wear, and Dain gave great thanks for the awful wooded herb Sable had made him chew last night. He knew Mo was headed for the poop deck, but he'd already been loitering in the hall for over an hour, waiting to talk. He was desperate. Dain moved to intercept. "Morning."

The first mate rubbed his temples gingerly. "Morning, Lad. Ye must have something on yer mind, or ye wouldn't be blocking my way."

Dain couldn't help smiling, Mo knew him so well. Still, his voice got awkwardly quiet in response. "I was wondering—say, if I kissed a girl, and then asked her whether or not she thought it was serious—and she responded that it remained to be seen—what do you suppose that might mean?"

The first mate gave a low chuckle, then winced as he

rubbed at his temple again. "I suppose it could mean a lot of things. Maybe she wants more security—"

"Security?"

Mo sighed patiently. "Aye, Lad, it's common for a lass to want security. And with the way things are at present . . ." The first mate's face started to look a little green. "Can we talk about this later? I am needing to—" Mo didn't finish, pushing his hulking form past Dain and heading fast for the upper deck.

Following slowly behind, Dain contemplated Mo's words, and wondered what exactly, at this stage, a relationship would look like for Sable and himself. They could make a temporary home together on *The Maiden* for whatever time they had, but Mo was right. After that, who knew what they'd be facing, or how life would change? It wasn't the best circumstances for beginning a relationship.

When he surfaced up on deck, a low-lying fog spun through the ceaseless drizzle. Dain could barely make out the glow of the spires in the distance. As he navigated himself toward the stern, his gaze landed on an approaching ship. He stared, jaw slack, as a glimmer of gold peeked through the morning mist and a billow of crimson sails buffeted on the breeze. It was the ship from his dream.

* * *

Dain wasn't surprised when Thornwalsh's missive arrived an hour later. He'd gotten so used to surprises over the past few months that he was pretty sure little would phase him anymore. The ship had been moored and registered with the port authorities, and the vessel he'd seen roll through the mist belonged to the Alloway Trading Company.

The company master requested that Dain meet him on the pier at high noon to begin formal inquiries. Dain's response to Thornwalsh was firm. He instructed the man to remain in the city, stay confidential, and wait until Dain investigated the ship himself. He knew Thornwalsh wouldn't be pleased by the order, but he'd find some way to fix that later. His father had never done anything without purpose. This ship was a mystery for a reason, and, quite possibly, it needed to remain so.

Yet, Dain knew he wouldn't be able to keep it a secret aboard *The Maiden.* Everyone would wonder where he was headed, and they'd never allow him to wander off alone. Plus, he had taken Sable's words to heart—none of this was a solo mission. He needed a team. Once informed, his miniature crew insisted on accompanying him to inspect the vessel. Dain felt gratified by their protective support, but he wasn't comfortable leaving *The Maiden* without guard. In the end, Casper offered to stay behind, and since Tars appeared indifferent, he remained also.

As they prepped to row out, Dain had very little time to think things through, but what he did know, now that this ship had arrived, was that in the future he needed to start taking his dreams more seriously. The ship's appearance seemed to confirm that prophetic vision was indeed one of his talents. While he still hadn't completely come to grips with the magic now in his life, he had to admit that seeing the future might be useful.

* * *

The mists shrouded the rowboat as they made their way through the rain.

Toff sat at the head of the vessel, whining about the chill in his bones and his throbbing headache. Before they'd cast off, Sable had offered the old sailor some of the wooded herb to help with the hangover, but he had taken one sniff and refused.

Mo still seemed a little worse for wear. He too had refused the herb, but, unlike Toff, he kept his complaints to himself as his enormous arms worked hard at the oars.

Lydia sat just in front of Mo, occasionally reprimanding Toff for his grousing, and then offering words of encouragement to the first mate as he labored.

Sable was at the back of the boat beside Dain. He could tell she was enjoying the trip away from *The Maiden*. Her wet hair stuck to her cheeks as she craned forward to peer through the fog in search of the mysterious ship. And as Dain watched her, he gave thanks that he wasn't going this alone. He looked forward to solving the mystery ahead of them, but he also couldn't shake the feeling that something bad awaited them as well. Perhaps his dreams were making him paranoid. The same nightmare had haunted him again last night. The horror of being trapped inside a body of stone was draining him. He knew exactly who he dreamed about, but the dream made it feel like the experience was entirely his own. He was becoming far more empathetic to Ileana and Elden's plight.

As though reading his mind, Sable nudged her knee against his. "It's the dreams, isn't it?"

Dain blinked quickly. "How did you know?"

She lowered her voice. "You thrashed around all night. I've nearly changed my mind about sleeping next to you. I figured it must be dreams, and I assume they are not so good?"

"No—no, they were not."

"Well, I think we should visit those soon, and do a bit more research—see what we can learn." Then she smirked at him sideways as she nudged his knee with hers again. "Otherwise, you'll be sleeping on your own again soon."

Dain definitely didn't want that.

As they floated over the waters, Dain felt every ebb and flow of the elements. They constantly called to him, and at times it took some presence of mind not to reach for the elements in return. The wind swirled around him relentlessly. Sadly, Dain was not immune to its ravages. His well-oiled cloak kept him mostly dry, but the cold was starting to set into his bones as well. He'd just begun to commiserate with Old Toff when the mists finally pulled up from the waters.

The ship came into view.

Dain sucked in a fast breath as he read the name inlaid along the side of the golden prow in common script. *The Wildflower.*

Sable saw it too, and her eyes grew wide.

The vessel was nearly twice the size of *The Maiden*, and it was not actually constructed of gold, but merely painted a shimmering ochre. The crimson sails had been secured, and in this state it looked like an ordinary carnival ship.

As they drew nigh, Toff hailed the ship. "Hi ho!" When no response came, he called again, and this time, a few suspicious faces peeked over the edge. Toff hailed again. "Captain Alloway of *The Maiden* requests permission to board *The Wildflower.*"

There was some rushing, scuttling, and movement up on deck as they waited. Finally, a rope ladder was released over the starboard side, and an older gentleman peeked over. "Permission granted to Captain Alloway."

Mo rowed alongside the hull, and Toff tied off the boat as Dain reached for the ladder, Sable and the others following directly behind him.

The sight that met his eyes when he surfaced on deck was unexpected. A crowd of faces stood staring at him in suspicious wonder, but they were not the type Dain expected to see on a carnival vessel. There were no gymnasts, nor clowns—instead, the ship was filled with hardened, weather-worn sailors, along with regular men, women, and children of all ages and nationalities. Dain couldn't help staring. His eyes roamed from one face to another as the old man who'd granted them permission made an announcement. "Make way for the first mate."

The crowd slowly parted as a slim woman walked toward them through the throng. She was flanked on one side by a child, and on the other by a—peacoline. Dain did a double take as the creature drew near. The peacoline was far more beautiful than the figurine resting back in his apartments at the manor. The animal's head, legs, and torso resembled a giant cat, though its ears were far bigger. The turquoise fur on the creature's back sloped down and shifted naturally into a long, feathered tail. Dain was certain that if the tail were to fan out, it would be thrice the size of any regular peacock's.

The animal was magnificent, and it seemed to know this, because it moved with its head held high, sauntering boldly up to Dain. After a quick sniff of his tunic, the beast turned back to sit idly by the woman. Tearing his gaze from the peacoline, Dain realized that the lady was far younger than he'd first estimated. She was perhaps only a few years older than him, and he immediately noted her Iandiorian features. Her onyx hair hung to her waist, and two delicately pointed ears peeked out from beneath the thick strands. Her skin was deeply tanned, and her dark, slanted eyes gazed at him with curiosity. Dain had met few Iandiorians; their kind were little welcome outside their own kingdom, but from all appearances she looked quite comfortable in her station.

The woman's mouth remained still as she lifted her arms and began to sign with her hands. The young girl at her side spoke in her place. "We welcome you aboard *The Wildflower*, Dain Alloway."

Dain briefly turned his gaze upon the young interpreter. The girl was an albino. Her fuzzy white hair barely grazed her shoulders, and her skin was so pale it appeared almost translucent. The child met his stare, and her fuchsia gaze made him swallow hard. These were not the eyes of a young one. Shivering, Dain quickly turned back to the first mate. "We expected to be greeting your father. Is he not among you today? Does he follow?"

Taking a deep, settling breath, Dain was careful to make sure his lips were visible to *The Wildflower's* first mate. "Sadly, my father passed several months ago. I am now Captain Alloway of *The Maiden*."

A murmur echoed through the crowds behind, and Dain saw a few people dab at their eyes while others began to cry more openly. The Iandiorian woman's brows creased as she raised her hands to respond. "We are grieved to hear this. My deepest sympathies for your loss, Captain." She moved forward, and the peacoline swirled affectionately around her legs. Her dark eyes stared deeply into his own as the albino child spoke for her again. "Many of us, myself included, owed your father a great debt. My name is Anira Alasternia-Grain. Your father saved my life in Eandor Vid."

Dain heard Toff cough in recognition behind him.

Anira. This was the prostitute his father had released from indentured servitude to Oswart Dulge. His head spun. This was it—*The Wildflower* was the safe haven. It made perfect sense. There was no place more secure than the sea. How had he not guessed? Dain's gaze fanned out over the crowd behind Anira as he now realized that most of the people aboard this ship must be adept. They were just like him. Turning to quickly glance behind at his friends, he could see by their faces that they also understood. His father had saved so many. Dain's breath picked up speed. The wooden princess would get to share her story about Derchar and Rectlor after all. And perhaps—perhaps with a boatload of adept, they'd have a real chance of winning this war. A real chance at freedom.

Anira turned, signing and motioning for Dain to follow. "The captain will see you now. Please, follow me."

Dain obeyed.

As his friends moved to accompany him, the child stepped

out to bar their way. "Only Captain Alloway is permitted."

Dain saw Toff stiffen, and he watched Lydia's hands hit her hips fast. He intervened. "It's alright. I think I'll be safe. Please stay here until I return."

Mo gave Dain a quick, obedient nod, but Dain could see by the first mate's expression that the man would plow straight through the throng at any sign of trouble. He gave Sable and Lydia a reassuring wink before he turned to follow Anira below.

Old Toff cursed. "Very well, we'll just stand here. In the rain. Until you get back."

Dain did hope someone took pity on his friends and found them a dry place to wait.

The captain's quarters were in the stern, and Dain marveled at the ship's size as they made their way. *The Maiden* could house a crew of fifty, but this vessel probably held at least two hundred and fifty people comfortably. Dain grew curious to know whom his father had chosen to captain this beauty.

Anira knocked soundly on the large double doors, but swung the two great oaks inward without waiting for a reply. The captain's quarters were as impressive as the rest of the ship, and triple the size of Dain's own quarters aboard *The Maiden*. The walls were painted the same shimmering ochre as the hull, and the large sitting room brimmed full of furniture.

To the left was an open door that led to what looked like an office space, and to the right was an arched entryway that framed a large dining space. At the back was a closed doorway that probably hid the captain's bedchamber.

Anira waved a hand for him to follow her through to the office.

The room was a disaster. Floor-to-ceiling shelves overflowed with vials and jars containing herbs, ointments, fluids, and all manner of pickled organisms. Dain read a few of the labels: Charred Densil Root, Illead Potion, Corpusc Gills. He involuntarily shivered when he spied the jar marked Human Fingernails. Why would anyone need pickled fingernails? Pulling his gaze from the shelves, Dain's eyes flitted around the rest of the room. Books lay scattered on every conceivable surface, including the floor—even the central desk was buried up to his nose in them. How could anyone work in a place like this?

Anira knocked on the wall behind them loudly.

Dain saw a woman's head pop up quick from behind the clutter. It was covered in faded blonde curls that flew wild in every direction. He squinted as she turned, and his chest tightened when a pair of stormy gray eyes fixated, with raised brows, on his own.

Dwarfed amidst this mountainous office mess stood his mother.

Chapter 29

Alis Lin Alloway navigated slowly through the piles. She rounded the desk with silver-lined eyes, and her voice was the barest rasp as she reached out toward him. "Dain . . .?"

He recoiled from her touch.

Alis stepped back hesitantly and lowered her hands. Turning to Anira, she signed and spoke at the same time. "Dismissed."

Dain turned to watch the first mate follow orders, and he almost reached for her as she closed the office door. His fists began to pump. This was impossible—this was—he couldn't bring himself to look back at *The Wildflower's* captain.

His mother's voice was barely audible over the roar now filling his temples. "Dain—Dain look at me. Son? Please?"

No, no, NO.

"Dain—please, where is your father?"

His palms stung as he slowly turned his gaze back toward the woman behind him. "He's dead." They were the only two words he could manage.

Alis's eyes grew wide, and her mouth opened and closed in silent protest.

The office door flew open. Dain glanced over his shoulder to see Mo, Toff, Lydia, and Sable burst in behind him. Apparently, they'd gotten suspicious. Perhaps the albino child had made them uncomfortable as well. Anira could be seen behind his friends, waving apologies to her captain.

Toff was the first to recognize Dain's mother. "Alis?"

Lydia started spitting and muttering half-religious, half-superstitious phrases under her breath.

The Wildflower's captain didn't look up. She didn't even answer. Apparently, the shock of Dain's news was still sinking in, but her reverie didn't last long. After a moment, the petite woman squared her shoulders and raised her chin. She ignored all of the unwelcome guests in her office, and she fixed her stern gaze on Dain. "Tell me what happened."

Dain could feel the tendons in his jaw stretch. His mother was alive—alive and well, and standing right in front of him. He suddenly felt small again, and an urge to run into her arms engulfed him. The feeling didn't last long, because he simultaneously recalled the boy outside her apartment doors— the boy who'd waited hours for her to come out and play. A heat rose, traveling up his chest, climbing his neck to sear his face. He tasted bile. Who did she think she was? This—this woman had lied to everyone who'd ever loved her. She'd abandoned her family. She'd abandoned him. He knew it was the wrong thing to say, but he couldn't help himself. "You don't deserve to know."

Alis Alloway bristled visibly. "I am your mother, Dain Hiram Alloway. You will answer my question, now."

Dain took a step toward the door, willing himself not to explode in response—he barely managed to keep his tone even. "My mother died long ago. The only family I have now are the people you see here behind me, and those who are waiting back on *The Maiden*."

It was evident that Dain's emotions were overriding his judgment. He knew what the appearance of *The Wildflower* meant. He knew that discussions were essential, but he just couldn't bring himself to do it. He was in no state to be rational.

It was an effort of will to even look Alis Alloway in the eye one more time. Somehow, he kept the shaking that permeated his body out of his voice. "My first mate and chief's mate will remain in my stead. I must return to *The Maiden*. They both have my complete confidence, and there is obviously much to discuss. Good day to you, Captain." Before Alis could reply, he gave a stiff nod, and turned.

When he caught Mo's eye, he could see the concern burning bright in the first mate's charcoal gaze, and it nearly sent Dain scrambling. Sucking in a steadying breath, he nodded his thanks to the man, and then to Toff. When he faced Lydia, he saw the same concern mirrored in her eyes, but something else too—an anger perhaps akin to his own. Her hands were on her hips again, and he knew she'd determined to stay behind as well. Dain gave silent thanks again for his friends. Then he felt Sable reach for him, her arm laced with his own. He squeezed her close in response, and without looking back, they left *The Wildflower* behind.

* * *

A rare winter sun greeted Dain as he climbed the bowsprit at dawn. The sky was a pale salmon as he watched the sunrise scatter the mists clinging to the waves. Despite the sunny glow, the air remained chill, and he watched his breath issue forth in wispy curls. Yesterday's shock had worn off, but Dain's anger still lingered. The current plague of nightmares only served to amplify his sour mood. He just needed one night of dreamless sleep.

Small footsteps sounded on the deck behind him. Glancing over his shoulder, he spied Sable walking up the steps to the prow. When she reached him, he offered her a hand up to where she could straddle the bowsprit facing him. She shivered, and he gently pulled her against himself as he wrapped his cloak around them both. She'd slept by his side all night, but they had conversed little since yesterday. She was giving him space.

She lay her head against his chest. "You're up early."

Dain breathed in her fresh scent. It soothed his mood a little. "I hardly slept . . ."

She pulled away, her large hazel eyes brimming with concern. "You once told me that it was all about choice. I—I hope you can reconcile with her, of course, but I understand. My parents were taken from me against their will. They had no choice, but your mother—well, she may have had her reasons, and I'm sure we'll hear all about them once everyone returns, and forgive me for saying it, but it does seem like she *chose* to abandon you. I think I'd feel angry too."

Dain's throat thickened, and he crushed Sable's slender frame hard against him as he kissed the top of her head. This girl's words, her practical spirit, her mind, her body, her gifts—everything about her soul made his own complete. Leaning into her hair, he brushed his lips against her ear. "*You* are my true home, Sable Cortham."

The girl's body relaxed against him. Then she pulled her face up fast and crushed her mouth firmly against his own. Dain responded with equal passion, tangling his fingers through her hair. His head was spinning when she broke off the kiss and set her forehead against his.

"Dain?"

"Yes?"

"That kiss was serious."

Epilogue

Another dawn, another night of internal hell. At least the birds were singing again, and the bleakness of winter had passed.

Motionless stone eyes—blank and dry.

A sound. Movement through the grass.

A woman with ebony skin, snow white hair, and eyes that shone like starlight. He stared, her beauty demanding it. He had never seen her in the garden before. Who was she?

She stared back, straight into his eyes. She saw. *She knew.*

It was the first time he'd been *seen* in centuries. He wanted desperately to cry, and the inability to shed a single tear only made the feeling well up in him further.

A male voice.

The woman's gaze never wavered. A tall man in twilight robes lined with silver, now by her side.

Elden knew him, hated him.

"I have come to find you myself, pet. Our guests from Iandior are here, and these savages must not be kept waiting. You are their hostess, guide to their powerful, immortal existence. You have work to do. The time has come for our army to meet its full potential. Everything we have worked for will come to pass after this momentous day."

The woman seemed unmoved by the speech—she did not look at the man. She simply continued to *see him*.

The man grabbed her arm, snatching roughly at her chin. He glared meanly into her face. "The statuary can wait on your admiration. You have a duty, my pet. I suggest you obey." His face twisted into something that made even Elden quake internally. "Perhaps it was unwise of me to give you extra freedoms. If you prefer, you can be put back into your tower."

Elden thought he saw the woman shiver before she took her master's arm. As they began to walk away, she chanced one last glance at Elden over her shoulder. He was sure he heard her speak—it resonated within him, but her lips did not move.

"We are the same, you and I. We are prisoners."

Acknowledgements

My firstborn was only three months old when I developed the story of *The Maiden Ship*. That was twenty-one years ago. The book didn't get far back then because the demands of a new marriage, a new child, and so many other life callings forced me to set the story aside. It wasn't until 2018 that I revisited *The Maiden Ship*. And that decision was brought on by several major life events: a mix of chronic health struggles, my firstborn leaving home for college (don't let anyone ever tell you it's easy when your children leave home—it is not), and a severely injured drawing arm. Art has always been my lifeline, and when my arm went, and that privilege was taken from me, a bout of depression inevitably followed. It was a tough season, and I was desperate for a creative outlet. I needed something to keep me sane amidst the chaos and pain.

So, I wrote.

Typing with my non-dominant hand took some getting used to. The process was arduous, and sometimes I used dictation when the pain was too severe. Yet, word by word, this book saved my life. This tale gave me a reason to wake up each day; it gave me a purpose. Is it appropriate to thank your own novel in the acknowledgements? I suppose I just did . . .

In the very beginning, there were a few select people who gave me feedback and encouragement—Meme Prier, Ryan Armstrong, Erin Kleveland, Tanner Eady, Emma Hamm, and my own daughter, Hannah Ryckman. They were my first readers; they were the ones who made me actually feel like I could do it. Thank you for your input and your time. You are all such a gift.

As mentioned above, my drawing arm was severely injured while I wrote most of this novel, and I wasn't able to create my own cover art or interior art at the time. However, it was with great confidence that I hired Gabriella Bujdoso to create the cover, and Diana Dworak to create the Four Kingdoms map. Both of these artists surpassed themselves, and I could not be more thrilled with how they helped me bring this book to life. Thank you, from the bottom of my heart, for all your hard work.

Speaking of artists, Hayden Wolf went above and beyond while creating my book trailer, promo videos, and cover art reveals for me. He is probably the most talented person on the face of the planet (well, along with his wife, Jayli), and my gratitude for him knows no bounds.

Can I just say that editors are my favorite people in the world? I actually wish I could have an editor to walk me through my everyday life. They could fix everything I say and everything I write. It would be awesome! My editor, Dylan Garity, didn't pull any punches while working on this book with me, and that was exactly what I asked him for. He took *The Maiden Ship* to a whole new level, and there is no way I could have had the courage to publish it without his expertise and skill. Thank you so much for all your hard work, Dylan. You are brilliant.

Not only could I not have done this without all those mentioned above, but I couldn't have done all this without supportive friends as well. To my dearest Macayla Radke, Caryn Krasnozon, and Ella Strong, you have been a life raft to me amidst the tumults of life, art, business, and writing. You are always there to inspire me, support me, and promote everything I do. There are no words to express how much all your love means to me. And, a special mention to Macayla for being the muse for my Ileana—she would not be the character she is without you.

The most important people in any thank you note should come last, don't you think? They should be the final thought in our minds, the ones we carry away with us after all is said and done. And so, last, but never ever least, I need to thank my family. To my husband, Shane, to my son, Hunter, and to my daughter, Hannah, thank you for being my greatest source of life and love. My true home is not any physical space here on earth. My true home is you.

About the Author

Micheline Ryckman lives with her family on a farm in beautiful British Columbia, Canada. She is co-owner of Whimsical Publishing, and an accomplished artist/illustrator in multiple mediums. *The Maiden Ship* is her debut novel, the first in an upcoming series. The sequel book, *The Lion of the Sea*, is already in the works. Stay up-to-date and connected with Micheline by signing up for her newsletter via her website/blog whimsicalpublishing.ca or connect with her on social media sites—Instagram: @whimsicalillustration, or Facebook: Whimsical Illustration.